WITHDRAWN

D1052950

Materials may be renewed
by telephone if not overdue
FREMONT COUNTY LIBRARY
332-5194

ALMOST GRACELAND

ALSO BY STEVE CARLSON

*Hitting Your Mark: What Every Actor Really
Needs to Know on a Hollywood Set*

*The Commercial Actor's Guide: All You Need
to Start, Build, and Maintain a Career*

*Hitting Your Mark, 2nd Edition: Making a
Life—and a Living—as a Film Actor*

Carlson
L

ALMOST GRACELAND

Steve Carlson

THOMAS DUNNE BOOKS
ST. MARTIN'S PRESS
New York

This is a work of fiction. All of the characters, organizations, and events portrayed in this novel are either products of the author's imagination or are used fictitiously.

THOMAS DUNNE BOOKS.
An imprint of St. Martin's Press.

ALMOST GRACELAND. Copyright © 2007 by Steve Carlson. All rights reserved. Printed in the United States of America. No part of this book may be used or reproduced in any manner whatsoever without written permission except in the case of brief quotations embodied in critical articles or reviews. For information, address St. Martin's Press, 175 Fifth Avenue, New York, N.Y. 10010.

www.thomasdunnebooks.com
www.stmartins.com

Library of Congress Cataloging-in-Publication Data

Carlson, Steve, 1943–
    Almost Graceland / Steve Carlson.—1st ed.
      p. cm.
   ISBN-13: 978-0-312-37398-6
   ISBN-10: 0-312-37398-8
   1. Presley, Elvis, 1935–1977—Fiction.   2. Brothers—Fiction.   3. Truck drivers—Fiction.   4. Memphis (Tenn.)—Fiction.   I. Title.
PS3603.A7533A78 2007
813'.6—dc22

                                    2007027634

First Edition: November 2007

10 9 8 7 6 5 4 3 2 1

To Mary Ann
My wife, best friend, and chief editor

ACKNOWLEDGMENTS

One thing is for sure, no writer is an island, either. A number of people have been beneficial to the genesis of this project. The first are my good friends Jim and Pam Smothers, who read a rough first draft of the concept and came up with some very helpful advice right from the beginning. My late friend Alan Pultz, by one simple observation, changed the format of the book. Chris Difraia has been the biggest cheerleader for this story ever since I started on it. The agent, Barbara Harris, believed in it, and me, when no one else seemed to. I appreciate that a lot.

Probably the most in-depth help came from my friend Ty Haller in Vancouver, who makes his living teaching folks how to write. His help was invaluable. You can find his suggestions scattered throughout the book.

All of this would be moot if it weren't for the wonderful eye of Ruth Cavin at St. Martin's Press, who picked this little story out of the incredible number of hopefuls that cross her desk. I will be forever grateful to her for that.

And, of course, my wife, Mary Ann. A writer's spouse is usually the first person to ever see anything written; all the early rough outlines, drafts, rejected concepts . . . all of it. They usually develop a good eye for separating the wheat from the chaff. I am very fortunate that Mary Ann is one of those.

Thank you all for what has been a most enjoyable ride.

1

RAY PACED THE TRAILER like an expectant father, more nervous than he could ever remember being. It was amazing to him how his perception of everything could change so quickly. Had it really only been an hour since the call came in? It seemed to only take a minute to shower away the grime and fatigue of the day. So what was he supposed to do now?

As tired as he'd been a few hours ago, the thought of resting now was out of the question. There was no way. He hoped he was dressed all right, but it wasn't like he had a lot of options. These were his cleanest jeans and his best almost-new shirt. Ray decided it was probably just as well that this was last minute. Any more time and he really would have been a basket case. What would he have done, gone shopping? How did one prepare for something like this anyway?

Suddenly, everything seemed inadequate. His trailer seemed smaller and dirtier than it had been yesterday, his life seemed like a joke (king of the underachievers), and he thought he looked like a hick. He was seriously questioning the wisdom of ever having started all this.

A couple of short months earlier, Ray's life seemed like it was actually going to, finally, work out. It was about time. At age forty-two, Ray Johnston had had his share of work problems, marriage problems, divorce problems, parental problems, identity problems, and, most definitely, financial problems.

But it seemed that perseverance may have paid off after all. Ray owned his own place, had had the same job for over a year, which he liked, and was anxiously anticipating the most important day of his life, promising a promotion and the end of his money shortages.

Marriage and divorce problems were over, including alimony payments that ended when Ray's ex-wife married her divorce lawyer. Ray always thought that was a cute move.

His dad had been dead for years and his mom was in a home, but since his dad hadn't really been much help to anyone ever and his mom couldn't remember her name anymore, Ray figured everyone was where they were supposed to be.

It had all seemed so simple. My God, how much had happened.

And then, now! It was really hard keeping all this in perspective. He really wished he had time to call Sheree. She had the ability to put a sane face on most anything. Even she'd have a tough time with this one, though, Ray thought. Actually going to Graceland, actually sitting down with Elvis, face-to-face, was beyond even her reasoning powers.

This was not reality stuff. This was . . . well, that was the problem. Ray had no idea what it was and there hadn't been enough time to figure it out.

Besides, the car was already on its way to pick him up. He knew he'd be right in the middle of telling Sheree about it, and she'd be going crazy, when the car would show up and he'd have to hang up on her because he knew she'd never hang up otherwise.

Ray smiled at the thought. He already looked forward to telling her about that night but, so far, there was nothing to tell except that it was about to happen. Everything else was yet to come. And how it was going to play out, no one knew.

Ray had no idea what to expect from Elvis. The few times they'd talked had not necessarily been friendly. Quite the opposite. They'd ranged from wary distrust to outright rudeness. Then out of the blue, some woman (Elvis's social secretary or some such, Ray figured) called to say that Elvis would like him to come to dinner. He was even sending a car for him.

What happened? Why the turnaround?

The sight of headlights through the window slammed Ray back to reality. Whatever was going to happen was starting now.

Ray looked a little closer and was surprised to see a long, white limousine pull up alongside his trailer. Talk about "out of place"! Ray's feelings of inadequacy came back again but not enough to rival the nervousness which overrode everything.

Since it was a warm night, Ray didn't bring a jacket as he stepped outside. Ned, a fellow Ray had met a couple of weeks earlier, was driving.

"How're you doin'?" Ned asked, exiting the limo.

"A bit of a surprise," Ray said as he walked stiffly around to the passenger door and started to open it. Ned beat him there.

"Oh no," Ned said. "You get the full treatment."

"Oh, c'mon," Ray said, getting embarrassed.

Ned opened the door to the back. "Hey, enjoy it. You're goin' where few have ever been."

Ray let that sink in a moment before taking a big breath and cautiously entering the plush, soft black leather of the Presley limousine.

Ned had been in Rusty's a few weeks ago, a bar and lounge where Sheree worked, and had casually mentioned how much Ray looked like Elvis, which he'd heard his whole life, but to later find out that Ned actually worked for Elvis! Well, that was just one of the bizarre happenings that had led to this moment.

They rode mostly in silence, Ray quite in awe of his surroundings. Needless to say, he'd never even seen a limousine up close, let alone ridden in one, especially Elvis's.

"Are there going to be a lot of people there?" Ray asked to break the silence as much as anything.

"Actually, no," Ned said. "That's how I can tell Elvis really wants to talk to you. He's practically always got a house full of people but he told everyone but me to take off. He doesn't meet too many people alone."

Ray didn't know if that made him feel better or not but it suddenly didn't matter. Before them were the famous musical gates of Graceland. Living in Memphis, Ray'd seen them a hundred times before but had never dreamed of actually going inside, except maybe with a tour.

Ned casually nodded to a guard as they drove through the gates and onto the property of Graceland. He parked the limo off to the side of the famous mansion, got out, and was back opening Ray's door before he could find the handle. Ray hesitantly climbed out.

"First time is through the front door," Ned said, leading Ray up the stairs, past the imposing pillars to the ornate façade.

"For me?" Ray was still having trouble grasping it all.

" 'Specially for you," Ned said, opening the wrought-iron screen door. Ned reached for the main door, put his hand on the knob, paused, and looked over at Ray. "You ready for your life to change forever?"

Ray looked at him a moment, took a big breath, and said, "Sure."

Ned smiled and opened the door.

Saturday, March 26, 1977

Only a month and a half earlier, life was a little simpler for Ray. At the moment, he was downright happy. It was a perfect evening for racing. As loud as the motorcycles were, the helmets mercifully cut the sound to a dull roar. Ray didn't mind it a bit. In fact, it seemed to provide the perfect background sound track for the battle that was currently transpiring.

The South Memphis scrambles track was hosting its regular Saturday Night Special, giving the local riders an opportunity to try their stuff against one another. Ray was currently embroiled in a neck-and-neck duel with one of his least-favorite people, Guy Stubbs.

Ray's 360 CC Bultaco ate this course up but, at the moment, it didn't seem to be bothering Guy's Yamaha much, either. Both men were about the same age but Ray was long and lean (except for a bit of a beer belly he vowed he was going to get rid of any day now), whereas Guy had always been much stockier.

Guy didn't have any love lost for Ray, either. The two men were being extremely rough, bumping, cutting each other off, just generally getting in each other's face.

Ray and Guy were out in front of three other riders when the last lap flag was waved. They both popped it up a notch. They were still close as duck feathers when Guy got a better position on a turn and took the lead.

Every time Ray tried to get around him, Guy would swerve over in front of him, cutting him off. Ray started setting up a rhythm. He'd try to pass on the left side—blocked, tried on the right side—blocked, back to the left side—blocked.

Ray then started to the right again, causing Guy to swerve over in front of him, but this time it was a setup. Ray didn't go right. As soon as Guy started to cut him off, Ray goosed it and flew by him on the left.

Guy was furious. He tried everything he could to catch Ray but it was too late. Ray only had to keep in front of him for one more turn, which he did to win it.

Guy drove up alongside Ray as they headed off the track toward their respective campsites.

"Piece of shit," Guy said in greeting.

"Love to stay and chat, Guy, but I've got to double-check my plans for Monday. Hope you're coming prepared to work."

"Yeah. What kind of sucking up did you have to do for that?"

"Oh, you know, basic stuff; showing up on time, putting in a full day's work. Stuff you wouldn't really know much about."

Guy gave Ray a gloved finger as he turned off to his camp. Ray laughed as he continued on to his own. Various motorcycle equipment was laid out around Ray's pickup, which made it look like a small war zone. A cooler was sitting prominently in the truck bed. Sheree watched as Ray rode up and stopped.

"You're crazy, you know that?" she said.

Ray laughed as he went to the cooler and popped himself a beer. "Just good, clean fun. Hell, Guy and I have been competing for girls and jobs for years. Don't much care for each other."

"No kidding."

Further discussion was effectively cut off as another pickup, with a motorcycle in back, pulled up next to Ray's. A tall, skinny cowboy type named J.D. stepped out wearing racing leathers similar to Ray's.

"What heat was that?" J.D. asked.

"Three."

"Good. I'm in the fifth. Runnin' late but I should have a minute or two to get loosened up." J.D. let down the back of his bed, pulled out the ramp, and started to roll his bike down it. Ray came over to help with the heavy Huskavarna.

"Oh, by the way," J.D. said, motioning with his head toward a young girl getting quietly out of his cab. "This here's Candy. Sheree and Ray."

Everybody said "hi."

Candy's mouth dropped when she saw Ray. "Holy smokes, you were right. He looks just like him!"

Ray looked dryly over at J.D., who was already trying to kick-start his bike, which he usually had to do a hundred times. J.D. stopped, leaned the bike over on its stand, excused himself from Ray, and took Candy aside. "Now, when I said it would probably be a good idea not to mention anything about that, what I meant was that it would probably be a good idea not to mention anything about that."

"Okay."

J.D. returned to Ray. "Sorry." Ray just nodded as J.D. resumed trying to get his bike started.

"How'd you do?" J.D. asked Ray between kicks.

"Won."

"Get out. Anybody else show up?"

"Just Stubbs and a few others."

J.D. started laughing. "Great. You beat Stubbs. You've got to be one of his favorite people about now."

"Right up there."

"Does he know he's working for you Monday?" J.D. asked.

"Oh yeah," Ray answered with a twinkle.

J.D. laughed. "You are bad. Not that he doesn't deserve it." The Husky finally came to life. J.D. pulled on a helmet, climbed aboard, and yelled over to Candy above the noise, "See you in a bit, darlin'!"

He then dug out and headed for some practice laps on the track, leaving Candy and Sheree together. "How long you known J.D.?" Sheree asked.

"About four hours," Candy said. "He seems pretty nice. How long have you known him?"

Sheree smiled. "About twenty years."

"Twenty years! You kidding?"

"Nope. It's been about that long," Sheree assured her. "And you're right. He is pretty nice."

"So's your guy. Wow!" Candy said quietly.

After a moment, Candy shook her head and started to laugh. "That's really something, knowing someone that long. That's like my whole life."

Sheree looked over to Ray with a "help me!" expression. Ray chuckled quietly to himself as he started putting his bike away.

Ray and Sheree waited around to see J.D. come in second in his heat while they exchanged monosyllabic conversational sound bites with Candy.

As everyone was getting ready to leave, Sheree let Ray know that she wouldn't be able to accompany him to his palatial estate that evening because of inventory at work early the next morning. But she did promise to make it up to him. Having every intention of holding her to that, Ray kissed her as they wished each other a good night.

Ray wondered if Sheree had any idea how much he cared for her. Oh sure, he'd let her know, but sometimes he could be a man of few words and maybe he hadn't quite made it as clear to her as it was to him. She was just so much fun and so easy to be with that he didn't want to think about it too much. It was so nice it was scary. Maybe if he didn't dwell on it or say much out loud, maybe the gods or the fates or whatever had been dumping on him for most of his life wouldn't notice. Maybe he could squeak by and actually be happy for a while. It was worth a try.

With the bike race behind him, Ray now had nothing to preoccupy himself with or prevent him from fantasizing about Monday. One more day to go before not feeling like a loser anymore. He was so ready he could taste it.

As much as he would love it, a restful night's sleep was probably not in his immediate future.

2

RAY'S FATHER, CHARLES JOHNSTON, had been a mailman in Tupelo, Mississippi, when Ray was born. Shortly after that, he packed up his family and moved to Memphis, where he continued to be a mail carrier but for more money.

Life seemed comfortably secure for the Johnstons until the day everyone learned that Charles's social drinking had gotten out of hand. On two different occasions he was found drunk on the job, even leaving mail at the wrong houses, a carrier's biggest sin. The first time carried a warning, the second time cost him his job.

Memphis, in the late 1930s, was not the time or place to be out of work. Nobody was hiring, especially not someone with a proven drinking problem. Ray's mother, Esther, started taking in laundry and anything else she could think of to keep them eating.

Charles looked for work diligently, then went to the bar at the end of the day when he couldn't find anything. He grew steadily more remorseful and saw no way out of his dilemma. He solved these problems for himself by driving his car off a forty-foot cliff. Insurance was a luxury they'd never been able to afford. Ray, age three, and Esther were left with nothing.

Ray grew up a poor kid but it seemed like everyone else was poor, too, so it wasn't that big of a deal. He graduated from high school but never even thought about college. He wasn't that great a student, had no money, and didn't know what he wanted to do anyway.

A bizarre element was added to Ray's life when Elvis Presley started appearing on the scene. No one could help but notice how much they looked alike. The more famous Elvis became, the more Ray was constantly reminded of this similarity.

Every once in a while, it was useful when he was trying to pick up girls but, generally, it was just a pain.

Ray's mother never remarried, had a colorless life of labor, then gradually lost all hold on reality. Although it stressed his meager finances to the bone, Ray had had his mother looked after in a home for nearly a year now. Since she was totally unable to take care of herself from moment to moment, he didn't know what else to do.

Ray was thrilled when he went to work for Covey Lumber Company. He worked there for fifteen years and would have been happy to have stayed there his whole working life. However, a big, mega-conglomerate came along and bought Covey and about ten other small lumberyards and turned them into one huge lumberyard chain, which lasted about two years before the whole thing went belly-up.

It was lose-lose. The big guys who'd never gotten it right lost everything. But then, so did all the people that worked for the little local yards that had been doing just fine. Ray had a tough time with that one. It just never seemed right.

Sunday, March 27, 1977

The sun through the window carved a bright slash across the floor, showing children's blocks being placed slowly, carefully on top of one another. The structure being created was precarious but did not fall. It was, however, getting dangerously high and teetering. The shadow of a hand coming to save it crossed over the blocks but stopped short. The blocks continued to weave. The hand poised above it all hovered, unmoving.

The battle was eventually won by gravity. The tower came tumbling down. The blocks cascaded from their heights, an avalanche crashing into itself on its way to the floor.

The poised hand remained there only a moment longer before it began, systematically, assembling and restacking the blocks.

The underpinnings of yet another block megatower were in place and starting to climb when the door opened.

"Oh, excuse me, Mr. Johnston," said Stephanie, one of the caregivers, as she stepped inside. "I just wondered why her door was closed."

"Just some quiet time with Mom," Ray said, looking down at the eighty-two-year-old woman playing on the floor.

"She surely does love those blocks."

"I was hoping she'd develop some interests in here. This wasn't exactly what I had in mind."

Stephanie laughed. "At this stage of dementia, these people plot their own course. All we can do is keep them as comfortable as we can on their journey."

"Well, thanks for it all," Ray said, standing. "I'd better hit it."

"It's ice-cream time. Would you like to stay for some?"

"Not today, thanks."

"How about you, Mrs. Sharp?" Stephanie asked the ninety-year-old woman who shared the room with Ray's mom. Mrs. Sharp lay in her bed and stared at the ceiling like she had for the past two years. Ray had never seen her with a visitor. She blinked a couple of times but made no other acknowledgment.

"I'll bet you'd like some, wouldn't you, Esther?" Stephanie said, leaning closer to the old lady with the blocks. "Are you ready for some ice cream?"

Esther looked up at her and gave a vacant grin at hearing her two favorite words. It was the first reaction Ray'd seen that day.

Stephanie helped the woman off the floor. Ray came over and kissed his mother on the forehead. "I love you, Mom. See you in a few days."

With the help of Stephanie and a walker, Esther was already out the door, unaware that anything had been done or said. Ray followed slowly behind. Mrs. Sharp stared at the ceiling.

"By the way, Mr. Johnston," Stephanie added, "I won't tell anyone you were here."

Ray nodded his appreciation as Stephanie wheeled his mother down the hall.

An old two-lane road wove through the foothills outside Memphis, Tennessee. A few miles up, a dusty dirt road turned off and ran for about a quarter of a mile to a knoll overlooking the city. Atop this knoll was a light blue trailer in need of paint. This trailer and the one-and-a-half acres of dirt around it was the "palatial estate" of Ray Johnston.

Ray knew that most people wouldn't care for this place but that didn't bother him a bit. He loved it. Just by driving down the country road back to his trailer, he could feel the tensions of the day fall off him. It was the most peaceful place he knew.

Dusk was approaching that late afternoon and the first of the city lights were coming on when Sheree arrived in her white Chevy. Ray was waiting for her exactly where she knew he'd be: outside, sitting in an aluminum lawn chair, tipped back against the trailer, looking out over it all.

He also held a bottle and had a lap full of papers.

"How's your beer?" she asked by way of greeting as she headed into the trailer.

"I'm good."

Sheree soon came back with a beer of her own, sat in the other lawn chair, tipped it back like Ray, and let herself relax. She found his place restful, too.

"Long day, huh?"

"Tell me." After a silent moment, Sheree asked, "How's your mom?"

"The same. Exactly."

"It's too bad she couldn't have seen this place. She would have loved this view."

"She'd also be glad about tomorrow."

"Yeah. I see you've been working on it again," Sheree said, acknowledging the papers. "You in good shape?"

"I've got it so nailed, it's silly. Poetry in hauling."

"So you've got a train full of lumber, five trucks . . ."

"And four hours to load, deliver, and unload. Precision!"

"Why would anyone put themselves in that position?"

"Because whoever planned it was an idiot."

"They should have had you do it."

"Oh yeah. I'm a wonder."

Sheree smiled. "Pretty much a wonder."

Ray was quiet for a while. "This is coming along at just the right time, you know?"

"Things getting a little tight?"

"Oh yeah." She didn't know the half of it. Ray didn't particularly want to get into it right then but he'd probably have to talk about it sooner or later.

"You seem tired," Sheree said after a moment.

"I am. Didn't sleep worth a damn last night. Sure as hell better tonight."

Sheree finished her beer and stood. "Well, c'mon. Let's see if we can find something to eat and get you to bed early."

"Yes, ma'am," Ray said as he got up and looked out over the city. Most of the lights were now on. "I don't think I'll ever get tired of this."

Sheree came to him. Their arms easily went around each other. She appreciated that her tough ol' macho man still had the sensitivity to appreciate things like city lights and was comfortable enough with her to say so. "Love you," she said quietly.

"Love you right back," he said, kissing the top of her head. They walked back toward the trailer door, taking one last look at the sparkling world below them before going inside.

*3

THE SUN SHOWN BRIGHTLY through Ray's bedroom windows. The cloudless day promised another perfect, crisp Tennessee day. Ray, at last, was sleeping soundly. The blanket on the other side of the bed was tucked up under the pillow the way Sheree did when she had to leave before Ray got up.

As Ray rolled over, adjusting his position, he moved right into a shaft of the sun, the glare hitting him in the eyes jolting him awake. He lay there a few moments, half-asleep, before squinting over to see what time it was.

The clock read 10:15.

Ray jerked upright, looked unbelievingly again at the clock, then outside, seeing the day in full swing. He could hardly believe what he was seeing.

"No!" Ray leaped out of bed and started dressing as fast as he could. "Damn it! Damn it! Damn it!"

He bolted for the door, ran to his truck, and dug out the entire way to the paved road, kicking up dust clouds in the air behind him.

As Ray squealed his truck into Thorton Creek's very busy lumberyard, he could see his project well under way. The train was there, two trucks were currently being loaded while two others waited. He was dismayed to see Guy Stubbs supervising it all, carrying Ray's clipboard.

Ray quickly ran over to another man nearby.

"Jer, God, I'm sorry," Ray panted. "You'll never believe . . ."

"You're talking to the wrong man, Ray." The man motioned with his head toward a distant office and moved away from him. Ray's heart sunk further.

Walking over to the office, Ray noticed Guy Stubbs looking at him, smiling broadly. Ray resisted flipping him off or throwing something at him. Instead he entered a door marked ANGUS FERGUSSON.

Angus Fergusson was a gruff, stocky, sixty-two-year old ex-fighter with the personality of a flamethrower. He looked at his watch as Ray entered.

"Mr. Fergusson, please, I am so sorry. I—"

"I was counting on you, Ray."

"Sir, I have been planning so hard for this, I haven't been able to sleep, so—"

"I don't want to hear it," Fergusson said, cutting him off.

"I can't believe this! This is all I've thought about for—"

"You know, I was wondering if you'd find a way to blow this opportunity," Fergusson said quietly. "You're good at that. Actually, I thought you'd finally gotten it together."

"Oh, I have sir. So much. You can't believe how much. "

"And you know what I found out, Ray?" Fergusson asked. "I don't even need you. Stubbs has got this place running like clockwork."

"Of course he does. I had all my notes in my clipboard and he's using them. I had everything planned down to the slightest detail."

"Too bad you weren't here to actually see it work. You're fired, Ray. Get out of here."

"But, sir, really. You can't just—"

"I can and I just did. Go!"

Ray knew it was over. More frustrated than he ever thought possible, Ray left the office slamming the door behind him. There was a slight tinkle of broken glass from the other side. Trying to avoid the looks of the workmen, Ray sped out of the yard as fast as he came in.

After he'd driven a block or two, Ray pulled over to the curb and parked. Where was he going? What was he going to do? He felt numb. He still couldn't believe what had happened. He just sat and stared. As angry and embarrassed as he felt, he also couldn't keep it in. It was too big. Unsure of practically everything, he slowly drove away.

His truck seemed to drive itself to Rusty's, where Sheree worked. He put his head in the back door and asked one of the busboys if he could let Sheree know Ray was out back.

Ray leaned, dejectedly, against the old brick wall of the building until Sheree came out. She was wearing her uniform of black slacks, white shirt, and a bow tie. Ray had always thought she looked sexy in that outfit but his mind was currently light-years away from those desires.

"Are you all right?" Sheree asked, concerned.

"Boy, I wish you would have woken me up this morning."

"I never wake you up. What happened?"

"I was so nervous and excited last night I couldn't sleep," Ray began, pacing around the alley as he spoke. "When it got to be about one, I started to worry. I needed a good night's sleep for today, so I took one of those little pills you take to help you sleep sometimes."

Sheree's face dropped. "My God, Ray, I take those for migraines. They don't put you to sleep, they knock you out."

"I didn't know that."

"You could have asked me."

"You were asleep. I didn't want to bother you."

"I can't believe this," Sheree said, as stressed as Ray.

"I don't even remember turning the alarm off."

"Are you out of work?"

"Oh yeah." That was the one thing Ray was sure of.

"I'm really sorry, honey, but I've got to get back inside. I'll see you later, okay?"

"Yeah."

She gave him a quick kiss, a sympathetic hug, and went back inside to work. Ray hung around the alley for a minute or two before deciding he'd better go home. Hanging around the garbage didn't seem to be helping his spirits any.

Garbage seemed to be what that day was all about. The trashman had been by earlier and left the cans laying out in Ray's drive after he'd emptied them. Ray got out of the truck to put them away. Well, that was the intent. What happened instead was that Ray lost it with the garbage cans. He kicked them, he threw them, he jumped up and down on them, and then he kicked them again for good measure.

Ray had never felt so dumb, so stupid. What the hell was he doing? Was this really going to help anything? After working up a good sweat he picked up a dented can and tried to straighten it out and put it away. But it seemed his cathartic frenzy wasn't quite over yet. Another bout of kicking, throwing, and cursing ensued until Ray'd finally had enough.

He left the cans where they were, went inside, got himself a beer, and went back outside to his "good ol' lawn chair," panting. He leaned back against the trailer and sat there quietly, holding his beer, staring off into the distance. What was wrong with him? Why did he have such a hard time just living? What the hell was he going to do now?

It wasn't supposed to have been this way. As a young man Ray hadn't been strongly attracted to any particular career but there were many that could have been possibilities.

He could have been a mechanic, a coach, a fireman (flat feet had kept him out of the military). He had thought about going to big-rig driving school but had never quite gotten around to it. He wondered if he was too old now? He might want to look into that.

He even toyed around with becoming a cowboy but he really didn't know anything about horses. He decided that probably wasn't a good fit.

Everything had been so perfect for so many years with Covey that he knew how life could and should be and it seemed to be headed back in that direction again with Thorton Creek. Damn it!

Ray was as confused as ever, back to square one, and had hardly moved when J.D. pulled up in front of Ray's trailer a couple of hours later. As he approached, J.D. gave a nearly imperceptible nod. "Ray."

Ray returned an equally effusive nod. "J.D."

J.D. entered the trailer and soon returned with a beer of his own. He grabbed another lawn chair and struck the pose that everyone seemed to end up in around Ray's place, leaning back against the trailer. A few moments passed before he spoke.

"The cans add a 'touch.'"

"Thank you."

After a silent moment, J.D. asked, "Feel better?"

"No."

J.D. nodded. "I understand you're looking for work."

"Never take pills unless you know what the hell they're going to do to you."

J.D. took a swig of his beer. "I guess Fergusson was really pissed."

"That makes two of us."

Sometimes there are just no words but neither man seemed to have trouble with that. They simply continued to sit, sipping their beers in silence.

J.D. and Ray had been friends since high school. They shared an easy-going philosophy and a seemingly ambition-free lifestyle. J.D. had found his occupational calling by almost getting killed.

He and Ray were working construction on a bridge when they were both about twenty-five years old. An iron beam had gotten away from the crane operator who was lifting it. The beam started careening wildly. Before anyone could shout a warning, the beam slammed into J.D., breaking his back.

After months of operations and all sorts of scares about J.D. never moving or walking again, he recovered perfectly.

When J.D. got home from the hospital, he was greeted by a check for twenty-five thousand dollars from the insurance company.

That was a lot of money for a young man to have and it was burning a hole in his pocket. He looked at new Jaguars, fancy pickups, five-hundred-dollar cowboy boots, but ended up doing the smartest thing he ever did in his life.

He bought a bulldozer and learned how to drive it. Now he rented himself and his 'dozer out for better than ten dollars an hour and was booked as far as he could figure. Life was good . . . for J.D.

The two men were probably as close as two friends could be but they were far apart in this aspect. Life had never looked bleaker for Ray. What was going to happen to his mom? He was already behind in payments out there.

For that matter, what was going to happen to him? He still had monthly payments for the land and trailer and he thought he was behind there, too. He wasn't sure, he'd have to check. But if he were to lose his place, God! Well, some things he'd rather not even think about.

J.D. finished his beer and said he was going to have to take off. He'd met a girl that afternoon and had a date but had to swing by his place first. He'd forgotten her name but was sure he'd written it down somewhere. He just wanted to say "hey" and see if there was anything he could do.

"I tell you, the only thing I need right now is a job," Ray said. "You hear of anything, let me know. Okay?"

"You got it," J.D. said as he walked back to his truck and left.

Ray sat and thought for a while before going inside and coming out with his old, beat-up guitar. He sat back down on the lawn chair and began playing lightly like he did when he needed to think, and boy, did he need to right then.

Ray's choice of music had always been the blues. He was an easy, laid-back kinda guy and the music just seemed to fit. Years ago he'd bought an old secondhand Harmony guitar for twenty-five bucks and he was still playing it. He wished he'd gotten his money's worth out of everything the way he had that guitar.

Ray had basically taught himself how to play except for asking occasional questions of friends who knew a couple more chords than he did at the time.

That was another thing Ray liked about the blues; you didn't have to be great to play them. Of course, if you happened to be a wonderful guitar player, like B.B. King or Muddy Waters or folks like that, you could get pretty intricate but it was also possible to play most blues songs with only a handful of chords.

Ray had worked up what he called a "walkin' blues riff," which was basically a variation of an E scale but when it was done to a good rhythm, with some chords thrown in now and then, it sounded pretty darn impressive.

When Ray was thinking or bummed or just wanted to play for the hell of it, he'd play that riff. He played it a lot. Perhaps the comparisons to Elvis that were always being made kept Ray away from rock 'n' roll. He never performed for anyone except sometimes Sheree (she liked his riff).

Mostly, music was just for him. He had a bunch of blues records and would occasionally try to sneak in to see someone like Memphis Slim play.

Ray never tried to belt out a song like Elvis but didn't think he sounded too bad with the blues. He'd gotten in a few discussions with his colored friends who thought of the blues as their personal art form, certainly nothing that a "white boy" like him would be able to understand. As a result, Ray never played for them.

Sometimes he felt like mentioning that rock 'n' roll had mostly been colored until Elvis came along and now this "white boy" was the greatest of them all, but he'd just be inviting more Elvis comparisons and he really didn't need that.

Ray also felt that colored folks weren't the only ones that could hurt. He'd known heartache, had lost what little he had in a divorce, never really knew his daddy, had been broke or damn near it most of his life, had no education to speak of, felt virtually unskilled in most everything, and whenever he got a chance to better himself, somehow or another he'd muck it up. Like today, damn it!

He was constantly reminded that his future prospects were based solely on how many hours he could put in and how many years he could keep working, if he could ever learn to keep a job. Currently, that appeared questionable.

Ray's retirement would probably find him in a cardboard box somewhere. Yeah, Ray figured he had the right to play the blues as well as anyone.

After an introspective hour or so, Ray cleaned up and headed back down to Rusty's.

Rusty's had pool tables, the obligatory TV on behind the bar with the sound turned off (which occasionally got turned up for a football game or fight), served a decent sandwich from a limited menu, but it was first and last a bar. Regulars like Ray and J.D. liked its no-frills, down-home, unpretentious atmosphere. Besides, they poured a good drink at a good price and, of course, there was Sheree.

She had to take care of a few things before she could talk so Ray was left at the bar with Sonny, another of the bartenders and the reason Rusty didn't need to hire a bouncer. Sonny also felt bad for Ray and bought him a drink on the house to show that he meant it. Ray thanked him and sat there nursing it as he mulled over the day and how he had effectively screwed his future. It was real hard not to get depressed.

*4

TEN MINUTES OR SO had passed and Ray was still waiting for Sheree to come back.

"Where'd you say Sheree went?" Ray asked Sonny.

"Just next door. She'll be right back."

It got quiet again. Ray started sinking into the abyss that was his life. He was so lost in his own thoughts that he didn't even notice that the bar's silent TV was showing an Elvis concert. He also didn't notice the man a couple of stools down from him doing double takes. He'd look at the TV, then over to Ray, then back to the TV, back to Ray.

Finally, the man couldn't take it anymore and scooted over to the stool next to Ray.

"Excuse me, but I couldn't help seeing that you . . . I mean, it's really amazing. I suppose you've been told that you look just like . . ."

It probably wasn't the best time for the man to bring that up. Ray spun around and faced him. "Do you mean that I look just like Ray Johnston?" Ray said brusquely. "Well, this is your lucky day, slick, because I just happen to be Ray Johnston."

Ray took the man's hand and shook it a bit too vigorously.

"Do you want my autograph? Maybe drop by Grace-fucking-land and say 'hi' to everybody? That what you had in mind?"

Ray was off his stool by this time, acting much more threatening than the situation called for. Sheree arrived in time to hear most of what was said and quickly went to Ray's side.

"Easy, cowboy. C'mere." She led Ray to an empty corner.

The man at the bar was still shaken. "Jesus, what did I say?" he asked

Sonny. "I was just going to tell him how much he looked like Elvis."

Sonny looked back at the man calmly. "I think he's heard that before."

Over in the corner, Sheree was trying to calm Ray down.

"You okay?" she asked softly.

"Yeah. Sorry."

"Sorry, bullshit!" Sheree said, not quite so softly. "I work here. I'm sorry you lost your job but that's no reason to come in here, be disrespectful, and cause me to lose mine, too! Now sit here and be a good boy, damn it. I'll be off in half an hour."

Ray mumbled an "okay" and sat in the empty corner, opting not to go back to the bar.

Later that night, Ray was once again propped up with his lawn chair back against the trailer. He was deep in thought, staring out at the city lights in the distance, when Sheree came out of the trailer and sat by him.

Ray silently continued to stare off into the night.

"Hey, c'mon!" Sheree said, trying to get Ray's attention. "I can hear those wheels turning in your brain from over here. Where are you?"

After a moment Ray asked, "How old am I?"

"Wow! This messed you up more than I thought."

"Do you remember?" he asked.

"Yeah. Forty-two."

"Damn. That's what I thought."

Sheree wasn't used to seeing Ray like this and it concerned her. When she asked what was going on, he had to think about it. He wasn't used to feeling like this, either. Finally, he thought he might have it figured out.

"You know what it is, Sheree?" Ray asked after a moment. "I'm just tired of being me."

"What are you talking about?"

"Well, look. I'm forty-two years old. I don't have a dime. I get the worst jobs in the world and I can't even hang on to them. I don't know what's going to happen to my mom." Ray paused. He hadn't wanted to tell her this. "And I might even lose my house."

"What?"

"Honey, Mom's payments have been killing me. Then I got curious about how I stood with this place and found out that I'm three months behind here, too. I don't know how much longer I've got. And then, of course, today tops it off."

"Ray, I'm sorry, baby. I didn't realize it was that bad."

"All I have in the world is this trailer and an acre and a half of dirt nobody else wanted, but it's mine, damn it! My goddamn castle. It feels good."

"You haven't lost it yet, Ray. You'll be fine. You know how you are when you decide to do something." Sheree thought quietly for a moment, then took Ray's hand.

"Could I help a little here? I've got some money saved and I know you're good for it."

"Honey, no, really. Please, thank you, but there is no way I'm going to take your money. That was sweet of you, though," Ray said, feeling even lower. "I got myself into this, I'll get myself out."

"You'll get another job. You know that."

He sat, staring for a moment. "It's just so damn sad what I've done with my life. After forty-two years, I have absolutely no future and a present that isn't worth diddly squat, either."

"Thanks a lot."

"Oh, baby, not you," Ray said, taking her hand. "That's part of it. I mean, you should have somebody buying you stuff and traveling around places. You're so much better than anybody around here, it's silly."

"Oh yeah. A thirty-eight-year-old bartender at Rusty's. I'm quite a catch, all right."

"Honey, that's what you do, not who you are." Ray paused. "I'm afraid this is who I am."

"Ray, having your ex-wife take everything didn't exactly help anything."

"Yeah, but see, that's part of it. The stupid choices I make. It's like I have this reverse Midas thing. Everything I touch turns to shit."

"Then keep your hands to yourself."

That brought Ray the first smile of the day. "Fortunately, not everything," he said as he leaned over and gave her a kiss.

Sheree let that sink in before turning to Ray. "Well, I will give you this. You can be a stupid bastard. In case you hadn't noticed, I would rather be with you than anyone, and I mean anyone. And, obviously, I'm not after your money.

"You're just a good guy, Ray," Sheree continued. "Sometimes you forget it and act like an idiot, like tonight, but you are." She stood, looked down on him. "Now, are you going to take me to bed or am I going to have to try to find it all by myself?"

Ray got stiffly to his feet. "I'm sorry, babe. I guess I'm just feeling sorry for myself."

"Losing a job will do that to you," Sheree said, putting her arm around him as they started for the trailer door. "You'll be back. Don't worry about it."

He walked her to the door. "Give me a minute, honey," Ray said and went back outside. He looked at the bright city lights and the full canopy of stars overhead.

"You sure make it look pretty, I'll give you that," Ray said, still looking up. "I guess there's a message here but I sure wish I knew what it was. You're making things pretty damn tough, you know?

"I try to be a good guy. I really do, then life comes and dumps on me again. In case you hadn't noticed, I could use some serious help down here.

"You know, there are an awful lot of people who aren't even trying to be good that are living a hell of a lot better than I am. Are you sure that's the message you want to send? You might want to look into that.

"Sure do want to thank you for Sheree, though. Anything else would also be appreciated, like a job? See what you can do, all right? Good night."

When he went inside, Sheree called from the bathroom. "Are you yelling at God again?"

"Just giving him a memo."

"You watch out for lightning."

Ray turned out the last of the lights. Tomorrow would have to be a better day.

Sheree was a statuesque, full-figured redhead. She was thirty-eight, lived in a rented bungalow, and was doing exactly the same work that she said she would never do—the same thing as her folks—bartending.

Anybody who knew anything at all about Sheree knew that one of her great joys in life was watching *It's a Wonderful Life.*

She was the only person anyone knew who wanted to watch it even when it wasn't Christmas. She identified totally with George Bailey. Hell, sometimes she felt like she *was* him. Her angel just hadn't shown up yet, that was all.

Like George Bailey, she had wanted to get an education, travel, and see the world. Maybe be a photographer. Actually, that was always a dream. She didn't really expect that, but what she did expect was to maybe be a secretary for some big shot in a really neat office, or to sell clothes in a fancy dress shop. You know, something classy.

Her family was a poor one, so going to college was going to be a problem. Sheree hadn't anticipated the biggest problem coming from her little sister, Amy. Amy was an artist and a damn good one. Everyone said the kid had talent.

Amy was a junior in high school when the scholarship offers started coming in. Sheree didn't get any offers. Like the Baileys, Sheree and her family decided to let Amy take advantage of the scholarships and go to school first. Since they just covered school expenses, not living expenses, they all decided they'd chip in and help support her while she was there. The plan was that Amy would then do the same for Sheree.

Amy graduated. She also got married that same week, was pregnant a month later, moved to the suburbs, and never used her education or her talent for anything. Amy said she felt real bad about not helping Sheree, but with a new husband and kids on the way . . . you know how it is.

A year or so later, Sheree's folks started to decline. Her dad had a couple of heart attacks and no one felt he could survive another. Her mother had fallen and broken a hip. She got around with the help of a walker but never quite mastered it. It seemed to be a balance thing with her: the very thing it was supposed to do actually made it tougher for her.

Having been a bartender his whole life, Sheree's dad didn't exactly have a cushy retirement set up. If it wasn't for Social Security and Sheree, they would have starved. Amy would have loved to help but she had another little one on the way and her husband just started a new job. It didn't pay real well but had great potential.

Sheree took care of herself and her folks the only way she knew how, in a bar.

She had a short marriage years ago with a charismatic cowboy trucker. Although Sheree had the distinction of being his wife, she soon learned that she certainly did not have any sole propriety as far as his female company went.

"You got a girl in every city in this country, don't you!"

"Hell no. I ain't been in every city."

It was an old joke but, unfortunately, it still contained the truth. The marriage ended badly, she got nothing, and her folks were still failing. Double shifts kept them all alive for years.

Her folks died a few years ago, three months apart. Amy said the timing sure was bad because she and her husband were just where they could have started to help some financially.

Sheree resisted the impulse to pull her sister's hair out. Ever since then, their reunions had been sparse.

She was basically a happy person, if a little resigned. Like Ray, she wanted to do more and be more but found herself approaching middle age without really being qualified to do anything but build a good drink.

It was a frustrating time for them both. Two middle-aged kids still dreaming and trying to figure out what they were going to be when they grew up.

5

RAY WOKE UP BEFORE Sheree the next morning, propped up his pillow, and lay in bed for a while, considering his options. He wished he hadn't blurted out all his troubles and insecurities like he had. He knew it bothered her when he was upset. He had meant what he said, though. He did feel like a flat-out failure.

Ray looked out the small window of his bedroom to a gray, naked sky. It would be nice to plant a tree out there sometime, he thought. But then he also realized that that wouldn't be happening soon. It had never occurred to Ray before but just the act of planting a tree implied the feeling, or at least the hope, that the planter would be around to see it grow. Faith and permanence, two feelings very alien to Ray at the moment.

When he got his mind back to his immediate future, like what to do next, it was really quite simple. He had to get another job as soon as he could and cut down on expenses. Since he was already living quite frugally, he had to think about that a bit more.

He usually used the high-octane gas in his truck. That's something he'd change. The truck pinged a little with the cheaper regular but it would just have to ping. That was a couple of dollars right there.

He was also going to try making more of his meals. He imagined that even hamburgers would be cheaper if he made them himself.

He also had to face the realization that his mom was never going to get better or leave that nursing home alive. He'd never wanted to think of it as bluntly as that but this was a time for realism, not hopes.

When Ray moved his mom out of her apartment and into the home, he'd put her stuff in a storage room that cost twenty dollars a month.

There was a real finality about clearing out and getting rid of her belongings but, realistically, she was never going to need any of it again. It just might be time to close it out.

Later that morning, Ray and Sheree talked about it all over a cup of coffee in his booth-type table in the kitchen. Sheree agreed with his assessments and offered to help any way she could. In fact, if he needed help with his mom's stuff, today was her day off. Did he want to act that quickly?

Ray thought that was a hell of an idea and jumped at it before she had a chance to change her mind. They made a quick breakfast, drove by Sheree's place so she could change into some grubs, and headed down to the storage room.

Ray hadn't really edited much at all when he put his mom's stuff in there. His thoughts at the time were much more on her and there was always the outside chance that she might get better. At this point, however, he didn't even feel guilty as he opened the storage unit and began assessing where to start. It was amazing how much worthless, unadulterated rubbish one accumulated during a life.

Equally amazing was how much one could pile into a four-by-eight-foot room. They were on the second story of a three-story building that consisted of corridor after corridor of doors leading to various-size storage units. Fortunately, no one else was using their particular corridor that day so they were able to take boxes out of the cramped room and go through them out there.

Soon piles were made to be thrown away, to be given away, a pile for Sheree (napkins, vases, and some jewelry), and a much smaller pile of keepsakes that Ray would like to hang on to.

Deep into the process, Ray noticed that Sheree was spending a lot of time with one particular box.

"What have you got there?" he asked.

"Books."

"Must be old. Mom wasn't much of a reader."

"Did you know she was a writer?"

"What?"

Sheree lifted up two cardboard-bound books. "They're journals, Ray. Your mom used to keep journals. These are from 1932 to around '35."

"I was born right in there."

"Do you want them?"

"I don't see why."

"Oh, they could be great fun. Do you mind if I look through them?

"Have at it."

Sheree set the journals aside and they both returned to the task at hand. They were only about halfway through what had already turned into a more daunting project than either had anticipated.

"You know, I really do want to thank you, honey," Ray said after a few minutes. "This helps so much."

"Hey, it's fun. A tromp down memory lane," she said as she put on one of Ray's mom's old hats, which looked quite silly on her.

"Cute."

"Seriously, babe, I'm glad I can help. I'd hate for you to be doing this alone. It's just too . . ." She suddenly stopped. "Wait a minute." She had found an old photo. "Oh my God!"

Ray looked up. "What?"

Sheree started to laugh. "You must have been about two! Look at that cute little butt. I'd know it anywhere."

"Let me see," Ray said, leaning over a couple of boxes to get closer. She held it up for him. Ray cringed.

"Sheree," he said seriously, "if anyone in the world ever sees that picture, I'm never speaking to you again. That's a promise. Never!"

Sheree was still laughing. "I've got a frame that's just perfect for this."

"Oh, no you don't," Ray said as he jumped over the boxes and tried to grab the picture from her. She squealed and ran down the corridor with Ray running after her.

A brief respite from the other half of the storage room, which still had to be dealt with.

Wednesday, March 30, 1977

Sheree awoke before Ray the next morning. Since she didn't have to be at work until later, she made a pot of coffee and settled down in the living room with Ray's mother's journals. The old lady had been pretty far gone when Sheree arrived on the scene so she'd never gotten a chance to know what kind of a woman Ray's mom had actually been. Sheree found herself greatly looking forward to what she might find as she got comfortable on the couch and started reading.

It was over an hour later by the time Ray finally got up and walked out of the bedroom and headed straight for the coffee, half-asleep. His hair was messed up and his morning stubble prominent.

Sheree was still on the couch, deeply involved with the journals.

"You're up bright and early."

Sheree looked up at him, unsure exactly what to say. After a moment, she just decided to go for it. "Did you know your mother had a miscarriage?"

"Had three of them, I think. Doctor told her not even to try anymore. Kinda glad she gave it one last shot."

Sheree gave him that apprehensive look again. "I'm not sure she did."

"What do you mean?"

"Are you awake enough to read?"

Ray sat down beside her. "What have you got there?"

Sheree turned back to a page in the journal that she had marked with a piece of paper. She handed it to Ray, pointed to a section. "There. About halfway down."

Ray started reading.

Friday, Dec. 21, 1934

I had another miscarriage yesterday. I talked with a nurse named Florence about adoption. She's all for it.

Earlier that day a young boy had died for no reason except that his parents were too poor and dumb to give him any medical attention until it was too late. That sort of thing happens all the time down there, Florence said. She was furious. She said her motto was "If you can't feed them, don't breed them."

She'll see what she can do for us.

Ray finished the page. Took another sip of his coffee. "That it?"

"There's more a couple pages on," she said as she reached over and turned to another page she'd marked with paper. "There."

Ray started reading again. Sheree watched him intently.

Tuesday, Jan. 8, 1935

Hallelujah! We have a son! Nurse Florence, who is also midwife, called earlier and asked if we would like to adopt a baby. It seems Florence was helping this unfortuante woman, giving birth alone in this two-room shack while her husband was out drinking. They were much too poor to support the child and wanted to give it to a worthy family. That's us!

She asked us to come down right then and to go to the back door of the hospital. She was doing us a favor by skipping all the red tape, forms and all, but if anyone ever asks, we have to say that we'd done all that. I guess she could get in trouble.

We are both thrilled. We have our boy! We're naming him Raymond Edward Johnston.

When Ray finished reading, he slowly lay the journal back on his lap. "I'm adopted."

"You didn't have any idea about this?"

"Not a clue."

"Wow."

"Yeah."

Ray stared into nothing, stunned.

6

RAY FELT LIKE HE was sleepwalking as he showered and shaved that morning. His mind never strayed far beyond the revelation that he wasn't who he thought he was. Then who was he?

He didn't even know how he should feel about it. Angry? Deceived? Grateful to the Johnstons for taking him in and raising him as their own? Mad at them for not letting him know?

The only feeling he was sure of was that of total confusion. Like a rug had been pulled out from under him. No stability. The foundation he always thought he had was gone.

Even in the worst of times, he could always rely on his nature. He knew what kind of a man he was. But . . . what kind of a man was he really? Whose blood was coursing through his veins? That, suddenly, was a mystery. Basic stuff.

Sheree went off to work, leaving Ray to decide in what order he wanted to get on with his life. He decided a trip to see Mom would start it out.

She was in her usual place on the floor when he got there, playing with the blocks. The only change was the rather comic addition of basketball knee pads that were put on over the pajamas that she always wore. Sliding around on the carpet so much was evidently giving her knee burns. Ray had to laugh but it was a good solution.

As usual, his arrival went ignored. He sat down and started talking like he always did. He told her about losing his job and that he'd start looking for another when he left there.

"Don't know what I keep doing wrong, Mom. It'd be a lot easier if I'd just get one and keep it, wouldn't it? Maybe I'll give that a try this time."

The end of Ray's thought was punctuated by the crashing of another mighty tower. Esther scooted around on her new knee pads, gathering the blocks to start yet another.

"Cleaned out your storage room yesterday. Didn't think you'd mind. Ran across some journals you'd written a long time ago. I didn't know you ever wrote journals, but then, I never knew I was adopted, either. I sure would liked to have known that, Mom.

"I know you usually don't tell little kids that right away but I haven't been a little kid for a long time. It would have been a good thing for you to do."

Esther continued with her task, seemingly unaware of anything or anyone.

"You used to say that we didn't talk enough. Boy, I wish we could talk now. Hey, you wanted to talk, you could have brought up the subject. You sure could have gotten talk."

Ray felt himself starting to get irritated and knew that that would accomplish nothing. He stood up and went to the door.

"Well, hang in there," he paused, "Esther. I'll see you soon."

Ray left the room feeling worse than when he'd arrived. He headed for the closest exit, hoping he wouldn't see anyone who worked there, when Mrs. Flatt, the manager of LifeCare, came around the corner. His heart sank.

"Mr. Johnston, good, I heard you were here. Could you come into my office, please." Not waiting for a response, she entered a nearby room and was already seated behind her desk looking at a folder when Ray followed.

"Mr. Johnston, I believe that you've been notified that you are three months in arrears in your mother's payment schedule—"

"Now, I made a payment just the other day," Ray interrupted.

"Yes. My apologies, Mr. Johnston. A partial payment was indeed received. That makes you two and a half months behind. You must realize that as much as we love Esther, we are not a charity. We get no help from the government or any other services. We rely solely on our allocated payments, your payments, Mr. Johnston."

"I know, Mrs. Flatt. I'm in the middle of some of the worst luck I've ever had. I thought I had it licked, but it didn't work out. I am looking, Mrs. Flatt. I truly am."

"I'm sure you are but I'm also sure you realize that good intentions are not going to care for your mother. As cold as this sounds, Mr. Johnston, it's not what you try to do or want to do, it's what you actually do that I'm interested in.

"We need a payment very soon," Mrs. Flatt stressed. "I don't think you'd be pleased with the alternative."

Ray stood, feeling like his hands had been slapped, thanked Mrs. Flatt, and assured her that she would be receiving a payment shortly. The how would be worked out later.

Ray got out of there as quickly as possible. He was very aware that the "alternative" she'd spoken of was the county loony bin. Ray had gone down to check it out before putting his mom in LifeCare but couldn't get past the chipped door of the run-down building. The sounds coming from inside scared the hell out of him. His mom, even if she wasn't biologically his mom, wasn't going in there.

Ray was having a hard time breathing. He walked around the parking lot a few minutes. When he felt a bit better, he got in his truck and took off in pursuit of a job that would hopefully solve all, or at least, a good bunch of his problems.

Nothing, it seemed, was going to be easy. The tone had been set with his first inquiry and continued practically identically to his fourth.

Bob was a contractor and old friend of Ray's. The men had always liked and respected each other. Ray thought that surely he'd have something. That was, of course, until he asked him.

"I'm sorry, Ray," Bob said. "I know you're a good man but I'm having trouble keeping the guys busy that I got."

"That seems to be the way it is," Ray said.

"Have you tried Sanchez?"

"He's in the same boat."

"Then I don't know what to tell you, buddy. If something comes up, you're on the list, but who knows when that might be, you know?"

"Yeah. Well, thanks, Bob."

"Sorry. Good luck." Bob went back into his office. Ray went home.

Ray was an emotional mess by the time he pulled into his place. It was too cold to sit out on the lawn chair, which always made him feel better, so he was forced inside. The first things he saw were the journals. He sat down and started reading the marked spots again.

When he finished, he tried to shift gears and get after some chores that needed doing but couldn't get into it. This whole adoption thing was hard to get his mind off. Well, maybe he shouldn't even try. He thought for a few minutes longer, then reached for the phone.

Two hours later he was at the bar in Rusty's talking to Sheree, who was on duty.

"Nothing, huh?" she asked sympathetically.

"Went to four places this morning. Guys I'd worked with over the years, but no. Nothing."

Sheree acknowledged the papers in front of Ray. "What's all this?"

"Well, this being adopted stuff kinda hit me. I mean, if my folks weren't my folks, I'd like to know who were. So I decided to see what I could find out." Ray had made some phone calls and looked over his notes. "There was only one hospital in Tupelo in 1935. They said records could be released to the person who the records are about. That's me. I'm going down there."

"When?"

"Oh, now. Might as well. It's only about a hundred miles. I'll be back tonight."

"Great. Let me know what you find."

"You know I will." He stood. "I'd kiss you but you're on duty."

Sheree looked furtively around, grabbed Ray by the shirt front, pulled him to her, and kissed him. "You drive carefully."

"Yes, ma'am," Ray said as he gathered his papers and left. Both he and Sheree were glad he was looking into this but neither knew what to even hope for as far as what he might find.

It had probably only been about forty minutes that Ray had been waiting but there was just something about hospital waiting rooms that made time seem to crawl. He had already read half the jokes in the two-year-old *Reader's Digest* that was sitting on the end table when he looked up at the people and the room surrounding him. He decided to go back to the jokes.

Ten minutes later a young clerk in his shirtsleeves and tie came over to Ray. "Mr. Johnston?" he asked.

"Yes."

"This way, please." He led him behind a counter to a ridiculously small office in the back. There was barely room for the desk, which was much too large for the office, and the two chairs they also managed to cram in. The clerk sat in one, Ray tried to fold himself into the other.

"We have your records right here," the clerk began. "Raymond Edward Johnston, son of Charles and Esther Johnston, January 8, 1935." The clerk then, proudly, handed Ray a small card containing that information.

Ray looked at it blankly. "That's it?"

"You wanted your birth record," the clerk said. "There it is."

Ray didn't quite know how to proceed. After faltering a moment, he said, "Well, actually, there's a chance that I was adopted. How would I find out about that?"

The clerk looked at his copies of the records. "There's no sign of adoption here. As far as the state of Mississippi is concerned, you're the natural son of the people on the card."

Ray thought a moment. He had not anticipated this at all.

"Could we see if Esther Johnston ever actually checked into the hospital around then to have her baby. Me? or maybe she had me at home?"

"I wouldn't have records like that," the clerk stated.

"Who would?"

"Probably Archives, but they don't release records."

"Could I talk to them?"

"They also don't deal with the public."

Stymied and frustrated, Ray thanked the clerk and left.

7

Wednesday, March 30, 1977

SHEREE CAME OVER TO Ray's after work that night to hear what he'd found out in Tupelo. They relaxed in Ray's small living room with a couple of beers as he related the frustrating tale.

"So then I went over to the adoption place and had them look up their records," Ray was saying. "Nothing there, either."

"It really sounded illegal, your folks coming to the back door of the hospital and everything. There might not be any records."

Ray sat back in the couch, thinking. That's exactly what he was afraid of. "I wish I could know everything that happened there that day. Maybe we could piece it together. I wonder if records like that even exist."

"I'll bet a cop could get them," Sheree said. "I wish I knew one real well."

They both sat quietly for a while. Yeah, Ray was thinking, he'd bet a cop could get those records, too. Now, what could he do about that?

Thursday, March 31, 1977

The next morning, after Sheree had left, Ray was pacing about his trailer in his underwear, sipping coffee, working on a script he'd been writing in his head all night. He felt self-conscious and nervous about what he was planning. He'd never done anything like this before but it just might work.

He was starting to get down on himself for being a coward, so he figured he'd better get on with it. It was now or never. He sat down by the phone, tried to compose himself, and dialed.

"Tupelo Hospital," the voice at the other end of the line said.

"Uh, Archives, please."

"One moment."

Ray cleared his throat and got himself as ready as he could while the operator switched him over.

"Archives," a young female voice said after a moment.

Ray took a big breath and went into his act. "Now, look! This is Sergeant Bailey from the Memphis police and I'm tired of getting the runaround," Ray said as gruffly as he could make himself sound.

"You're the fourth person I've talked to and if I don't get some help I'll have to bring in your local law enforcement and that can get pretty damn sticky. Are you listening?"

"Yes, sir," the young lady replied, "I'll help you if I can."

"Thank you. I like you already, miss," Ray said. "We've got a case of mistaken identity, possible illegal adoption, and a whole can of worms I won't bore you with. I need to know everything that went on that had anything to do with maternity on the date of January 8, 1935. Births, stillborns, everything."

"I can give you what the records say, sir, but I don't know how complete they'll be from that far back."

"That's all right. Don't worry about it. Just give me what you've got."

"I probably won't be able to get that for you until Monday. Is that all right, sir?"

"If that's the best you can do, I'll deal with it."

"Will you be picking these up yourself, sir?"

"Uh, no." Ray tensed up. He hadn't even thought about that. If he went in to get them, she would know immediately that he wasn't a cop. He looked around, trying to get a clue as to what to say.

His eyes settled on the morning paper, the *Examiner*, and the headlines: "Blue Flu Strikes."

"Uh, a Mr. Blue will be by. He's our, uh, examiner."

"Fine, sir. Will that be all?" the clerk asked.

"Yes, I think that will . . ." Suddenly another thought hit him. As long as she's willing and able to look info like this up . . . "Wait. There is one more thing, if you wouldn't mind. Could you see if a Mrs. Esther Johnston was admitted to the hospital within a couple days of that date?"

"Esther Johnston? Yes sir, I can do that."

"Thank you very much, miss. I appreciate it."

Ray hung up, took a big breath, and grinned. That was pretty good. He pulled it off. He stood and walked around, suddenly feeling much better. He finally did something that actually worked. He wished someone was there to share it with.

Ah well. What was he going to do until Monday?

The answer to that turned out to be not a whole hell of a lot. Friday and Saturday were spent, fruitlessly, looking for work. Sunday was chores. He had a small butane leak at the trailer that he had to fix and Sheree needed a cupboard door rehung.

About this time, Ray needed a diversion badly. He managed to scrape together enough change for a couple of tickets and took Sheree to the movies. It certainly was no big deal but it was nice for them to feel like they were out steppin'.

Ray tried not to think about what the next week would bring or put too much pressure on it. There was enough already. Sunday had already lost any luster it was supposed to have. He could do nothing whenever he wanted to now. Sunday was just a day when there was no chance at all that he would find work. And as for talking to God, he certainly didn't need Sunday or a church to do that.

Monday, April 4, 1977

Before driving to Tupelo that morning to get his records, Ray tried to put together a wardrobe indicative of an "examiner," whatever that would be. A suit would have been good if he'd had one. Choices were severely limited by his personal wardrobe. What he ended up with was his only pair of nonjeans slacks, a sport coat that was a bit too tight, and a tie that didn't quite work with anything.

Once there, he tried to look and act his most official best as he asked directions and finally found a door marked Archives. Inside a young girl was behind a desk surrounded by bookshelves filled with labeled boxes. She was typing intently when he entered.

"I am Mr. Blue from the Memphis Police Department," Ray said in his best *Dragnet* voice. "Do you have our records ready?"

The girl pivoted in her chair from her typewriter to a folder, hardly glancing at Ray at all. "Sure. First off, that lady the sergeant mentioned, Esther Johnston, was admitted a few weeks earlier with a miscarriage but was never checked into the hospital after that."

That was certainly what Ray expected but it was still startling to know it for sure. It also hit him strange that no one noticed that a woman who had had a miscarriage was credited with having a natural-born child weeks later.

"This is kinda neat," the young girl said, opening the file. "It was a fun day to look up, as it turned out, because . . ."

For the first time the girl looked up and actually saw Ray. She froze.

"What?" Ray asked, wondering why she stopped so suddenly.

"You're not him, are you?" she asked, not taking her eyes off Ray.

"Who?"

"You know, Elvis."

"Oh, right, I'm sure," Ray said. Not this again.

"Well, you really look like him and he was born here, too. Actually, the day y'all asked for, January 8. It's his birthday!"

Ray just stared.

8

Monday, April 4, 1977

RAY'S MIND WAS RACING a mile a minute as he drove back to Memphis that afternoon. The information of that day in 1935 had given him much more than he'd bargained for, but it'd also accomplished what he'd hoped. By seeing the events of the day, it was not difficult to figure out what happened. It's just that the conclusions were so startling!

The moment Ray got home he called Sheree and asked her to come over immediately. She started asking questions but he would have none of it. "Come over, now!"

It took her twenty minutes to get to Ray's place, during which he was reading, checking, figuring, and pacing. He was already a wreck by the time Sheree got there.

Sheree knocked twice, then let herself in, as she usually did. Ray was in the center of the floor, still pacing.

"Hi. What's so important?" Sheree said as she came up and gave him a quick kiss hello. "What'd you learn?"

Ray asked her to sit down. "Now, don't get all excited and make this a big deal or anything because I don't—"

"Oh, you can get excited but I can't?"

"I'm not getting excited! I'm just—"

"Are you kidding?" Sheree interrupted. "You're more excited than I've ever—"

"Do you want to hear what I've got to tell you?" Ray topped.

"Sure," Sheree said as she sat down demurely and waited. "Fire."

"Okay," Ray began, resuming his pacing. "There's a chance, an outside, really weird chance." He paused. "That I might be Elvis's twin brother."

Both were silent for a long moment.

"What did you find?" Sheree asked softly.

Ray got the folder from the table and sat down next to Sheree. "In 1935, Tupelo wasn't that big a place," he began. "There wasn't much going on in the maternity ward, so everything was pretty easy to track.

"Actually, the only thing going on that morning," Ray continued, pointing to corroborating documents as he talked. "Was when a Mrs. Townsend had a still-born baby boy at 7:30 AM.

"Here's where it gets weird," Ray said, pausing to get his breath. "Also sometime that morning, in a home birth, Vernon and Gladys Presley gave birth to a son, Elvis Aron Presley and a still-born male twin they had named Jesse Garon Presley. Now, what do you suppose the odds are of a little, podunk town like that having two stillborns in the same morning?" Ray let that settle in for a moment, excitement creeping back into his voice. "Plus, there was no record of an Esther Johnston checked into the hospital any time that week when she was supposed to have been having me. And God knows, I do look like Elvis."

"Wow" was all Sheree could say as the implications started to come to her. "That's too many coincidences, isn't it?"

"Yeah."

"What do you think happened?"

"That's what I've been trying to figure. Nobody mentioned a midwife but that might not be in the records anyway. A lot of people used them back then, especially if they were too poor to afford a doctor."

"And the Presleys were really poor, weren't they?"

"I heard so."

"Remember your mom wrote about how mad that nurse got at poor people having children they couldn't take care of?"

"Yeah, the one who was also a midwife. You can just imagine how poor the Presleys must have looked that morning in their two room shack." Ray paused but then had to say out loud what he'd been thinking. "I don't know exactly how, but I'll bet the Presleys ended up with the Townsend's stillborn while I was being shuttled off to the Johnston's."

"Wow" was all Sheree could say.

They looked at each other for a moment, trying to fathom what it all meant. Ray had asked Sheree over primarily to ask this next question. He didn't have a clue. "What do I do now?"

Ray and Sheree spent the rest of the day musing over the ramifications of this rather stupendous news. Try as they would, now and then, to shift the conversation toward some other subject, it never lasted. No matter what they chose to talk about, they always ended up back on Elvis. It was becoming increasingly obvious to both of them that the possibility of Ray and Elvis being brothers, quite simply, changed everything.

The twin brother of Elvis Presley. Ray could hardly believe it, even with the plausible evidence. He'd spent most of his life trying to get others to forget how much he looked like Elvis. He sensed all that was about to change.

Being the twin brother-thought-dead of the most famous man in the world would make Ray rather an instant celebrity, too, wouldn't it? He wondered if they'd want him to sing. He might have to practice a song or two and maybe work on his riff some. Why couldn't Elvis Presley's brother be a blues singer? It could happen.

But would he like being famous? Having everyone know his business, not being able to lead the quiet life he now enjoyed, and if he did something wrong, to have it plastered on every newspaper in the country? He had never really thought about being famous but now that it was a possibility, he wasn't sure that he wanted it.

Of course, he could easily avoid the whole issue simply by not telling anyone about what he learned, but that didn't seem right, either. It was just too big to sit on. Sure, it would probably change everything but Ray just might have to deal with that. It was just . . . too big!

He also had to think of how Elvis would react to this. Welcome him? Resent him? And what about Vernon Presley, who would actually be Ray's dad? What was he going to say?

As curious as Ray was about these questions, he wasn't looking forward to getting face-to-face with Elvis and telling him all this. Twins or not, Elvis was still Elvis and even thinking about being in the same room with him made Ray feel nervous.

These grandiose possibilities seemed light-years away from Ray's current station in life; out of work, in debt, flat broke. Sure, Ray thought sarcastically, Elvis would love having a brother like him.

The evening warmed up a bit so Ray and Sheree got a couple of beers and went outside to their favorite places, propped up against the trailer and looking out over the world.

"It's been kind of an amazing couple of days for you, hasn't it?" Sheree asked after a contemplative moment.

"Only changed everything."

"It's enough to find out you're adopted, but to learn that you might actually be the brother of Elvis Presley. My God!"

"Funny," Ray said. "Yesterday, I didn't think anything could be bigger than me blowing the best business opportunity I've had in fifteen years. It's still a biggie, but I think this tops it."

"Are you going to tell Elvis?" Sheree asked.

"That I lost my job? No, I don't think so."

Sheree gave him a playful slap on the shoulder.

"I suppose I should, shouldn't I?" Ray said, then laughed nervously. "Right," he continued. "And just how, exactly, am I going to do that?"

"He might be thrilled, Ray."

"He might."

"Maybe invite you over for some brotherly chats."

"Maybe I could invite him out here for a barbeque? It's . . . almost Graceland."

"Sure, and you could go see some concerts."

"I don't know," Ray said, playing along with her. "If I have time, of course. I might be busy."

Sheree laughed. "Oh, c'mon. You can make some time for Elvis. Your own brother!"

"Well, since you put it that way . . ." Ray's fantasy was broken by the ringing of the phone in the trailer. He went inside to answer it while Sheree stayed outside, trying to fathom what could happen next.

Ray soon reappeared in the doorway. The twinkle he had when he entered was gone.

"Mom died."

9

WHAT WAS IT ABOUT death? We're all aware that nobody gets out of here alive, so why was it that nobody ever planned for it? Actually, Ray supposed there were people who did plan ahead, just not anybody he knew.

So, here he was, faced with death, trying to figure out how to feel about the whole thing and what to do, when all the technical stuff got dumped on him. Did she have a plot? Of course not. Did she wish to be cremated? He had no idea. Choice of cemetery, et cetera, et cetera? The subject had never been mentioned in Ray's lifetime. He literally didn't have a clue.

And the salesmen, they just gotcha, don't they? Picking out a casket was a unique experience. Various colors, different metals, moisture-proof, dampness-proof, different color linings, pictures painted on the inside. Maybe the whole ordeal was designed to make you forget about the fact that the people aren't really there anymore. They'd checked out. The secondhand body was left behind but was far from caring about the color of the casket lining or looking at a picture. She was dead, for Christ's sake!

Whenever Ray would spend too much time looking at a cheaper model casket that he might actually be able to afford, the salesman would give him a silent look that screamed, *If you're looking at that model it's apparent that you didn't really love your mother very much!*

Ray couldn't decide whether to tell him to stuff it or punch him in the mouth. It was probably for the better that he decided on neither. He ended up buying a midrange coffin, a midrange service, and a plot at the bottom of a rise, forsaking the one on top at twice the money, but with a view. (A view? Did the salesman really say, "She would have liked that"? Actually, yes, he had.) Ray, once again, fought back the impulse to punch him out.

This plot was also closer to his dad's. Ray didn't know for sure how his mom had felt about his dad, all these years later (more of this "not talking"), but he figured he'd put them in proximity of each other and let them deal with it. Even if she never quite got around to forgiving him in life, maybe she could in the hereafter. If not, his dad was in for a bumpy eternity.

Ray finished that morning considerably more in debt than he had been the day before, sad because his mother was dead, also sad that he never had a chance to talk to her about all the weird Elvis stuff, and really pissed off at the funeral business for preying on people when they have no defenses.

The whole process seemed to have nothing to do with his mother and that didn't feel right. It should have all been about her.

Thursday, April 7, 1977

It was a gray, overcast, gloomy day, in keeping with the business at hand. A handful of people attended the graveside service, huddled against the chill around the small casket of Esther Johnston.

Sheree and J.D. stood with Ray next to a minister who had never known Esther Johnston. He skirted that fact by reading generic passages from the Bible dealing with forgiveness, the prospect of heaven, and the promise of eternal life.

On the other side of the minister stood three ladies from LifeCare. Stephanie, the rather large woman who had been Esther's primary caregiver, LuEllen, another aid, and the tenacious Mrs. Flatt.

All in all, Ray felt it was an unsatisfactory service. The minister seemed all right with it, though, as he wrapped up the well-rehearsed spiel, shook hands reverently with everyone, and left.

Ray went over to the LifeCare ladies and thanked them for coming.

"Well, your mother was a sweetie," Stephanie said. "She was never really any trouble at all. We all liked her very much and will miss her."

"Me, too," Ray said, with a knot in his throat. "Thanks again for everything."

As the ladies started walking off, it looked for a moment as if Mrs. Flatt was going to say something to Ray but changed her mind. That was just fine with Ray. The woman had a one-subject vocabulary and he definitely did not want to get into that with her today.

Ray walked back to Sheree and J.D., who asked what he'd like to do now. Was he ready to leave or did he want to stick around for a while? Ray asked them to give him a minute and he'd meet them at the car. They told him to take his time and walked off toward the parking lot.

Ray went over to his mother's casket, still suspended over the pre-dug hole, waiting to be lowered. He stood there a moment, then began speaking softly, intimately. "The minister kinda missed the part about what a wonderful lady you were, didn't he?"

Ray waited another moment before he could continue. "Life dealt you a pretty tough hand, Mom. Loosing Dad so long ago, having to work as hard as you did, then just when you should be able to relax some and enjoy what you'd worked so long for, you find that you've outlived all your friends and your mind gives out. A crummy way to end a life.

"But you were never a complainer. Not you. I hope I can be as good and as strong a person as you were."

Ray paused, looked up into the sleet, trying to collect his thoughts. "I do think we both did our best, Mom. I know you did your best to raise and take care of me and I sure tried to do my best for you. I hope what I did was right and that this place is okay with you."

Ray paused for another moment. "About all this adopted stuff, it's a whole different thing. Whatever happened happened forty-two years ago and you probably never even knew exactly what took place.

"But you know, Mom, it don't matter. It really don't. Not where you're concerned. In my heart, my mind, and my life, you are my mom and you always will be.

"I hope there are angels in heaven and that one of them has her arms wrapped around you right now. Rest well, Mom. I love you."

Ray walked back toward his friends. The lone casket with its frail cargo waited, glistening in the last sunlight it would ever know.

The three friends sat at a back booth in Rusty's for a few hours that evening, reminiscing about Ray's mom.

Growing up, Ray had never had any money but he also had never felt poor. His mother, very creatively, always found ways around it. When Ray as a child would be pestering her in the kitchen, she would make him a treat and send him away with it. She would take a leaf of lettuce, pour a healthy trail of sugar across it, and roll it up like a tube.

Sheree and J.D. made faces and Ray had to admit it didn't sound too appetizing right then but he sure had loved it as a kid. They also used to make water wheels out of sticks and tin cans and set them up in the irrigation ditch. They'd spin all summer.

Stories progressed into the night, only ending when they became more sad than nice. Like the time they were all going to take Mom Johnston out to dinner for her seventy-ninth birthday.

She had put on a new blouse, did her hair, put on earrings, a necklace, and makeup. There was only one small problem when she came into the living room ready to go. She had forgotten to put on a skirt. Her standing there so nicely quaffed on top, but wearing only her panties and shoes was quite a sight.

That was also when Ray realized that she was getting dangerously close to needing more attention and care than he could give her.

They laughed, but it was a gentle, sentimental laughter. She'd had a hard life but had made the most of it. They vowed to try to do the same with their lives.

Ray went home alone that night. A blue folder addressed to him had been stuck in his trailer door. Ray threw it on a chair in the living room, definitely not in the mood to look at it then. Probably just an ad anyway. If anyone knew Ray's situation, they sure as hell wouldn't be sending him any ads. What a waste of money.

It frustrated Ray when he realized he couldn't spend even one night simply mourning his mother without practical day-to-day problems intervening, like this folder, reminding him of how broke he was, but intervene they did.

When his mother had started forgetting things, one of the first things she forgot was to pay the insurance payments when they came due. All her insurance had been canceled years ago. The back payments to LifeCare loomed large, and now there was the funeral (such as it was), the casket, and the plot.

Then he remembered he was only weeks away from losing his home. Damn it, what was he going to do? He went outside and started walking around his dusty hilltop. After a moment, he looked defiantly up to the star-filled sky.

"I want to thank you for taking Mama. She'd been ready for a while. You take care of her, you hear? You gave her a tough life and all she did was worship you and your son. She didn't ask for much and you didn't even give her that. I know all about the 'mysterious ways' bit and maybe you do have a plan, but give her a rest before you do anything else with her, okay? She's been through a lot. Listen to her, she'll tell you."

Ray paused a moment before continuing. "Not much has changed since we last talked and I got to tell you, I'm not real happy. You're kinda beatin' us up down here. Remember we had talked about being nicer to good folks? Well, if you want to start turning this thing around and help people who are, at least, trying to do right, you could start here with me. I could use a little boost right now and 'mysterious ways' don't exactly cut it. You know what I mean?

"Sorry to take this out on you but you're the only father I've ever talked to, and you're supposed to be 'benevolent.' I always thought that meant that you're supposed to act kindly toward people. Well, you sure blew it with Mom, you're not doing a great job with me, and there's a few million other people on this planet who aren't doing real well, either.

"Tell you what, you get busy and I'll get busy, too. Let's see what we can do together. Looks like we both have some work to do." Ray started to leave, then added, "Say good night to Mom for me."

Ray went inside and went to bed.

10

RAY HAD THE HELP wanted section of the classifieds spread out over his kitchen/booth table, the blue folder that had been stuck in his door momentarily forgotten. He was on the phone with what seemed like his thirtieth call.

"No, I don't have any donut-making experience but I sure can learn," Ray was saying, then listened a while, not overjoyed with what he was hearing. "Well, sure. I might be interested in the janitorial position. Please give me a call if that does come open."

Ray hung up disgustedly, wondering who in hell actually had donut-making experience.

He had hardly put down the receiver when the phone rang, causing him to jump. It was Sheree, wondering how the job search was going.

"Oh, just great. Lots of supervisors and managers of stuff I don't know anything about, and I think I'd make a really crappy receptionist."

Sheree laughed and agreed. She basically wanted to check with him to make sure he'd be in that night. She had some good news. Needing some, Ray tried to wheedle it out of her but she stuck to her guns. Later.

As he hung up, Ray noticed the time. Damn. He wasn't looking forward to this. He put on his cleanest dirty shirt and the jeans without the hole and prepared for yet another friendly chat with the abominable Mrs. Flatt.

As Ray was admitted into Mrs. Flatt's office at LifeCare, he wondered if she was ever in a good mood. He even wondered if she was ever even not in a really pissy mood.

"Mr. Johnston, as sorry as we are about your mother, her passing does not alter our agreement in any way," Mrs. Flatt said, getting immediately to the point. "There are now three and a half months of payments outstanding."

"What about the deposit I paid?" Ray asked.

"I explained that at the time. The deposit had nothing to do with monthly payments."

"Mrs. Flatt, my life just got turned upside down, but I'll get things back on track soon. I promise."

"I think that would be a fine idea. As much as I hate to pressure," Mrs. Flatt said while looking over some papers on her desk, "I see here that we could put liens on a 1949 Ford pickup and a 1945 Stratoliner house trailer." She looked harshly at Ray. "Unless we hear from you in a timely manner, we will do just that."

"No, it won't come to that," Ray said, trying to keep the panic out of his voice. "Look, I have a job interview in a few minutes. It won't be long."

"I would hope not," Mrs. Flatt said with an icy stare.

Ray got up and left, mouthing the word "bitch" to himself as he went.

The interview was at Big Sam's used cars and Ray had had the dubious pleasure of talking to Big Sam himself. Ray felt the interview had gone fairly well and was currently waiting by a table containing papers and magazines while big Sam got him an application form.

Ray noticed one particularly tasteless magazine called *Dish*. The cover headline read: "Valley of Space Aliens Discovered." Ray was amazed. Another headline read: "The True Stories of Celebrities' Real Lives. Page Three."

Big Sam, wearing a rather absurd-looking checked suit, arrived back with some papers and noticed what Ray was looking at.

"Can you believe people read that crap?" Big Sam said. "They seem to love it, I guess. They make millions."

Ray put the magazine down and shook his head as Big Sam handed him the papers. "Anywho, here's the forms. Just fill them out and we'll see what we can do. Now, you do realize this is commission only?"

"Yes, sir."

Ray started to leave when Big Sam called to him. "Have you got plenty of good suits?"

"Uh . . . sure."

"Good. We like our boys to look nice around here."

Ray nodded and waved as he walked back toward his truck. On the way, he passed a trash can where he deposited the forms.

Desperate times called for desperate measures. Ray even thought he'd try to get back on the good side of Mr. Fergusson. He figured hearing "no" would be about the worst thing that could happen and he was sure getting used to dealing with that.

Still, Ray was surprisingly nervous as he drove into the lumberyard. He knocked politely on the office door and was told to come in by a voice on the other side.

Mr. Fergusson was working at his desk when Ray walked in and was not particularly pleased to see him. "What the hell are you doing here?"

"Sir, it's been a while since we argued and I just wanted to ask again about a job. You know I really am a good—"

"Shut up!" Fergusson said harshly, cutting him off. "Before I throw you out of here, I'm going to tell you why. Did you know I was voted bowler of the year by the Lumberman's League in 1975?"

"Of course, sir. We were all very happy and proud of you. You got that great trophy." Ray looked over to the wall by the door where the trophy had stood. It was gone.

"Do you remember slamming the door as you left that day, Mr. Johnston?" Mr. Fergusson was glowering at Ray while holding a humorless smile. A strange effect. "Do you know what happens when a fine crystal globe hits the floor, Ray? It shatters."

"Oh sir, I am really sorry. I never meant—"

"In a million goddamn pieces!"

"Really, sir, I—"

"Get out!"

Ray went knowing that hell would indeed freeze over before he'd be working there again.

★ ★ ★

"How would you like to make a hundred dollars?" Sheree asked that evening from the comfort of the lawn chairs.

"Who do you want me to kill?"

"Remember when my cousin Cindy got a job with the *Outlook*?" she continued. "Well, they're hurting for stories."

"Because it's a terrible paper."

"Ray, they'll pay you a hundred bucks if you let her write about you and Elvis."

Ray thought for a moment. "Do you really think I should do that? I mean, I don't know anything for sure."

"Then tell it that way," Sheree said. "They just want your story."

"Well, hell, I guess I could do that. Thank you, darlin'." Ray leaned over and gave her a kiss.

"You're welcome. Just for that, I'll steal one of your beers."

"Steal away," Ray said. Sheree went inside. Ray thought a moment, smiled, then laughed to himself. "I'll be damned."

Wednesday, April 13, 1977

Cindy was twenty-three, overweight, and not particularly attractive except for a pretty smile and the flaming red hair that identified her as Sheree's cousin. She seemed very determined and businesslike, if a little manic, as she set up her old tape recorder on Ray's living room table.

"Thanks so much for doing this, Mr. Johnston," she said. "This is really neat."

"You bet, Cindy," Ray said from the kitchen. "And it's Ray. Sure you don't want some coffee?"

"No thanks. I've already had a bunch," she said, settling back with her pad and pencil. "Well, I'm ready when you are."

Ray grabbed his living room chair, swept the blue folder off it onto the floor, and scooted the chair over to the coffee table, opposite Cindy and her tape recorder. "You just tell me what to do here. I never done this before."

"Just talk to me, that's all. You'll be fine. Okay, let's start at the beginning. Do you remember anything when you were really, really young?"

"Not much. After Tupelo we lived in Boonesville but my dad got a better job here. Better, at least, until he lost it."

"Sheree mentioned your dad had an accident, didn't he?"

"Weren't no accident. Mom said he was a real good driver. He wouldn't of ended up down there if he hadn't meant to. Things were going bad and he couldn't handle it, that's all."

"Where's your mom now?"

"Heaven. She waited tables and did laundry her whole life. Just when it got time for her to relax some, her mind kinda went."

"Oh, that's right," Cindy said, talking note. "Sheree said that just happened. I'm sorry. When do you first remember hearing about Elvis?"

"I don't know. When he started making records, I guess."

"Did people always tell you that you looked like him?"

"Only every day of my life. Especially years ago, Jesus!" Ray laughed, remembering. "Got a little sick of it, to tell you the truth."

"Did you ever wonder about that?"

"No. Some people just look like other people, that's all. Happens all the time."

The interview lasted about two hours. It ended when Cindy ran out of questions and Ray couldn't think of anything else to say. Ray fondled the five twenties reverently as he thanked Cindy and showed her out.

He couldn't help thinking it had been the easiest hundred bucks he'd ever made in his life. That wasn't all he couldn't help thinking about, though. Going through it all over again reminded him what a strong case there was for him being that Jesse. My God, Elvis Presley could really be his brother! Wouldn't that be something! It was still a tough concept to actually believe.

Ray got up to get himself another cup of coffee. On the way to the kitchen, he passed a mirror. His reflection almost startled him, given where his mind had been for the last few hours. He stopped, turned, and studied himself for a moment.

A wave of confidence came over him, which he felt he should act on real quickly before it left. He crossed to the phone, sat down, and dialed. When the information operator answered, Ray wished he'd thought out what to say a little better.

"Uh, I know this is going to sound kinda funny, but do you have a number for Elvis Presley?"

"As in *the* Elvis Presley?" the operator asked.

"Yes, ma'am."

'Well, let's see. We've got an Elvis Fan Club. Would you like that?" the operator asked.

"No. I really need to reach *him*, like in person. I know I can't just call him at Graceland, but—"

"Now, Graceland," the operator interrupted, "I think we have that number."

"Really?"

"Yes sir, and here it is."

Ray could hardly believe it when she gave it to him. He hung up, looked at it a moment, and figured he'd better keep it up while he was on a roll. He took a deep breath and dialed.

"Graceland guard gate," a man answered.

"Yes sir, I wonder if you could get me in touch with Mr. Presley."

"Is he expecting you?"

"No."

"What's your business?"

"Actually, it's a personal matter," Ray explained.

"Then you'll want his personal secretary," the guard told Ray on the phone.

"I don't know how to reach her. Look, there's a chance that I might be his brother! Jesse!"

The guard hesitated on the phone a moment. "I'll save you some time, pal. You know what you'll get from the secretary?"

"What?"

Ray found himself listening to a dial tone. The guard had hung up on him. Ray slammed the phone down in frustration.

*11

SHEREE CAME OVER AND woke Ray up by bonking him on the head with the morning's paper.

"Up and at 'em, sleepyhead. You're on the front page."

That got his attention. Soon they were sitting in the living room with cups of coffee while Ray read the article that had come out that morning. He could hardly believe it. There it was, on the bottom of the front page:

THE GHOST OF GRACELAND
THE JESSE GARON PRESLEY STORY

The article began;

> *An amazing discovery has just been made that could rock the world. It has long been thought that Elvis Presley's twin was stillborn. New evidence is showing that may not have been the case.*

The article went on but Ray had to catch his breath. "The Ghost of Graceland. My God!"

"Kinda catchy," Sheree said, reading over his shoulder. "Looks strange seeing it in print, doesn't it?"

"Real strange. I didn't expect all this."

"Ray, Cindy really thinks you are Jesse Presley."

"I think we're heading in that direction, too, but . . ." Ray paused. "What if Elvis sees this?"

"Then I think you're going to need a better answer than 'somehow baby Jesse got switched.'" Sheree said. "Do you know how that really could have happened?"

"Yeah, I do. I also needed a definite there." Ray thought for a moment. "Nurse Florence had to have talked to Mrs. Presley before the delivery day. I think she knew exactly what she was getting into out there, and everybody knew the Presley's were expecting twins. Vernon was gone to the bar at that time, as fathers-to-be did back then.

"So, it was just Mrs. Presley and Florence, alone at delivery time. I'll bet money that Mrs. Presley lost consciousness during the birth, either naturally or with some help, and woke up with one baby and a stillborn. I'm sure nurse Florence was very sensitive and left Mrs. Presley soon with her new born and her grief. Vernon came back some time after."

"Ray, I'll bet that's exactly what did happen," Sheree said after a moment, amazed. "Wow." Sheree sat silently thinking, then abruptly stood. "I got to go to work. I'll talk to you later." She bent over and kissed him, then stopped in the doorway and looked back, smiling, "It's going to be interesting."

"Yeah."

"Good luck this afternoon."

Ray thanked her as she left. He didn't move much for a while, reading and rereading the article over and over, still having trouble believing it all.

The more he read it and thought about it, the more it made sense. Elvis was going to have to find out about this somehow. Ray thought for a while, then called information again. This time he took the number of the fan club and called them. Maybe he'd have better luck there than with the guard.

"Elvis Presley Fan Club," a young girl's voice answered the phone.

"Hi, this is Ray Johnston. I'd like to get in touch with Elvis, if I could."

"Wouldn't everybody?" the girl replied, laughing.

"No, I mean really seriously. You talk with him, don't you? See him?"

"I wish. We just take care of his fan mail and send out a monthly bulletin. Would you like to be put on the list? I could do that for you. It's really boss!"

"I really need to *talk* to him," Ray tried to clarify. "I'm kind of . . . a relative."

"Really? Oh my God!" Ray suddenly had the girl's attention. "What kind of relative?"

"Well, I might be his twin brother, Jesse."

This information was met with a long pause. When the girl spoke again, the lightness in her voice was gone.

"You know, that's not even funny," she said as hard as she could make it sound and hung up.

Ray put down the phone, frustrated. Damn! There had to be a way.

It was practically noon before Ray got dressed. He was just putting on the finishing touches when J.D. came in the front door, carrying a newspaper.

"Excuse me for interrupting. May I sit down, Mr. Presley, sir?"

"I think you should stand."

J.D. sat. "How about giving us a sample of those golden tones."

"Hey, did you read this or just look at the pictures? This could be true."

"You been smoking them funny cigarettes again? C'mon, I know you."

"What's that supposed to mean?" Ray questioned.

"Forget it. It's all bullshit." J.D.'s level of patience had just been maxed out. "Listen, they got the Scrambles track open again. Want to hit it?"

"Can't do it. Got an interview over at Fields in a few minutes. Looking for drivers, finally! Jesus, I got to get a job." Ray noticed the time. "In fact, I'd better get over there. C'mon."

Ray grabbed a jacket and started to shuttle J.D. out the door when he noticed another headline in the newspaper.

ELVIS TO HELP IN THEATER OPENING TONIGHT
PERSONAL APPEARANCE AT 8:00 P.M.

Ray stopped for a moment, thinking. "What do you think the press would do if I showed up at the same place where Elvis was?"

"Probably go crazy. Why?"

"Just thinking." Ray and J.D. left. Time to take care of the task at hand. But later?

Well, maybe this would be the day that got everything going, Ray thought as he returned home that afternoon. He felt good about his interview with Fields Construction and Elvis appearing at the new theater downtown just might be the place to actually meet him.

Wouldn't it be great if the two biggest concerns in his life could be dealt with in one day? As nervous as Ray was at the prospect of actually coming face-to-face with Elvis, he also knew it would have to eventually come to that, one way or another.

Ray dug through his closet looking for the loudest, most Elvis-like outfit he could put together. He wasn't sure that what he ended up with worked exactly, but his wardrobe and Elvis's weren't even close. His jeans, cowboy boots, and a red shirt someone had given him would have to do.

As Ray was driving down to the theater that night, he realized he didn't have an idea as to what he was going to do. He hoped the situation would take care of itself. With him looking so much like Elvis, somebody with a camera would have to pick up on that. If not, maybe he would have to point it out.

He wondered if it would help if he dyed his hair black and grew some sideburns. He didn't much care for the look, but . . .

Ray parked two blocks from the theater and made sure he had his copy of the article in his pocket before starting to walk over. A stage had been built outside the new theater and the speeches had already begun. Some second-tier celebrities were seated on the stage, waiting their turn to speak.

Elvis was not there, though many signs were around touting the fact that he would be. Ray wasn't worried. Nobody expected Elvis to sit around on a folding chair waiting his turn. No way. He'd show up when it was time, do his thing, and leave. Classy.

Ray worked his way through the crowds to where most of the press and cameras were. So far no one had paid the slightest bit of attention to him. He walked back and forth in front of and around the press people. Nothing. What was wrong with these people? And they call themselves reporters? What were they, blind?

Damn, he was going to have to do something to get it started. He was already embarrassed and he hadn't even done anything yet, but if he could get an introduction out of it, it would be worth it. He was just a guy trying to meet his brother, Elvis. Right.

He pulled the article out of his pocket, took a deep breath, and walked up to a three-man news team with a camera.

"Excuse me. I'd like to introduce myself. I'm Elvis's brother."

"What's that?" one of them said over the noise of the crowd and speakers.

"I'm Elvis's brother," Ray said louder and started to show the man the article.

The man started to laugh and got the other guys to look over at Ray. "This is a new one. We got a blond Elvis."

"Listen, buddy," another one of the crew said, "take it from one who knows; grow the hair, get yourself a dye job, and show some creativity with the clothes. You might have a shot."

Ray then noticed a sign advertising that an Elvis impersonator contest would be held that night, also.

"No, you don't understand. I'm not an impersonator. I might be his brother, Jesse! What I really need is to meet . . ."

Whatever he was trying to say didn't matter. The screams of the crowd had buried Ray's words. Elvis had arrived. Everything else was forgotten.

Elvis stepped on the stage cool and calm, as though he did this sort of thing every day. Ray hid himself in the crowd in the very unlikely chance that Elvis might see him and recognize him. If he wasn't going to get a chance to meet Elvis properly, being seen as a fan in a crowd wasn't the way Ray wanted to start out this relationship.

The cameras were so busy they sounded like a swarm of crickets. As Elvis stepped to the microphone, a hush spread over everyone.

"I want to thank you all for coming tonight," Elvis started out with that unmistakable twang of his. "This here is a good and great cause and I'll tell you why. Bob Neal, who's behind it all, has been my friend forever. There's no finer man in Memphis. And there's no finer theater than this one.

"A *theater,* ladies and gentlemen," Elvis continued. "Now, you never heard this from me, but there is more to life than rock 'n' roll (laughter), and here's where you learn it. Here's where you grow.

"You take good care of Bob Neal and this theater, you hear? And he'll take good care of you, I know that. It's times like these where we all win. Good times.

"Now, you go and enjoy yourselves. Thanks very much for coming out. God bless you."

Elvis left the stage amid cheers, whistles, and screams. It had been short and sweet but nobody seemed disappointed. Even at his heaviest, Elvis could still charm the socks off anyone he chose.

As soon as Elvis left, the news crew started packing up, too. Ray had not made much of an impression, had immediately been forgotten, and was now being ignored. He tried to run backstage where he might have a chance to meet Elvis face-to-face but couldn't get close due to the crush of people.

On the way back to the truck, Ray passed two serious Elvis impersonators. They had the hair, the sunglasses, and each wore a white sequined jumpsuit. They saw Ray and acknowledged him as one would a kindred soul. They also knew they had him beat all to hell.

An Elvis impersonator! Was that what people were going to think about Ray? He'd spent all his life distancing himself from this whole Elvis thing. It sure was a hell of a lot easier doing that than it was trying to get next to the big man.

It was frustrating to have people think he was some kind of hustler. Of course, how could anyone even possibly suspect the truth, if, in fact, that's what it was? It sure seemed like it but Ray supposed there could be other ways to look at the information. Maybe he was just . . .

No, damn it! Now he was just being a coward. He wasn't going to let himself back out of this. Like Sheree had said, there were too many coincidences. He was going to have to find out positively and somewhere along the line that meant meeting Elvis. They were going to have to meet face-to-face. Period. Ray was just going to have to deal with that and not chicken out.

The rest of the way back to the truck, he carried his head a little higher, walked with more resolve. He was an honorable man on an honorable quest. All right. Now all he had to do was convince Elvis of that.

12

LATER THAT EVENING, RAY sat at the bar in Rusty's with Sheree. He had just told her the tale of the ill-fated attempt of meeting Elvis.

"Sorry, babe," she said.

"Yeah," Ray replied, still feeling a little down. "It probably wasn't the time or place, but at least it was a possibility. I never thought about how hard it would be to actually meet someone like him."

"There aren't many people like him to practice on."

"Yeah, especially in Memphis." Ray laughed. "Oh well, I just hope Fields comes through."

"But you felt good about it, right?"

"Yeah, we had a good talk. It's just driving a truck, for Christ's sake. How could I blow that?" Then he thought on it. " 'Course, I've been known to do some pretty amazing things. Monday will tell."

"Well, I've got a good feeling," Sheree said. "The world's going to look a lot better once you get working again."

"Yeah. A couple more bucks wouldn't hurt, either," Ray said.

"Keep good thoughts. Your guardian angel might be working overtime here," Sheree said as she got off the stool and kissed Ray quickly. "Work time. I'll catch you later."

"I'll finish up here and split," Ray said as she went into a back room to get ready to start her shift.

Soon Ray was lost in a myriad of thoughts as he sipped his drink and stared off into nothing.

Neither Sheree nor Ray had noticed a man sitting a couple of stools away from Ray. Ned Coleman, short, stocky, and fortyish, had been listening intently to Ray and Sheree's conversation. Now he was quite blatantly studying Ray. Finally, he scooted closer.

"Excuse me," Ned said, "I heard you mention Elvis. Quite a resemblance you got goin'."

"So I've heard."

"You the guy they wrote that article about?"

Ray looked over at him, surprised. "How'd you hear about that?"

"Word gets out, I guess." Ned studied Ray a little closer. "I'll be damned. Are you really his brother?"

"Hell, I don't know. There's a lot of stuff that points to it." Ray pulled the already worn clipping from his pocket and handed it to Ned. "It does make sense when you read it."

"Yeah. I heard about this," Ned said as he scanned the article. "All this true?"

"Yeah, but it don't matter. Nobody believes it anyway." Ray thought for a minute and smiled. "You know, if it's true, it's funny. That old nurse thinking the Presleys weren't anything and that the successful ones would be the Johnstons. After Dad killed himself we were a welfare family until I started making enough money to get us off it. I wonder if she ever knew that that Presley baby grew up to be one of the most famous people in the world?"

"Your folks never mentioned anything about it?"

"Nothing." Ray thought for a moment. "I wonder if Mama ever put it together? If this is true, she might not even have known the name of the other family; in fact, she probably wouldn't have."

After another silent moment, Ned handed Ray back his clipping and asked, "Do you know Elvis?"

"Oh, hell yes! Just had him over for dinner last night. Are you kidding me?"

"Do you think he'd like to meet you?"

That's a question Ray had been wrestling with himself. "I don't know. If he thinks I'm trying to rip him off he'd probably be mad, but . . ." Ray paused. "You know, if I'm not his brother then I can see him being pissed, but if I am . . . you'd think he'd want to know that, too."

Ned considered that and had to agree with Ray. "Yeah, you'd think that, wouldn't you?"

Ned finished his drink and stood. "Well, nice talkin' to you. Take care."

"You, too."

Ned left. Ray looked at the article before putting it back in his pocket, wishing again that he could have had an in-depth conversation with his mother about all this. He sat there a while longer, wondering what his next step was going to be.

Monday, April 18, 1977

Ray was awakened at 8:00 a.m. by the ringing phone. He ran out to the kitchen in his underwear, vowing for the hundredth time to get an extension in the bedroom.

"Hello . . . yes . . . well, that's great . . . you bet. I'll be there. Thanks a lot."

Ray hung up, smiling. Finally! He thought he deserved a congratulatory cup of coffee and was starting to put some on when a car drove up to the trailer. There was something about strange people driving up his road onto his property that he didn't like.

Ray threw on a bathrobe, opened the door, and stood there as a man in his midtwenties with a cheap suit and an armload of papers got out of his car and walked over to him.

"Ray Johnston?" the man asked.

"Who wants to know?"

The man laughed. "You know, that's the perfect response. Why more people don't do that, I don't know." He paused a moment. "Actually, I'm from Tennessee Federal and I'm supposed to give you this."

The young man handed Ray a folder full of papers.

"What is it?" Ray asked, taking it.

"Well, it's a few things. Actually, you were supposed to have been given a blue folder a week or so ago that would have allowed you to take care of this much easier but since we didn't hear from you, here I am.

"Mainly it's a court order," the process server continued. "Telling you to vacate these premises in three weeks or pay your back debts, which I think comes to about fourteen hundred dollars. There's also a summons to appear in court, in case you don't make the deadline."

"Did Mrs. Flatt send you?"

"Who?"

"You know, the LifeCare lady?"

"I don't even know what that is. Like I said, I'm from Tennessee Federal."

"You son of a bitch."

"Hey, I'm only the messenger," the young man said, stepping back toward his car.

"And I suddenly have the urge to punch someone in the face," Ray said threateningly.

The young process server figured he'd been there long enough, quickly went to his car, and drove off.

Before Ray had a chance to come back inside, his phone started ringing again. What the hell was going on today? Ray wondered as he went to the phone.

"Hello."

"Mr. Johnston?" said a female voice on the other end.

"Yes."

"Please hold for Ms. Almeada."

Ray was put on hold before he had a chance to say "who?" He just stood there in his bathrobe, wondering what life was going to throw at him next.

Early afternoon that same day, Ray was straightening up his trailer when he saw Sheree drive up in front. He went out to meet her. "Hey, babe. What's up?" he asked, not used to seeing her there in the middle of the day.

"Just have a little surprise." She kissed him hello and led him to the trunk of her car. "I got excited and couldn't wait."

She opened her trunk and motioned for Ray to look in. He did . . . then looked back to Sheree questioningly.

"I got them at a garage sale yesterday," she said, proudly lifting out one of a pair of two-foot-tall porcelain lions with one paw raised. "Aren't they neat?"

"Well, yeah . . . but why?" Ray wondered.

"Why? For many reasons," Sheree began, admiring the lions. "The lion is the king of beasts and since you are my very own personal king, you should have them. Also, as you've told me many times, this is your castle. Your very own personal Graceland . . . almost.

"And this . . ." she said, indicating the dirt road leading to the trailer "This is the very fashionable drive over your grounds to your castle. Elvis has lions at his Graceland, you should have them for yours. Actually, they should be on top of the pillars by your gates, but since they haven't quite gotten built yet, I'll just put them by the turnoff."

"Aren't they going to look a little strange out there?"

"They might look a little silly, which is exactly what you need, my friend, a little whimsy."

"Whimsy?"

"Every time you look at them you'll think of having fun. Whimsy." Sheree then switched gears. "What were you doing inside?"

"Just cleaning up a little."

"Good move. How come?"

"God's screwing with me, Sheree. He really is."

"So you clean your place?"

"I had kind of a busy morning," Ray began. "First, I get a call from Fields telling me that I got the job. I start tomorrow."

"Ray, that's wonderful. What's bad about that?"

"Nothing. But then I get a process server telling me that I've got three weeks to get off my property because they're foreclosing."

"My God, Ray. Is this that Flatt lady?"

"No, that's what I thought but this is the bank. They're beating the nursing home to the punch."

"What are you going to do?" Sheree asked, concerned.

"I don't know . . . but there's more."

"Do I want to hear this?" Sheree asked, knowing Ray couldn't take much more bad news.

"Actually, yeah, it's kinda neat. A couple of writers saw the article and are coming out this afternoon to interview me. Get this . . . they're from *Life* magazine."

"You're kidding!"

"Honest to God."

Sheree put down her lion and gave Ray a hug. "Oh, honey, that's wonderful. See? People are believing it."

"Well, might be a little early for that, but we'll see."

"I got to go but call me and let me know how it went. Better yet, come down."

"Okay."

Sheree called out "good luck" as she got in her car and drove off. Ray returned to his chores, quite aware that that afternoon could change everything.

13

A COUPLE OF HOURS later, the fruits of Ray's labors were beginning to show. The trailer was as clean as it had been in years. Ray had even tried to make himself more Elvis-like. He tried to get his dirty-blond hair to flop down over his forehead but it wasn't quite long enough. He also tried to find a better Elvis suit than the one he'd worn to the theater, but couldn't. So there he was in his jeans and red shirt, hoping it would work better today than it had then.

Ray checked himself out in the mirror, looking from every angle he could. He practiced an Elvis sneer, which he thought he did pretty well. Getting into it, he tried an Elvis stance . . . then did some Elvis moves . . . then went into his very best "thankyouverymuch."

He struck another pose and tried it again: "Thankyouverymuch." Ray was so involved with all this he hadn't noticed a car drive up and park outside. A knock on the door startled him and slammed him back to reality.

A man and woman in their early thirties stood outside his door. Ray quickly opened it and invited them in.

"Are you Ray Johnston?" the woman asked.

"Yes, ma'am."

"I'm Jackie Almeada and this is Harry McNeal. Thanks for giving us some time," she said as they entered.

"You bet," Ray said, shaking hands. "Sit yourselves down."

"Saw the lions," Jackie said with a twinkle as she pulled a notepad and pen from her purse. "Nice touch."

"Oh yeah. A bit of whimsy."

"Whimsy?" Harry questioned. It wasn't a word that fit with his initial impression of Ray.

"Yeah, you know . . . fun?" Ray explained. "You're both from *Life* magazine, right?"

"That's correct," Harry replied. "I must say you certainly do look an awful lot like Elvis."

"Well, we should. We're . . . uh . . . twins."

"About that." Jackie began placing a small, expensive tape recorder, quite different from Cindy's, on the table and turning it on. "Do you really feel that you are Jesse Garon Presley?"

"Well, sure . . . yeah."

"Other than your looks, what do you base this upon?"

"Well . . ." Ray reached into his back pocket and pulled out the newspaper clipping. "You see, my folks were real poor and there was this nurse—"

"We've read the article, Mr. Johnston," Harry cut him off. "Would you happen to have these journals that seem to be the basis for this?"

"Sure. They were my mom's . . . well, my adopted mother . . . sorta of."

"May we see them?" Jackie asked.

"Yeah," Ray said as he got the journals from where he had put them, under an end table. He showed them where the pages had been marked and sat back as the writers read the passages, wondering how he was doing.

When they'd finished, Jackie said, "These are dated but not signed."

"They were just hers. Nobody else was even supposed to read them."

"How do you know?" Harry asked. "Did you discuss this with your mother?"

"No. My girl and I just found them. Mom . . . uh, Esther . . . wasn't able to talk for quite a while. She'd kinda lost it."

"We also understand she died recently," Jackie said. "As sorry for you as we are, it certainly would have been nice to corroborate this information. You realize, Mr. Johnston, not only can anyone say anything, anyone can write anything. That doesn't make it true."

"Just as dating something 1935 doesn't necessarily mean it was actually written then," Harry added, pointedly.

Ray just looked at them. "I don't know what you want me to say to that. We found the journals just like the article said. I sure didn't write them myself, if that's what you're trying to get at."

"Do you have any memories or recollections of the Presleys?" Jackie asked.

"How could I? I was just a—" Ray held up the article as evidence when Harry again cut him off.

"Have you even met Elvis?" he asked.

"No . . . no, but—"

"Mr. Johnston, do you know how he has reacted to this?" Jackie asked.

"I didn't even know he'd heard about it," Ray replied, surprised.

"Indeed he has," Jackie said. "And from what I've heard, he's not pleased. The memory of his dead twin is precious to him. He doesn't like anyone trying to capitalize on it."

"Hey, I ain't asking for—"

"Had it ever occurred to you that you could be Elvis's brother before 'finding' these journals?"

"No. I never really . . ."

Jackie noticed Ray's old guitar in its usual spot, leaning in the corner. She motioned toward it. "Do you play?"

"Yeah. A little. Always have."

"Can you sing?" Jackie asked pointedly.

"As a matter of fact, I can," Ray said decisively, realizing that the interview was not going well. "I'm more into blues than rock 'n' roll, though, but I imagine I could probably . . ."

Ray saw Jackie and Harry exchange looks as his voice trailed off to nothing. Jackie turned off the tape recorder, stood, and started for the door.

"Mr. Johnston, I think that's all we need," Jackie said. "We've taken up enough of your time."

"Thanks very much," Harry added. He shook hands quickly with Ray and followed Jackie outside.

"Yeah," Ray replied to no one as the door closed behind them.

Ray went to the window and watched the reporters drive away. "Damn!"

Later that evening, Ray was once again at the bar in Rusty's with Sheree. He had just told her the tale of the ill-fated meeting with the reporters.

"That's a shame," she said.

"Yeah," Ray replied, still feeling a little down. "'Course, I don't know what would have happened if they had written a big story on me. That would have been weird."

"You would have been a celebrity."

"Oh yeah. What a claim to fame, that I look like someone famous."

"How about being the twin brother of someone famous?" Sheree suggested. "How are you feeling about that?"

"I don't know. Actually, I kinda believe it, but . . . anyway, it don't matter, nobody else does. Let's let it go. I'm just glad I got that job."

"That's got to be a relief."

"Well, not really," Ray said, taking some notes out of his pocket. "I figured up what's going on. I'm really screwed."

"What do you mean?"

"I got to rob a bank or something. I'm four months behind on the trailer. At three hundred fifty a month, that comes to fourteen hundred bucks. I owe LifeCare three and a half months at four hundred dollars a shot, that's another fourteen hundred. And it cost an even grand to get Mom buried. That's thirty-eight hundred bucks.

"If I took the whole hundred and fifty a week that Fields is paying me," Ray continued, "I could get it paid off in a little over twenty-five weeks, that's over six months! Of course, that's if I don't do anything else that costs money, like eat. And they want to take it away in three weeks! Jesus!"

"Boy, am I sorry, Ray," Sheree said. "I sure wish I could help. Actually, I could help a little. I've got some money saved in the—"

"Sheree," Ray interrupted. "Thank you. I love you and am real glad you're in my life but I'm not going to take money from you. I'll deal with it. You just stick around and give me a kiss on the nose every once in a while, okay?"

"I can do that," Sheree said as she leaned over and kissed him on the nose. That brought about the first smile on Ray's face since early that morning.

14

Thursday, April 21, 1977

RAY WOKE UP THE next morning feeling driven. He was sick and tired of being broke and was totally determined that he was not going to lose what little he had. The fact that it wasn't much made it all the more important that it be saved. If he was going down, he was going down fighting, not whimpering.

He made sure work went well at Fields. He was the first to show up and the last to leave every day. After a few days, Ray asked the foreman if he could take on any double shifts that might come up, filling in for someone that might get sick, or even if anybody needed anything extra at night or over the weekend.

At lunch and after work, Ray went down to unemployment and grocery stores that had bulletin boards and put up cards he'd made, saying that he was strong, not afraid of work, and was available at night or on weekends to do most anything.

And they worked. He got a job as night custodian at Nedermeyer elementary school. It was just basic sweeping and occasionally waxing the floors, removing crayon marks from most everywhere, and, fortunately less frequently, cleaning up where someone had gotten sick or "had an accident."

He even got his own shirt with *RAY* over the pocket. The twenty bucks a night added up to an extra hundred a week, which was great, but his goal was still a long way off.

On his way home from his day job one afternoon, Ray turned onto the dirt road that led to his trailer and smiled as he always did when he drove past Sheree's lions flanking the road. As he approached the trailer, he was surprised to see a long, white limousine parked in front.

Ray drove up, got out with his lunch pail, and went to see about the limo. Ned got out of the driver's seat.

"Hey, remember me? Ned Coleman. We were talking about Elvis a few nights ago in the bar?"

"Hey, how are you?"

"I guess I didn't mention that I worked for Elvis, did I?"

"I think I would have remembered that."

"Well, I do. Elvis is pretty interested in this. Could we talk a little? You got a minute?"

"No, I don't," Ray said strongly. "I got another job I got to get to. Look, I'm sorry this Elvis stuff ever got started in the first place. Let's just let it go, all right?"

Ray turned away, then started for his trailer.

"Wait a minute," Ned called out. "Please!"

"I mean it," Ray said, getting upset now. He turned back to Ned. "I'm tired of . . ."

Suddenly, Ray felt his entire body go cold. The back door of the limo opened and out stepped Elvis. He wore a blue jacket with the collar turned up, a baseball hat, and mirrored sunglasses that hid his eyes.

Still, the sideburns gave him away, along with . . . everything. He was the same height as Ray and heavier but there was something about the way he moved, the way he stood there looking at Ray . . . a power . . . and the most famous face in the world. Ray could hardly breathe.

"Mr. Presley, I'm sorry," Ray said nervously, having no idea what else to say. "I really didn't mean any . . ."

Elvis walked up close to Ray, which shut him up immediately. "So, you're supposed to be my brother?" Elvis asked straight out.

"I really don't know, sir. Finding all those records . . . it seemed like a real possibility. Look, I'm sorry if . . ."

Elvis stepped closer and took his glasses off, studying Ray. Ray got a chance to study back and was amazed. He really did feel like he was looking back into his own eyes.

"Could you be?" Elvis asked after a moment.

"*Could* I be? Did you read that article? I mean, it made sense . . . to me, anyway. I . . ."

Ray decided he didn't need to ramble on anymore as Elvis turned away, had a silent exchange with Ned, then turned back to Ray.

"If I find you're jackin' me around, it's goin' to be your ass."

"Look, I just told the paper what I'd found out," Ray said, not backing down even though he was scared to death. "I was kinda surprised that I was adopted, that's all. I don't want anything from you. As far as I'm concerned, we can just forget about it."

Elvis and Ned exchanged another quick glance before Elvis said, "I tell you what I'm going to do. I'm going to look into it. Till then, I want you to shut up about it and I mean that."

Ray said nothing, then, after a moment, he nodded his agreement. Elvis looked at Ray a beat longer, then put his glasses back on and walked back to the limo. Ned had the door open for him. Before Elvis stepped in, Ray stopped him.

"Elvis?"

Elvis paused in the doorway, then looked back at Ray.

"What if I *am* your brother?"

Elvis showed no reaction to this. He just stoically looked at Ray a moment longer and silently got into the limo. Ned nodded a farewell to Ray as he also got in and drove away.

Ray watched them drive off in the dust and tried to digest what had just happened. He then sat down in one of his lawn chairs to catch his breath, as the reality of it all started to hit. My God, he thought. What just got started?

Well, now, that was interesting, Ray thought. He felt numb the rest of the evening. Even though Elvis acted like an ass, seeing him in person, talking with him, at Ray's own castle, for crying out loud! It was pretty amazing stuff.

The weirdest thing of all, though, was how Ray felt when he'd looked into Elvis's eyes. Face-to-face, not two feet apart, the years, the totally different lives, and the weight suddenly didn't matter. It was the same face.

Ray couldn't know how Elvis felt but for him, there was no longer a question. They were twins.

A strange calm came over Ray as he mulled this over. He'd been so upset about finding out he was adopted, then the possibilities went crazy when the Elvis connection was first made. He had worried considerably about what was going to happen.

But it was all right. Whatever happened would be okay. What was important was that Ray, himself, knew. If it worked out that the world also found out, he'd deal with that. If it stopped right there, he'd deal with that, too.

At least he now knew who he was. He knew why he was adopted. He knew who his real folks were. He also knew that his real mother was dead and wondered if he'd ever have a chance to meet his father. And he had a brother. And a niece!

All right. Ray felt proud of himself. He was truly handling all this like an adult (something he was very seldom accused of being). Now he could concentrate on what was really important: trying to save and preserve his life as he knew it.

Yet, down deep inside, there was still a part of him that was so nervous and excited about all this that he could hardly stand it.

15

PROBABLY THE HARDEST THING Ray had ever done in his life so far was not tell anyone that Elvis had come out to see him, but he had given his word and he intended to stick by it. He assumed that he'd hear from Elvis somehow, either to welcome him into the family or to punch him out. Ray had to admit that both those scenarios seemed unlikely but he didn't know what else could happen. But, as Ray told himself, he was putting all that out of his mind for now.

A few days later, Ray was driving a Fields Construction truck down a rural highway when the rather unforgettable white limousine passed him, then slowed down. When Ray started to pass, the driver motioned for him to pull over. He did.

A nurse in a white uniform got out of the limo with a medical kit, walked back to the truck, and got in the passenger's side.

"Excuse me," the nurse said. "Mr. Raymond Johnston?"

"Yeah. What are you. . . ?"

"I realize this is rather odd, but I need to get a blood sample from you."

"Blood? Are you crazy?"

"Do you recognize the car?"

"Sure."

"All right then, roll up your sleeve," she said as she pulled a needle and cotton swab from her kit.

Ray looked with fear at the needle but did roll up his sleeve. Even though Elvis hadn't been particularly nice, it still didn't even occur to Ray to say no to him.

* * *

When Ray returned home that evening he was surprised to find Sheree there, cooking.

"Hey, babe. What are you doing here?" he asked as they shared a quick kiss.

"To celebrate your first week at Fields. I thought I'd give you some home cooking before you took off for the school."

"Well, ain't you somethin'?"

"Want a beer?" she asked, already reaching in the fridge.

"Damned straight," he said as she handed him one. "Hell, I'm going to have to work more often."

"There's an idea," Sheree said with a twinkle. They both laughed.

Ray took off his long-sleeved work shirt, sat back in his T-shirt, and took a good long swig of his beer. Sheree noticed the cotton ball taped to his inner elbow.

"What happened?" she asked.

"Oh, nothin'," Ray said, not wanting to get into it. "Gave blood today."

"The hell you did."

"The hell I didn't!"

"Damn it, Ray!" Sheree wasn't kidding around anymore.

"What? Is it so hard to think I could do that? You told me yourself I was one of the good guys."

"You also forget who you're talking to," Sheree explained patiently. "As macho and studly as you are, I also happen to know you're the biggest baby in the world when it comes to needles. Now, what happened?"

Ray was caught and knew it. "Sheree, if I tell you something, will you promise to keep it to yourself? I mean, really. It's important."

"Sure, honey. Nothing's wrong, is it?"

"Elvis wanted it done," Ray stated simply.

"Damn it, Ray!" Sheree blew up. "This is not the time for that. It's not funny."

Ray went to her, held her, trying to calm her down. "Elvis was here."

"What?" That got Sheree's attention.

"He was, really. Him and a long white limo . . . last Thursday," Ray explained. "You know, there might be a chance that I actually am his brother. That's what the blood test's all about."

Sheree sat down, trying to take all this in. "Wow. He came out here?" Ray smiled and nodded. "All this time and you didn't tell me? You rat!"

"He asked me not to."

"How'd you feel?" she asked.

"Oh, like I couldn't breath real well."

"Was he nice?"

"Not really. It was kind of a 'if you aren't my brother, I'm going to kick your ass' sort of thing."

Sheree smiled. "I can picture that," she said. "What if you are?"

"Don't know."

"So you really might be?"

"Sheree, remember, you promised," Ray said seriously. "He asked me as a favor, personally. Okay?"

Sheree still sat, overwhelmed. "Sure." Then added to herself, "Wow."

16

RAY GOT HIS MIND back to his problems at hand and became a working machine. The long hours, hard work, and going from one job to the other was exhausting but strangely satisfying. He really felt he was doing everything he could and that he was going to turn this whole financial nightmare around.

That was until he got home from working at Fields Construction and got a phone call before he could change and jet over to his night job. He learned that a gas leak had been discovered at the school that day and they had evacuated everyone. No one was allowed inside until it had been satisfactorily dealt with. They imagined it would be fixed tomorrow. They'd let him know. Until then, he had the night off.

Damn! That definitely put the brakes on the momentum he was starting to feel. Right then the phone rang. Ray answered.

"Hey, babe." It was Sheree. "Just thought I'd get you before you took off to become Mr. Janitor Person."

"Actually, you got me hanging around. The school got evacuated today. A gas leak, I guess, so I'm off, damn it!"

"Oh, right. I heard about that today. I didn't realize it was your school. Well, listen, instead of moping around, why don't you come down later? I just found out that today is Sonny's birthday. After we close a bunch of us are going to stick around and raise a glass or two. How'd you like to join us?"

"How old is he?"

"He's not telling."

Ray chuckled and thought a minute. Rusty's didn't close until 2:00 a.m. but he'd always liked Sonny and could definitely use the diversion.

"Sure. Should be fun. I'll see you later."

Sheree said she was happy he was coming. Ray hung up, looked around the trailer, and saw nothing that needed doing that he felt like doing so he decided, what the hell, he'd go a little early. It didn't matter how old Sonny was. He'd give him a hard time anyway.

Ray went outside, hopped in his pickup, and turned the key. The engine turned over but wouldn't start. That was strange, it had been running fine. He turned it over and over. He pumped the gas, being careful not to flood it, but nothing happened.

Damn! He climbed out, popped the hood, and took a look. All he could see was a large, black engine compartment. It was already getting dark and the one small bulb outside Ray's door was too far away from the pickup to do any good. It would have to wait until tomorrow.

He slammed the hood down in frustration, stormed back into the trailer, and called Sheree back.

"Damn it, honey, my truck won't start. I don't know what the hell's wrong with it. Could you come pick me up?"

"Oh, Ray, it takes me a half hour to get to your place. That's an hour before we could be back here and I don't know if it'll even go that long. It was just for a drink."

"Yeah. Well, hell. I hate to miss it."

"Me, too, honey. Sorry. I'll give him a 'happy' for you. Look, we're kinda busy right now but I'll catch you soon, okay."

"Hope so."

Ray hung up. The trailer seemed more quiet and lonely than before. That sinking feeling of failure came back as he realized, once again, he was heading in the wrong direction. Now how much was the truck going to cost to get fixed? Jesus!

Dejectedly, he called J.D.

"Hello."

"Hey, partner, I got a problem. This piece-o-shit truck of mine decided to stop working. Can't get the sucker to catch. Could you give me a tow into town?"

"Tonight?"

"Well, yeah. Then Chris could jump on it first thing in the morning."

"Ray, you know there is nothing I'd rather do than help out my old buddy . . . well, that's not exactly true. There's one other thing. I got a date, pal, and you ought to see her. Outstanding! Name's Brandy or Dandy or Gandy, something like that. Anyway, she's a piece of work but I've got to go by the job site 'cause I left her name and address there . . . I think. How about first thing in the mornin'?"

"Sure, but aren't you working?"

"Supposed to be starting a new job but I'll put it back a day. People expect us laboring types to act like that anyway so, ain't no big deal."

"Well, thanks, partner. Have fun tonight. I'll see you then."

Ray then called Chris the mechanic at home to tell him he wouldn't be able to get his truck down there until the next morning but would appreciate it if he could get right on it. Chris the mechanic, not known for his big personality, said he'd do what he could do and hung up.

He then called his foreman, told him about the truck and that he'd be a bit late the next morning. The foreman told him to take the morning off, just come in at one o'clock. Easier for bookkeeping that way.

Ray did not want to lose any more hours but couldn't really do anything about it. He pulled his guitar out of the corner and strummed and sang for an hour or so. He hadn't played for a while and it felt good. Finally, though, the disappointments of the day got the best of him and he decided that, early as it was, he might as well go to bed while he still had one. Even Johnny Carson didn't sound good.

★ ★ ★

Ray was sound asleep when the phone rang later that night. He glanced at the clock, which read 11:30, before running out to the living room to answer it.

"I thought you promised to keep quiet about all this," a man's voice on the phone angrily said when Ray answered.

"Who's this?" Ray asked, his head starting to clear.

"Who the hell do you think it is?" Ray now knew who it was and sat down. "So I've already learned that you lie and I can't trust you to keep your word," Elvis continued on the phone. "What else am I going to find out about you?"

"Bullshit!" Ray said, awake enough to not like being put down by anyone. "C'mon, I've been real quiet about everything. My girlfriend finally got it out of me but she wouldn't—"

"Great. Why didn't you just put it on the radio."

"You don't know her. She wouldn't tell anyone."

"Then how did my people hear about it?" Elvis asked.

"I don't know. Ask them."

"Listen, just have her shut up until we figure out what's going on. Try to handle that," Elvis said with a cutting edge.

"Hey, I'm doing the best I can here and I don't like you telling me wha—" *Click.* Dial tone. Elvis had hung up on him. Ray slammed the receiver down.

Great. Just great. As if the day hadn't been terrific enough, now Elvis was pissed at him. What was Sheree doing? He was sure she wouldn't have told anybody. She promised. She wouldn't have . . . would she?

17

KNOWING J.D.'S PENCHANT FOR promptness and inability to sleep in the mornings, 6:00 a.m. found Ray outside, hard at work trying to fix his truck. Two or three times he thought he'd figured it out and turned the ignition hopefully. The engine still turned over but didn't catch. Actually, the only change at all was that the engine was turning over slower each time as the battery was starting to wear down.

J.D. arrived just in time to stop Ray from going crazy and putting a bullet into the engine block. J.D. tried to tinker a bit with the truck also, but the battery was so low he couldn't really do much.

They tied a rope from J.D.'s trailer hitch to Ray's bumper, leaving about fifteen feet between trucks. Slowly and carefully, they caravaned off Ray's hill to his mechanic's shop. The mechanic said he'd get to it when he could get to it and would let Ray know. Expecting nothing else from Chris the mechanic, Ray and J.D. just nodded and left.

They got a cup of coffee from a vendor down the street and got each other caught up with what was happening. Ray told J.D. about the wolf biting at his door. That no matter how many hours he worked, he was hardly getting close to what he needed to keep his place. J.D. commiserated but could only identify so much. His main problems in life had to do with getting anyone to go out with him twice.

J.D. was going to drop Ray off at work that noon but had to stop off at the market for a minute first. He was out of beer, out of coffee, and something else . . . oh, yeah . . . food.

Ray hung out near the checkout stand, looking at the girls on the covers of the magazines while J.D. shopped. Suddenly, Ray stopped.

Among the *TV Guides* and *Glamour* magazines was that tawdry magazine he had seen earlier, *Dish* magazine. The headline was different this time:

"SOAP STAR GIVES BIRTH TO TWO-HEADED BABY!!"

J.D. came up about that time with his groceries. Ray pointed out the copy of *Dish* magazine. "You ever seen one of these before?"

J.D. bent over, read the headlines, and laughed. "A two-headed baby?"

"The magazine."

"Not so's I remember," J.D. said, still chuckling. "But it looks like a quality piece of work, bro. I think you ought to pick one up."

"I hear they make a fortune."

As J.D. checked his food, Ray read further about all the "inside scoop" on various celebrities, which started his mind churning.

At work later that afternoon while Ray was on break, he looked up the number of *Dish* magazine. When the receptionist answered, Ray asked, "You pay money for stories, right?"

"Well, it depends," the receptionist said. "Most of our stories come from our reporters but they have been known to pay for very important stories. You know, big scoops."

"How about unknown stuff about Elvis? Really big stuff?"

"Well, possibly. Would you like to speak with one of our reporters?"

"Yeah, your best one," Ray said. "I think that's just what I need, your best reporter."

After work that night Ray bummed a ride home with a buddy but talked him into swinging by Chris the mechanic's place first to check on his truck. Chris said it "weren't no big thing." Something with the solenoid and his carburetor was mucked up. It'd be ready in the morning. One hundred twenty-five dollars.

"One twenty-five! Really?" Ray asked, recoiling.

"It costs what it costs," Chris the mechanic said by way of explanation as he walked away.

Ray knew it could have been a lot worse but there went a full week's pay. Damn it! He'd also checked on his elementary school and they hadn't gotten rid of all the gas yet, so there went another night without making a dime. They assured him that everything would be okay tomorrow and would like him back on the job that evening. Still, Ray was going quickly from being mad to being scared.

Saturday, April 30, 1977

Thankfully, Ray was able to work that Saturday. J.D. came by to take him to his truck and arrived with his usual promptness. He was also angry.

"So when were you going to tell me?" he asked Ray, who was still trying to wake up.

"Tell you what?"

"Oh, nothing real important," J.D. said sarcastically. "Only that Elvis came out here to see you in person. Did that really happen?"

"Where'd you hear that?"

"Only all over town. C'mon, slick, people are coming up asking me about it and I'm standing there with my finger up my nose because I don't know nothin'! Hell, a date I had last night knew about it and she don't even know you!"

"Damn it! *Nobody* was supposed to know."

"Then how did they?"

"Sheree caught me. She was the only one I told," Ray said, heading back into the bedroom to get a jacket.

"You did what? And you were trying to keep this a secret?!"

"Yeah. I guess that didn't work out, did it? And Elvis is pissed."

"So it's true? He was really here?"

Ray was actually bursting to talk to him about it. He needed to talk this over with someone. He'd had a chance to with Sheree after she had caught him, but J.D. was his best friend. He had been the hardest to keep it from but, since it was already out . . .

Ray had J.D. sit down and told him the whole tale, about meeting Ned, the limo, talking with Elvis, the blood test on the road . . . and that's all. He didn't know if he'd hear from Elvis again or not. He guessed it depended on the results of the blood test.

Ray repeated that he'd promised Elvis he'd keep it quiet so he asked J.D. not to further blow it for him. Please. It was important. He'd deal with Sheree later.

J.D.'d gotten over being mad by the time he'd driven Ray to his truck. But he wasn't out of questions. "What was he like?" "Did you look like twins?" "How big was he?" and on and on. Ray fended them the best he could and was grateful to pick up his truck, get to work, and think about something else for a change.

After work that day, while he was changing into his custodial uniform, Ray got another response from his card at unemployment.

A farmer called telling Ray he needed a field cleared. It was going to take more than just weekends and it was going to be hard, but if Ray was as good a worker as he said, he could make a hundred a day for a week or so. Was he interested?

Ray could hardly get "yes" out fast enough. He took down directions and would meet the man tomorrow.

On the way to his janitor job, Ray stopped by Rusty's and took Sheree aside.

"You let me down, kid."

"What? What did I do?" Sheree asked.

"I asked you to not say anything about Elvis coming over and you said you wouldn't. Elvis called, his people heard about it, and he's pissed. I hadn't even told J.D. My God, what'd you do?"

"Oh, I'm sorry, honey," Sheree said. "It was just too much. I couldn't keep it all inside. I just talked to Charlene, that's all, and she promised that—"

"Charlene!" Ray interrupted. "Sheree, what were you thinking?"

"I know, I know. I really am sorry. It was just too big."

"Damn it, Sheree. Of course, it's big. That's why it's important that it be handled right. So now Elvis is mad at me, which is definitely not the way I wanted to start this off."

"I'm sorry it leaked out, Ray, but they're going to find out anyway. It's been in the paper, for crying out loud," Sheree said in her defense.

"Yeah, but nobody was believing it. We could have left it right there and let it fade away. Besides, I asked and you promised you'd sit on it. Elvis doesn't think he can trust *me*. Can I trust you?"

"Evidentially not," Sheree said contritely. "I'm sorry."

"Look, I'll try to make it work out," Ray said, still upset. "But please, don't tell anybody else, okay? For now?"

"Yeah," Sheree said quietly.

Ray told her about the other job he was going to be doing and that it might be a few days before they saw each other. Sheree just nodded as Ray left, wondering if that was really the case or if he just didn't want to see her anymore.

Ray wasn't real happy, either, as he walked out to his truck. Between his finances and Elvis, the last thing he needed was to have a fight with Sheree. They hardly ever disagreed about anything and Ray didn't like the feeling at all.

Somehow it seemed fitting that this most marvelous of days be topped off by mopping out the toilets in Nedermeyer elementary school.

18

THAT SUNDAY, BEFORE MEETING the farmer, Ray did something he never thought he'd do. Bolstered by the fact that he had survived the needle episode with the nurse, Ray gave blood at a blood drive that was going on that weekend. Actually, Ray sold blood. Another five dollars in the kitty, and he did it without screaming.

He figured if he could give blood every other day, that would be . . . not nearly enough. But everything helped.

The farmer was a small, raw-boned, weathered, ornery little cuss in his midfifties and was right where he told Ray he'd be. Still, Ray was surprised at what he saw.

The farmer didn't actually lie, except maybe about it being a field. He should have said that he wanted it to be a field. Right then it looked more like a forest. The farmer wanted the trees cut down and trimmed, the stumps dug up and removed, and the dirt graded back smooth. A field.

Ray's back hurt just looking at all those trees. "Alone?" he asked.

"Of course not," the little farmer said. "You crazy? There's too much here for one man to do. I'll help you."

Ray still stared at the trees. Two people were definitely better than one, but a crew of twelve would be better yet. Ray took a little side look to the heavens as if to ask, *God, what are you doing to me now?*

The farmer wanted to start on it the next day, Monday. Because the money was so outrageously good, Ray said he'd do it, then drove by his foreman's house and caught him outside raking his lawn.

Yes, it was strange, Ray admitted, first to be asking for double shifts, then requesting a leave of absence for a week, but it was important. The foreman okayed it, just this once.

Ray sped home to change into his custodial shirt and fainted in his bathroom. He woke up a few minutes later with a bruise on the side of his face. He must have hit the rim around the shower bottom when he fell.

Damn! Then he remembered that after giving blood, he was supposed to drink a lot of fluids to replenish himself. He'd forgotten all about it. He hadn't had any.

Ray was in the process of downing two eight-ounce glasses of water when a yellow Chevy unfamiliar to Ray drove up. A nicely dressed man in his middle sixties climbed out.

"Hi, there. I saw the lions out front. Are they some kind of 'Elvis is king' kinda thing?"

"No," Ray replied bluntly.

"Oh well," the man said, coming over to Ray. "I'm Morgan Bates, a writer with *Dish* magazine. I understand you gave us a call."

"Oh yeah."

"I read that article you told my secretary about. Pretty interesting stuff. How much of it is true?"

"All of it."

"Well, from the look of you, I can see why you'd think you were Elvis's twin."

"Actually, I didn't until we ran across those journals," Ray said. "You pay money for stories, right?"

"It depends. How familiar with our magazine are you?"

"Not very."

"Let me fill you in," Morgan said. "What we deal with are behind-the-scenes stories of celebrities. How do they *really* live? What are they *really* like? That kind of thing."

"I don't know any of that stuff."

"That's all right, but you might. We're always looking for more information on Elvis. There aren't very many people who get on the inside of his life. Now, personally, I'd be real surprised if he went for this brother thing, but if you ever get a chance to actually meet him—"

"Hell, he was out here the other day," Ray interrupted, not liking being talked down to like that.

"He what?" Morgan asked, surprised.

"Yeah. He's curious about all this, too. He's looking into it."

"Excellent!" Morgan could barely contain himself. "Listen, you may find yourself in a position to make some very serious money . . . I mean seriously serious."

"You want to buy my story?"

"Your story! You already gave that away to the newspaper. It's old news already."

"How could I make big money then?"

"Get as close to Elvis as you can, then let me know what happens. I want to know everything."

"Look, I don't really want to do anything like that," Ray said. "I thought you might want to interview me. Take my picture. Show everyone the similarity. Something like that, maybe."

"It's a little late for that, pal. That could have been worth a couple of grand if you'd come to us first, but I'm not going to pay you for something that's already out there. We handle things a little differently: 'Elvis Contacts Possible Twin Brother.' See? I could start right now. That should sell a mag or two," Morgan said, laughing.

"You're not really going to do that, are you?" Ray asked, suddenly wishing he had not called that magazine.

"I could. Why? Don't you want me to?"

"No, I don't. Look, I don't know for sure if I'm Elvis's brother or not, but one thing I do know is that I don't want to make him mad. I really was just thinking of interviews, pictures. Stuff like that. I don't want to spy for nobody."

"It's not quite like that," Morgan said. "Let me explain. What we're really interested in is what Elvis does with his days when he's not performing. His interests, his friends, like that. Now, why's that going to make him mad?"

Put that way, it didn't sound quite so bad to Ray.

"Of course, what's important to any magazine is getting information that no one else has. If you can truly get inside," Morgan continued excitedly, "and give us really good information over a period of time, this could be worth major bucks to you. Hell, if you can actually *prove* that you are Elvis's twin, there's no end to the money you could make just for talking with us. You could end up a millionaire, son."

"Excuse me?" Ray was stunned.

"Hey, if it sells magazines. That's what it comes down to, but remember, nobody gets that kind of money for nothing. We'd need stories and information that nobody else has and that people will want to know. Headlines, exciting stuff, you know? Can you do that?"

"I don't even know if I'll ever see him again but if I do, I don't think he'd like me telling stories about him."

"You'd be surprised, Mr. Johnston," Morgan said seriously. "He just may thank you."

"How do you figure that?"

"Think about it. Presley has always been so aloof that more information on him would just make him more identifiable, more appealing. Let's face it, he could use some help. His reputation is sliding seriously, all this weight, rumors of drugs and everything.

"He could use a major PR turnaround," Morgan continued. "You just may be the one to put him back on the front pages again. He'd like that, and a publication like *Dish* is the perfect place to do it."

Ray thought for a moment before Morgan went on. "Also, you've got to think of yourself. If you are, in fact, Jesse Garon Presley, you are a very special guy. That's too big to keep under wraps."

"So I've heard."

"It's not fair to you," Morgan stressed. "Or to the public, or even to Elvis, because something this big will eventually come out anyway and it would look like Elvis lied to the public. His reputation would be hurt even more. The public doesn't like being lied to.

"It would also look like he wanted to keep the limelight all for himself and not share any with you. That would make him look small and petty in the eyes of the world.

"You can stop all that from happening and make a great deal of money at the same time. I don't know about you, but that sounds like one of the sweetest deals in the world to me. What do you think?"

After a moment, Ray said, "Let me think about it."

"You got it," Morgan said as he reached in his pocket and pulled out a business card, which he gave to Ray. "Just give me a call when something happens."

Ray put the card in his back pocket and watched Morgan drive away. When he was out of sight, Ray took the card out again and looked at it. He then took stock of his used pickup and the barren, treeless hilltop that held his old, faded, third-hand trailer that was home, and he did allow himself to think, just for a second, about what life would be like out of debt and maybe be able to take Sheree to the places she'd like to go.

As he left to go be a janitor, he couldn't help but imagine how a million dollars might just change a few things.

Monday, May 2, 1977

The next week was the hardest in Ray's life. The skinny, little, wiry farmer could do the work of two men. Of course, since he was paying Ray so much money, he wanted him to do the work of three.

They sawed, chopped, sorted, hauled, dug, loaded, unloaded, graded, and started all over again. Every muscle in Ray's body burned. He would come home, stand in a hot shower as long as he could, dreaming all the while of having an actual bathtub someday, then he'd go back out to his janitorial job.

Physical labor, while it occupied the body, left the mind free to roam. Ray kept reliving his talk with Morgan Bates over and over. As badly as he needed the money, what Bates was asking didn't feel right, yet he had made a good case for it. Maybe Elvis wouldn't be mad. Maybe it would help him.

Wouldn't that be something, to be able to help Elvis and make a pot full for himself at the same time. But he wasn't sure.

Finally, after spending an entire afternoon worrying about it, he decided he'd ask Elvis personally. It just seemed the right thing to do.

Before work that night, Ray went back to his place, cleaned up, changed clothes, and set out for Graceland. His custodial uniform with his name on it was in the backseat. He didn't really want to talk to Elvis wearing that.

Ray had been by Graceland and seen the gates before. You can't live in Memphis without going by there at least once. On this day, however, they took on an entirely different meaning. He never dreamed he might actually have an opportunity to go inside.

The gates somehow seemed bigger and even a bit ominous as Ray drove his truck up to them and parked. He was amazed at how nervous he was as he got out and walked up to them. A guard soon met him.

"You can't park there," the guard said.

"I need to talk to Elvis for a minute."

"Is he expecting you?"

"No, but he knows me. Just tell him Ray Johnston is out here. It'll just take a second."

The guard looked at Ray closer. "Are you a . . . relative?"

"Yeah, sort of . . . I think," Ray stammered.

Normally, the guard would just tell people to get lost but there was something about this guy. He told Ray to wait a minute, went to his guard shed, and made a phone call. A couple of minutes later he returned to the gates.

"I'm sorry, sir, but he's not going to be able to see you today," the guard said politely.

"But it's really important. He'll want to know this stuff, he really will."

"Please move your truck. Parking is not permitted there."

"Listen, damn it," Ray said, not liking being dismissed like that. "He knows who I am. He'll want to talk to me. Ask him again."

"Listen yourself, buddy," the guard barked back. "I'm trying to be nice to you here. You want to know what he *really* said?"

"Yeah."

" 'Get rid of the son of a bitch and don't bother me with any more crackpots,' " the guard quoted. "Does that sound like someone who wants to talk to you? Get out of here!"

Realizing there was no further reason for arguing, Ray got back in his truck and left. What the hell was with Elvis? Maybe he didn't remember his name or something. Or maybe he did and didn't give a damn. Either way, it hurt. Ray felt embarrassed. He was just trying to help, for Christ's sake.

The more he drove, the madder he got. By the time he got to his school and changed into his uniform, Ray was livid.

All right, Mr. Presley, he thought, if that's the way you want to play it, you're fair game.

Ray didn't know if he'd ever see Elvis again or have anything amazing to report but if he did, he was one "crackpot" who didn't have any reservations about making a couple of bucks from it.

Ray's life returned to labor and cleaning. He was absolutely exhausted and had time for nothing else.

A couple of grueling days later, J.D. called him, wondering what was going on. The two friends hardly ever went over three days without seeing each other. Ray didn't want to go into it too much so he just explained that he was doing a little extra work.

Being the old friend he was, J.D. read between the lines and asked Ray if he could use a little financial boost. Business had been good for J.D. lately and it would be no problem. Again, Ray was quick to thank him for the good thoughts but paying his own way was something he felt strongly about. It was nice to know he had such good people in his life but this was something he'd take care of himself.

Ray had never slept better in his life, though not nearly long enough. As he told J.D., he was also, finally, starting to put away some money, which felt good. He was beginning to make some headway.

The little farmer liked Ray's work so much he offered to hire him on full-time (at considerably less money, of course). Ray thanked him but declined. He'd finish this job and that was it. The thought of working that hard for the rest of his life didn't appeal to him at all.

Ray tried selling blood again but fainted in the forest/field. He'd forgotten about the liquids again. Fortunately, the farmer hadn't seen him. Ray had to admit that, generally, he had never felt this bad in his life.

Friday, May 6, 1977

At the end of the week, the little farmer figured there were still two more days of work to wrap up his "field." He told Ray to take the weekend off, rest up, and come back on Monday. As much as Ray dreaded it, he said he would because that was two hundred dollars more.

As soon as he finished work that Friday, he sped over to Fields and asked for two more days off. He finally talked them into giving him Monday and Tuesday off if he agreed to come in Saturday and Sunday to do general maintenance around the construction yard. Ray had been hoping to have two days in bed, but maybe next weekend.

Ray went home, prepared to take a hot shower and go to bed immediately, feeling more tired than he could remember. He'd put in a TV dinner, popped himself a beer, and had just started to relax when the phone rang.

Ray answered, "Hello."

"Mr. Ray Johnston?" a female voice on the other end of the phone inquired.

"Yeah."

"I'm calling from Graceland. Mr. Presley was wondering if you'd like to have dinner with him this evening."

Ray managed to laugh even though his side hurt when he did. "Oh, at *his* place. I thought he was coming over here tonight."

"Excuse me?" the lady asked.

"All right, all right. Let me talk to Sheree." Ray knew she was there. Actually, he was just about to call her anyway. She didn't do anything so bad that he couldn't forgive her. Actually, as he thought about it, she didn't do anything that Ray hadn't done also. For their own reasons, Ray broke his promise to Elvis; Sheree broke her promise to Ray. It was definitely time to make up.

"I'm afraid I don't know anyone by that name, sir. I assure you—"

"If Sheree isn't there," Ray interrupted, "I'm not going to play anymore, but you can tell her that I miss her anyway." Ray hung up. If it wasn't her, it was probably somebody still making fun of the article. Oh well, hopefully they'd forget about it soon.

The phone rang again.

This time, Ray answered with "Sheree?"

"Mr. Johnston, will you please do all of us a favor and call me back at this number? My name is Velma," the lady said.

"Yeah. I can do that," Ray said, playing along, reaching for a paper and pencil. "Shoot."

He wrote down the number, thanked the lady, hung up, and dialed the number, wondering what kind of a game Sheree was up to.

"Graceland switchboard, how may I direct your call?" a different female voice asked.

This surprised Ray. "Graceland? As in . . . Graceland?" he stammered.

"As in Mr. Presley's residence. Yes sir. Who did you wish to speak to?"

"Uh . . . Velma?"

"One moment please." Ray could hear the lines being clicked over.

"Mr. Johnston?" Velma asked. "Can we talk now?"

"Yes, ma'am. I'm sorry."

"That's quite all right. As I said, Mr. Presley would like to have you over for dinner this evening. Would that be convenient?"

"Tonight?" Ray's beaten body cried out *no!* "Uh . . . sure, I suppose."

"We'll send a driver to pick you up in a couple of hours. Would that be all right?"

"That'll be fine, ma'am. Thank you." They hung up. Ray gazed ahead, looking at nothing. He then happened to glance to the side and saw himself in the mirror. His dirty, worn, crusty self. "Oh God!" he cried and ran for the shower.

After showering and changing clothes, Ray paced another hour or so before a long, white limousine pulled up outside the trailer.

Ned hopped out as soon as he saw Ray leave the trailer. "How're you doin'?" Ned asked, exiting the limo.

"A bit of a surprise," Ray said as he walked stiffly around to the passenger door and started to open it. Ned beat him there.

"Oh no," Ned said. "You get the full treatment."

"Oh, c'mon," Ray said, getting embarrassed.

Ned opened the door to the back. "Hey, enjoy it. You're goin' where few have ever been."

Ray let that sink in a moment before taking a big breath and cautiously entering the plush, soft black leather of the Presley limousine.

He could hardly believe this was actually happening until he saw the gates of Graceland opening for them. Ray looked to see if the same guard he'd talked to was there. He wasn't. Ray's nerves were so much on overload he started to forget about how tired and sore he was.

Ned parked the limo off to the side of the mansion, got out, and was back opening the door before Ray could find the handle. Ray hesitantly climbed out.

"First time is through the front door," Ned said, leading Ray up the stairs, past the imposing pillars to the front door.

"For me?" Ray was still having trouble grasping it all.

"'Specially for you," Ned said, opening the wrought-iron screen door. Ned reached for the main door, put his hand on the knob, paused, and looked over at Ray. "You ready for your life to change forever?"

It wasn't without a large dose of trepidation that Ray took a big breath and said, "Sure."

Ned smiled and opened the door.

19

RAY STEPPED INTO A plush, mirrored fantasyland, the likes of which he had never even imagined. He barely got a chance to start gawking when a fiftyish woman in a white uniform met them.

"Good evening, Mr. Coleman. This must be Mr. Johnston."

"It is. Ray, meet Velma," Ned said. "She knows more about the running of Graceland than anybody. She'll take you from here."

"Hullo" was all Ray could muster.

"I believe we talked earlier on the phone."

"Yes, ma'am. I'm sorry about that, but . . ."

"That's quite all right. I fully understand," Velma said. "Invitations from Mr. Presley don't occur every day. Follow me, please."

She started to walk off. Ray turned to thank Ned before following her but he had already gone. Ray quickly caught up with Velma as she walked through this most elegant house.

Ray heard Elvis singing a gospel song with a piano accompaniment. He'd heard some of Elvis's gospel records before and knew this was on one of them. However, he wasn't quite ready for the fact that this was Elvis live, sitting at his shiny black baby grand in what he would learn later was called the music room.

He and Velma waited in his sumptuous red, white, and mirrored living room, looking through a doorway flanked by stained glass peacocks as Elvis played and sang.

Ray thought Elvis looked even heavier in person than in the recent pictures he'd seen of him but there was no mistaking that voice. It hadn't seemed to falter a bit over the years.

Ray was hoping he'd keep singing for a long time because he had no idea what he'd say to him when he stopped. What did somebody say to Elvis? He had no idea.

Suddenly, the song was over and Velma led Ray to the music room doorway.

"Mr. Presley, Mr. Johnston."

"Ray, c'mon in," Elvis said, still sitting at the piano. "Been warming up the pipes. Got some gigs coming up."

"You sound great," Ray said as Velma silently disappeared.

"Well, I'd better. Seems like I'm touring this whole damn year," Elvis said with a little smile as he swung around on the piano seat and took another good look at Ray. "Little surprised to be here?"

"Uh, yeah. Just a little," Ray said, trying not to seem as overwhelmed as he really was.

"A wild hair came over me, you know?" Elvis asked as he got up and crossed to the bar. "Just wanted to talk to you some."

"Good. That's fine."

"Pepsi?"

Ray couldn't remember the last time anyone offered him a Pepsi. Although he could certainly use something a little stronger than that right then, it probably would have been rude to ask for a beer. "Yeah, sure."

Elvis popped a couple, handed one to Ray, and walked into the living room. He sat in an easy chair and motioned to a nearby one for Ray. "Take a load off."

Ray sat, never remembering enjoying sitting down so much in his life. "Actually, I wanted to talk to you the other day. You told me to 'get lost.'"

"When'd I do that?"

"I don't know. Couple of days ago. I talked to your guard."

"Oh, well, that never works," Elvis said. "Do you know how many people try to get in here every day? It's ridiculous. Everybody tries to get a piece of me, you know? After twenty-some-odd years it gets pretty old. What'd you want to talk to me about?"

"Oh, just this whole thing, I guess," Ray said, knowing this was not the time to mention *Dish* magazine. "No big thing."

"Yeah, sorry I got a little hot the other day. I get so much grief from these guys around me . . . I don't know. I love them, but sometimes I want to throttle 'em, too. Anyhow, I shouldn't take it out on you. Sorry about that."

"It's all right."

They sat quietly for a moment, each wondering what to talk about. Elvis took a big swig of his Pepsi and started to laugh at the same time. This caused him to start choking. He coughed a couple times but recovered quickly. He cleared his throat, then chuckled a little more.

"Hope my nurse didn't scare you too bad."

"It was pretty strange," Ray admitted.

"Now, you understand this test can't prove that we're related. All it can do is prove we're not."

"Heard anything yet?"

"You're here, ain't you?"

Ray had no idea what to say to that, which was fine. He never got the opportunity. A gray-haired man came into the room and walked over to Ray.

"This here is my daddy, Vernon Presley," Elvis said from his chair. "He'd like to meet you. I guess we'll just call you . . . Ray."

Ray quickly stood and shook hands with Vernon. Ray had seen pictures of him in the past but thought he was taller than he actually was. This was getting to be very heady stuff. "A pleasure, sir."

"The same. Sit down," Vernon said as he sat on the sofa looking at the startling similarity between the two men. "Johnston, wasn't it?"

"Yes, sir."

"From Boonesville, I understand?"

"When I was a baby. We moved here when I was two."

"Your dad, Charles?"

"Yes, sir. Did you know him?"

"Not personally," Vernon said. "Died, didn't he?"

"He did, yes."

"Your mother?"

"Esther. She died just a couple of weeks ago."

"Sorry," Vernon said.

"It's actually all right. She'd been sick for a long time. It was probably kind of a blessing."

Vernon nodded and silently looked at the two men a moment more, then looked over at Elvis. "Hungry?"

"You bet," Elvis said as he got up. "Over here, Ray," he said as he started off toward the dining room. Vernon followed them in.

Things kept getting harder for Ray to casually accept. The marble-floored dining room was a place where a sultan would feel at home. The chandelier probably cost more than Ray had made in the last five years. Yet he sat down at the eight-foot table with its priceless china trying to pretend that he did this all the time.

They were served their dinner by two of the kitchen staff. The meal seemed simple: steak, potatoes au gratin, and creamed corn. Simple, but probably the best steak Ray had ever tasted. He *knew* they were the best potatoes he'd ever had. Wonderful.

It was all Ray could do to try to act normal while sitting with Elvis Presley and another strange man who might actually be Ray's father.

At first it seemed no one knew what to say so they ate mainly in silence. Elvis and Vernon seemed as interested in Ray as he was in them. Ray was looking from one to the other but as soon as he did, he would catch them staring at him and they would look quickly away. They couldn't stop looking at him but didn't want to get caught at it.

Finally, Ray gave up. He just let them stare.

After a few moments, life in the Presley house seemed to return to what seemed more normal. Elvis started talking and just kept on. Dinner was obviously where the King held court, even if it was just Vernon and Ray.

Elvis had run into Jerry Lee Lewis earlier at a studio. Elvis seemed to like him and thought he was a good musician, if a bit limited in scope and range, but everytime they ran into each other, Lewis was after him to do something together. An album, a duet, go on tour again . . . something.

A mouthful of food didn't stop Elvis from laughing or talking. "Can you imagine going on tour with a wild man like that? It damned near killed me. Things are crazy enough on my tours, believe me. I don't need that kind of an influence any more. No, sir!"

As Elvis continued on, Ray noticed that Vernon was staring at their hands, going from Ray's to Elvis's, back to Ray's. Ray looked to see what was so interesting and practically froze. My God! Ray had always held his fork a little differently. Most people held it between their index and middle fingers, like a pencil. Ray had always held his between his middle and forth fingers, more like how a drummer held his drum sticks. He didn't know why, he wasn't trying to be different or anything, it just felt right.

Elvis was holding his fork the same way. Vernon obviously noticed this. What were the odds? Another coincidence?

Elvis had changed the subject to the exploits of a couple of his police buddies when Vernon started to mist up—tears were starting to form in his eyes. Suddenly, he scooted back from the table and tried to excuse himself but the lump in his throat wouldn't let him. Vernon motioned for Ray and Elvis to continue and quickly left.

After a moment, Elvis said "happens" by way of explanation and continued his stories. "So two of my guys decided to patrol a local lovers' lane. Sure enough, here's a car parked off to the side. Knowing they were going to catch a couple of teenagers, they quietly snuck up to the car, then jumped out and zapped them with their flashlights.

"There was a young man in the front seat reading, and a young girl in the backseat knitting. My friends were puzzled. One asked, 'What are you two doing?'

"The young man replied. 'Well, I'm reading and she's working on a sweater.'

"Still confused, my other friend asked the young man, 'How old are you?' He said, 'Twenty-two.'

" 'And how old is she?'

"The young man looked at his watch and said, 'She'll be eighteen in six and a half minutes.'"

Both men laughed. Even though it was his joke, Elvis seemed to get just as much of a kick out of it as Ray. They then resumed eating and Elvis told another story or two but Vernon never came back.

When they finished, Elvis offered to give Ray a tour. He said he enjoyed showing people Graceland. It was quite a place. It deserved to be shared.

They avoided the private, upstairs rooms but Elvis showed Ray around the main floor and basement, even the kitchen. Ray's favorites were the striking yellow and dark blue TV room, the multicolored, draperied pool room, and Elvis's African-themed den, complete with waterfall.

It seemed to Ray that Elvis was having trouble walking. He relied heavily on the railings when they went up or down the stairs and seemed to get winded easily. He gave a hell of a tour, though.

One of the many things that struck Ray that evening was that Elvis was a total television freak. There was at least one TV in every room, most of them were turned on with the sound down. He also noticed that his love of TV, like everything else in Graceland, just seemed to fit. This was, indeed, the King's lair.

"You've probably got the greatest place in the world here," Ray said when they arrived back at the living room.

"Yeah. I probably do," Elvis agreed.

"I should have shown you around the trailer," Ray quipped.

Elvis laughed. "Next time." Ray laughed, too.

"You play racquetball?" Elvis asked.

"No."

"Good. I'll whip your ass. C'mon," Elvis said, already on his way. Ray fell in behind, not even wanting to think what running around a racquetball court was going to feel like to his trashed body, but refusing was not even anything that crossed his mind.

Ray did wonder, since Elvis had such trouble walking, how could he possibly play racquetball? He didn't look well at all.

Elvis led the way outside, over to a two-story building not far from the main house. Inside was a two-level lounge, workout area, dressing room, Jacuzzi, and a glassed-in racquetball court. He loaned Ray suitable workout clothes (which, ironically enough, were Elvis's when he was a little thinner and they fit Ray perfectly), and proceeded to give Ray a lesson, literally.

It was interesting. Elvis would get winded, cough, lean against the sides for support, then attack the ball. His innate competitiveness was enough to handle Ray easily. Elvis thanked him for helping him. He had to get some weight off quick!

Generally, Ray was impressed by how well Elvis moved, even with his additional weight. Then he remembered the black belts in karate. Ray imagined one would have to move pretty good to earn those.

Ray was also surprised how well his own body came through once he got it moving. Elvis definitely gave Ray a workout, which was the last thing he needed but since Elvis tried to chase down all the errant balls Ray hit, Elvis worked up a good sweat, too.

Afterward, they relaxed in the lounge with another Pepsi and told stories. They started trading high school stories and found that they each had the ability to crack the other up.

Ray was wrapping up a story and was laughing so hard he could barely get it out. "And I couldn't believe it. I was as sick as a dog but everytime I'd get back in the car, her tongue was right back down my throat again. It was horrible!"

Elvis was laughing, too. "I'm with you. Get a woman on a mission, look out!"

Their laughter was interrupted by Velma, who came into the lounge carrying a tray of pills and a glass of water.

"Excuse me, Mr. Presley," she said. "You asked me to remind you about tomorrow morning."

"Oh, right."

"Should I leave these?" she asked, bringing them over to him.

"Yeah. Thanks Velma," Elvis said, already starting to take a pile of pills four and five at a time. Velma left. Elvis resumed talking while still taking the pills.

"Excuse me. All the years on the road's made me into a night owl. It's a real pain in the butt when I have to meet someone in the morning, but tomorrow's one of those mornings."

"Well, I should probably be going," Ray said. The bottom had actually dropped out a while ago. "Let you get some rest."

"Hell, I haven't been able to sleep for years."

"Couldn't you make the meeting for later in the day?" Ray wondered. "I mean, what are they going to tell *you*? No?"

"You don't know me, Ray," Elvis said, then motioned to their surroundings. "All this didn't happen by accident."

He scooted over a little closer to Ray and held out his hand so Ray could see the large ring on his finger. The initials TCB were on it with a lightning bolt in the background.

"Do you know what that means?" Elvis asked.

"No."

" 'Takin' care of business.' We have fun, we fool around, but we don't screw with business."

Elvis stood, seemed to lose his balance, and almost fell over. "Whoa there, mama," Elvis said as he caught himself. Ray got to Elvis just as he regained his balance.

"You all right?"

"No, not particularly. Happens sometimes," Elvis said lightly, then looked at Ray silently for a moment. "You know, no matter what happens here, I'm glad you came over. Had a good time."

"Me, too," Ray said. "Is Vernon going to be okay?"

Elvis thought before answering. "You're kind of a shock, you know? We didn't see you coming. He doesn't quite know what to do with you. Hell, neither do I!"

"Hell, neither do I!" Ray added, laughing.

Elvis shook Ray's hand, looking at him closely. "Maybe I'll know more when I come back, maybe I won't. We'll see. But let's try to keep this quiet for a while, all right?" Elvis smiled. "I realize things get out of hand every once in a while but let's try to keep a lid on it as much as we can. All right?"

"Sure." Ray tried to sound casual but was hoping Elvis would want to see him again.

"Now, get your clothes on and get out of here. God bless." Elvis started to leave.

"Thank you. Uh, mind if I call a cab?" Ray asked.

"Ned's back at the house. Probably in the kitchen. He'll take you home."

"Still?" It surprised Ray that Ned wasn't included in any of the evening's happenings but still was there.

"Yeah." To Elvis, that was simply the way things were. He turned, waved, and walked away. As Elvis left, Ray was left with an uncomfortable feeling of dread. Elvis was really sick. There was no question about it. As impressive as he was, there was a pervasive unhealthy pallor about him.

Ray stiffly changed into his own clothes and went over to the main house. It felt strange to be walking through the Graceland property alone at night. Strange, but also exhilarating. He hoped he'd be coming back again.

Ned was indeed in the kitchen, at the table, drinking coffee and reading the paper. He saw Ray come in.

"Hey, ready to go?"

"You been here the whole time?" Ray asked.

"Takin' care of the boss is a rare privilege," Ned said, getting his jacket. "But the hours suck." They laughed. "C'mon."

Ray followed him out to the limo. He looked back before getting in, already savoring his first night in this new, totally amazing world.

Ray was asleep before they cleared the gates. Ned woke him when they reached the trailer.

20

IT SEEMED AS THOUGH Ray's head had just hit the pillow when his alarm went off at 6:30 a.m. Every muscle in his body screamed *no!* when he tried to get out of bed. He had a major desire to say screw it and go back to sleep, but the thought of losing his home, his job, and further trashing what was left of his credit rating was just too much.

The amazing occurrences of last night came to him and, despite his aches and pains, he had to smile. He also decided not to make the same mistakes he'd made before and gave J.D. a quick call, knowing he'd never been able to sleep past six o'clock in his life. Ray told him to get his butt over there quick before he went to work. "Big news, will explain when you get here."

Ray hung up, staggered into the shower, and let the merciful, God-given hot water flow over his aching body. He was still in there when J.D. arrived about twenty minutes later, scaring the hell out of him. Ray had fallen half-asleep in the shower and probably would have stayed there another hour or so if J.D. hadn't pulled back the curtain, saying, "Hey, what's up, bro?"

Ray jumped so much he practically fell down. He told J.D. to get a cup of coffee while he dried off. J.D. did, and called out, "What's the smell?"

Ray put on his bathrobe and came out into the kitchen. He hadn't been out of the shower long enough to notice anything, but J.D. was right, something had burned.

Then he found it and started to laugh. The TV dinner he'd put in before the invitation to Graceland the night before was still in the oven, which was still turned on. As Ray's mother used to say, it was "a little brown." He smiled at the memory, even if she might not have been his real mother.

Getting back to reality, he showed what looked to be a lump of charcoal to J.D. "TV dinner. Forgot all about it last night."

"How the hell couldn't you have noticed that?"

Ray sat on the couch half-dressed, suddenly very awake. "All right, listen. What I'm about to tell you stays here, understand? Really, if this gets out anywhere, I'll know you let it out and I'll never tell you another secret in my life. Agree?"

"You got it," J.D. said, anxious to hear what was so big that Ray had to go through all this buildup.

Actually, now that Ray got the preliminaries out of the way, he was quite anxious to share it all with his best friend.

"Well, you see, I was gone most of last night. Jesus, I can hardly believe this myself. J.D., last night I had dinner with Elvis at Graceland. Hell, we played racquetball till three in the morning."

"Get out!"

"And I met Vernon Presley, who might be my dad. This is all very strange."

J.D. sat down. "Are you kidding me? All right, seriously. Talk to me!"

"Can't do it. Got to work today. We'll talk later. God, my mouth tastes like hell."

Ray started brushing his teeth in the kitchen sink, which gave him a lot more room than the tiny one in his bathroom.

"You bet your ass we're going to talk," J.D. said as he tried imagining Ray in Graceland. "Can I meet him?"

"No," Ray said emphatically with a mouth full of toothpaste.

J.D. laughed. This was all just too amazing. "I'll be damned."

The next few days were filled with questions and answers. Ray shared his experiences, his observations, and his feelings and together he and

J.D. hypothesized about the various things that could happen. It was an enjoyable time of "what if?"

Saturday, May 14, 1977

Ray worked his last weekend for the farmer, went back to work at Fields, and was still cleaning the elementary school at night. Progress had been made, leaving Ray totally exhausted and still about twenty-eight hundred dollars short.

But the time was up. Even though he didn't have the whole thing, he did have over a thousand to distribute and he did. Five hundred bucks each went to LifeCare and his land/trailer payments and fifty bucks went to Chris the mechanic. Everybody promised not to do anything bad to him for at least a month. He'd catch the funeral home next time.

Ray had just come home from dispensing his extremely hard-earned money when the phone rang. It was Elvis.

"Dad blame it, Ray, I'm getting all kinds of shit here."

"Why? What? What's going on?" Ray asked.

"That damned article got more attention than you think. My guys are back at me again, pestering me about it all the time, wondering what I think, when they can meet you, if I think you're for real. Some even wonder why you picked now to get in touch, wondering if you're going to be hitting me up for money or something. That kind of thing."

"That's bullshit. I don't want anything from you and you know damn well why I didn't get in touch before now. Because I didn't know anything about it before we found the journals."

"Yeah, I know the story," Elvis said.

"Are you telling me you don't believe me?"

"I don't know what to believe. All I know is that I was having a hard time before you came along and now I'm having an even harder time. Look, I hate to say this but as far as I'm concerned, my twin died when we were born. I never had a brother and I don't want one now." Elvis hesitated. "And now the colonel's all over me, too."

"Why would he be upset?" Ray asked, suddenly feeling cold.

"For about a million reasons you don't know nothing about," Elvis barked back. "I owe everything to him. We built something pretty darn great here, I think you'd have to admit that, and he don't want anything to distract from it. Things are tough enough. I got to listen to him. Besides, when he gets pissed it all gets dumped on me and then I get pissed."

"So what do you want me to do?" Ray asked after a pause.

"Hell, I don't know. Just don't go thinking that the other night over here meant anything. I was just curious, that's all. You just get on with your life and I'll get on with mine."

That came as a surprise to Ray. It was almost as surprising as the fact that he wasn't mad, not at all. He was profoundly hurt.

"Sure," was all Ray could muster. The lump in his throat prohibited him saying more.

"Good. We'll just leave it be, then," Elvis said with finality, then seemed to soften a little as he said, "You take care." And hung up.

Ray just looked at the receiver for a while, stunned, before he, too, hung up. He sat in his little living room for the longest time, just staring. His world suddenly seemed much smaller and bleaker. All the wonderful possibilities of the past few weeks were gone, just like that.

The momentary joy he'd gotten from staving off his creditors for a bit seemed quite pale. He felt very alone. The family that he knew was dead. And now, it seemed, the family he never knew about didn't want him.

Ray came as close to crying as he had in years.

Saturday, May 21, 1977

The next week got back to normal for Ray—working. He questioned God's motives for bringing Elvis into his life, then taking him away. That seemed a little mean to Ray, not at all "benevolent," but he guessed it fit in nicely with the "mysterious ways."

After Elvis called, downplaying everything, Ray shared his night with Elvis with Sheree. She could hardly believe it but promised repeatedly to keep it to herself, for now. He chose not to tell either her or J.D. about the phone call that ended the dream. They were having such a good time hypothesizing about it all, and besides, it was embarrassing. It was as though he hadn't measured up. Would Elvis feel differently about him if Ray had been more successful? More interesting? Was he ashamed to be related to this truck driver? This janitor?

Yeah, maybe.

Ray also told J.D. the full story of why he had been killing himself for the last couple of weeks and had answered most of his questions about Elvis.

J.D. felt bad about the hole Ray was still in but was happy that Ray had, at least, bought himself some time. J.D. was sure the future would work itself out and be just fine. Ray wasn't so sure, but kept it to himself.

As stiff and sore as Ray felt, he still let himself get talked into an evening of pool. Even though he just wanted to sleep the whole weekend, he also realized that he hadn't had any fun for much too long. That night the two old buds went off to their old haunt, the Take a Break pool hall, and proceeded to kick back. It was a busy night. It felt good to be out among 'em.

As much as Ray tried to minimize and underplay anything to do with Elvis, J.D.'s questions were never far under the surface.

"He got a pool table?" J.D. wanted to know.

Unless he wanted to go into Elvis's phone call calling the whole thing off, which Ray didn't want to do, he had to keep answering questions as though nothing was wrong.

"God, you ought to see his pool room. It's all made out of material, every color you could imagine. It's pretty neat."

"Yeah, I think I've seen pictures of it," J.D. said as he set up a shot. After making a fairly easy shot and starting to set up another, J.D. asked a rare question that didn't have anything to do with Elvis.

"How's working at Fields?"

"They're being real good to me," Ray answered. "It'll probably get boring after a while but it's a good bunch of guys. I owe them big time."

Just then Sheree came in, found them through the smoke-filled room, and came over to their table.

"I thought I might find you two in here."

"Well, hi, darlin'," Ray said, giving her a hug and a kiss.

"Hey, babe," J.D. said, giving her a hug and a kiss, too. "Perfect timing. I was just going to make a run. Want a beer?"

"Sure. Thanks, J.D.," Sheree said and she sat down on a stool by Ray as J.D. left. "Got the message you left with Sonny. I'm glad they're not going to be hauling you off to debtors' prison in the next month or so."

"Yeah. Got a little breathing room," Ray said, giving Sheree an extra hug. "Paid like hell for it, but at least I got it."

Sheree relaxed into Ray's arms for a moment before saying, "I don't like it when we fight."

"Wasn't much of a fight."

"Well, you were mad at me. I didn't like that."

"I didn't, either."

"Trust is a big part of a relationship and I really want you to feel you can trust me," Sheree said. "And you really can, you know? Can you forgive me?"

"Actually, I already have, but don't tell Sheree," Ray said playfully.

Sheree bopped Ray on the arm, causing them both to smile.

Just then J.D. arrived with the beers.

"Thanks, J.D. You're a good man," Sheree said as she took one of the cool ones.

"Damn straight," J.D. agreed.

Sheree's face suddenly paled as she noticed three men enter the place and head over toward their table. The tallest was Guy Stubbs, flanked by a couple of his friends. Sheree knew that this would be the first time Guy and Ray had seen each other since the debacle that cost Ray his job and gave it to Guy.

Ray hadn't noticed Guy until he spoke.

"Well, if it isn't Mr. Presley."

Ray turned around and saw red. "I wondered how long you could keep avoiding me."

"You make it sound like I give a shit." Both men stared hard at each other.

"Yeah, I guess that would be giving you too much credit, wouldn't it? You enjoying my job?"

"Yeah, I am, as a matter of fact."

"How'd my planning work out for you? Hope I didn't use too many big words so you didn't have any trouble stealing every bit of work I'd put into that day."

"No, it was just fine. Too bad you couldn't have been there to actually see it."

"Wasn't it now?" Ray stated coldly.

"Hey, it's a good thing you got Elvis to fall back on." Guy laughed and looked over at Sheree. "How does it feel, hanging out with a liar? Elvis's brother, my ass."

"Shut up, Guy," Sheree said.

"He's really more of a fraud," Guy continued, taunting. "Sucking up to that pathetic, bloated joke."

"Easy, Guy," Ray said. "This ain't something going on behind my back, like you're used to."

Sheree didn't like the way this was going at all. She grabbed Ray's arm, tried to lead him away. "Let's get out of here, Ray. C'mon, right now."

"What are you trying to milk him for?" Guy continued. "A new car? He does that, doesn't he? Maybe you could get a nice pink Cadillac."

Ray put down his pool cue and looked as though he was going to leave with Sheree, but suddenly turned and punched Guy in the face, knocking him down. Guy's two buddies then jumped on Ray, which brought J.D. into it.

The rest of the players in the pool hall came over and watched the melee. Ray and J.D. were both pretty handy with their fists, but so were the other guys, all three of them. The quick surge of energy Ray had gotten at the beginning of the fight was sapped out of him quickly. His body was definitely not quite up to this yet. Needless to say, he and J.D. got the worst of it.

Sheree watched with disgust before the owners of the pool hall came over, broke it up, and sent everybody off through opposite doors and threatened to call the police if it continued outside. Not needing any more trouble, everyone decided to go home.

On the way, Ray thought to himself that it was a bit ironic that he'd gotten beat up in defense of a maybe brother who didn't want anything to do with him. Then he thought about it some more. Nah, that wasn't true. He got in the fight because he didn't like Guy Stubbs and he was acting like an ass.

All right. It was good not to fool yourself. If Ray didn't feel any better outside, at least he did inside.

21

THE NEXT DAY A beat-up, thoroughly wiped-out Ray was asleep on the couch, while an equally trashed J.D. slept in the chair. Sheree, looking fresh and rested, came out of the bedroom.

"Aren't they cute at that age?"

Ray managed a grunt.

"Are you awake?" Sheree asked.

"Mornin'," Ray managed to say.

"I'll come back later and make you guys something to eat. You shouldn't be trusted with anything sharp today," Sheree said as she started to leave.

" 'Bye, baby," Ray said. Then, as she closed the door, "Damn!"

"Yeah," J.D. muttered, waking up also.

"Don't say anything with a 'b' in it," Ray said, trying not to move his lips.

"Why not?" J.D. asked. "B-b-b . . . Oh God."

"You never listen, do you?"

"Damn," J.D. also said, in pain again, holding his mouth.

It was another much-needed day of sleep, rest, and healing for Ray and now for J.D., too. Sheree was a girl of her word as she came back a couple hours later and made the guys some toast and eggs, sent J.D. home, and put Ray back to bed. She then left again, allowing Ray to sleep.

Ray woke up in the afternoon, was tired of laying around, so he gathered up his bills, put them in a pile on the kitchen table, and was in the process of discovering exactly where he stood with everybody when the phone rang.

It was Vernon Presley. He seemed to know that Ray and Elvis had "talked some" but said that Elvis was out of town. Vernon wondered if Ray would like to come over, have a bite and chat a little. Ray thought for a moment, wondering how Elvis would react to this, then agreed, not knowing how he could ever say no to any of these people even if he wanted to, which he didn't.

Ray described his pickup when asked, and gave Vernon his license plate number to permit him to drive into Graceland.

When they hung up, Ray stiffly got up to see what clothes he had that were clean enough to wear over there. He caught a glimpse of himself in the mirror. He'd momentarily forgotten about the fight but his reflection reminded him: a black eye, small cuts around the face and mouth, swollen lip, et cetera.

He started to panic. He couldn't go to Graceland looking like that! Then he got an idea and called Sheree.

"Hey, babe, it's me. Could you come over right now? I need a favor . . . no. Not that kind of favor . . . good, and listen, if this one gets out, we're through, understand?"

She said she understood, so Ray went on to tell her what he needed. She was on her way.

A couple hours later, Ray was sitting with a towel over his bare shoulders as Sheree admired her handy work.

"God, I'm good," she said as she handed a small mirror to Ray.

He looked over the makeup job she had given him. "Actually, you are," he agreed. The black eye and cuts were simply gone and the swollen lip was hardly noticeable.

"Nervous?" she asked while putting her stuff away.

"Wouldn't you be?" Ray asked, feeling bad that he wasn't telling her the whole truth but he knew he would soon. Just not now.

"Hell yes!" Sheree admitted. "But still, are you sure I can't come with you?"

"I sure wish you could, honey. Maybe someday. Who knows?"

As she cleaned up, Sheree noticed Morgan Bates's business card from *Dish* magazine that Ray had taken out of his pocket when he changed clothes.

"What's this?" she asked, reading. "Do you actually know some-body at *Dish*?"

"Yeah, met him the other day," Ray said.

"Do me a favor and don't introduce me. My God, they're the worst. They're not going to do a story on you, are they?" she asked, worried.

"I don't know. I don't think so."

"Please, don't let them. Really, Ray, any credibility you may have would be lost. They're really awful."

"Aren't they just about celebrities and what goes on backstage and stuff like that?"

"More like 'behind closed doors,'" Sheree corrected. "Even that's giving them credit. If they don't know something, they'll just make it up. Everybody knows they do it but they still have the power to hurt people, and boy, do they!"

"You really think they're as bad as all that?"

"Worse! They're the sleaziest magazine in the world but there are a lot of people who like that stuff. They sell millions of copies. They make millions of dollars! I *really* don't like them!" Sheree bundled up her makeup kit and got ready to leave. "Anyway, sorry about my little tirade. Just please don't have anything to do with them. You look great, by the way. Good luck."

"Thanks, honey. You're terrific. I owe you, big time."

"Yeah, you do. Call me tomorrow and tell me everything."

Ray agreed. They had a lingering good night kiss until Sheree pulled away. "Easy," she said playfully. "We don't want to smudge your makeup." She smiled, blew Ray another kiss, and left.

Ray went back to his bedroom to finish changing. Sheree's verbal attack had had the exact opposite effect she would have liked. Try as he did, suddenly, he couldn't get his mind off of *Dish* magazine.

It was too bad that Sheree thought so little of it but it sure sounded like they could afford the million. Ray didn't even want to think about it anymore, there were just too many sides. Still, just knowing it was there . . .

As Ray approached the Graceland gates, he saw a group of teenage girls hanging around there, hoping for even a glimpse of the King. Ray thought that these were probably not hard-core fans because they didn't know Elvis was out of town. He was sure that Elvis's die-hard fans would know his every move. At least every scheduled appearance.

The guard compared the look of Ray's truck and license plate to what he had on the list, then did a bit of a double take when he actually looked at Ray. After hesitating a moment, the guard decided to say nothing. When the gates opened, Ray drove through, trying to hide his face from the girls, who suddenly went into a frenzy.

The guard had to hold them back until the gates closed again.

Ray parked his pickup where Ned had parked the limo. That same strange, privileged, weird feeling came back to him as he walked up to the front door, past the famous columns and Elvis's lions that were a little more formidable than Ray's, and rang the bell. Again, it was hard for him to realize he was actually doing this.

The door was soon opened by Velma. "Good evening, Mr. Johnston. The Presleys are expecting you."

"Thank you, Velma," Ray said as he entered and followed her to the living room where Vernon was sitting, reading a magazine. He stood when he saw Ray and went to him.

"Ray, thanks for coming," Vernon said as they shook hands.

"My pleasure, sir."

"I want to apologize for the other night . . ." Vernon started.

"No need to at all, sir. I . . . I understand," Ray said.

Dee, Vernon's second wife, came in the room. She was a nicely dressed, attractive woman in her sixties.

"Oh, darlin', this is . . . Ray. My wife, Dee."

"Nice to meet you, ma'am," Ray said.

Dee was obviously taken aback as she shook his hand. "Oh my . . . excuse me. Hello. Nice meeting you, too." Still amazed, she looked over at Vernon. "I see what you mean. Heavens!"

"Now, don't go staring at him like he was a trained seal. Sit down," Vernon said. They all sat.

"Elvis is on tour again. Gone practically this whole month," Vernon explained.

"This has been a very busy year for him. He really is working way too hard," Dee said, then added, "Our place is being painted. Elvis said we could stay over here while he's gone."

Ray nodded, having no idea what to say to that.

"I understand you and Elvis had some . . . words," Vernon said tactfully. Ray nodded as Vernon continued. "Colonel Parker only knows how to look at things one way, and that's his way. Any possibilities that may exist here for all of us don't fit in with his plans, therefore they don't exist. He can be pretty hard on Elvis every once in a while but the boy adores him. Thinks he owes him everything."

Vernon paused for a moment. Once again, Ray didn't know what to say so he just sat and listened.

"Sometimes I think he'd be better off having someone else manage him but the Colonel surely did get him started. Made him the biggest thing in the world and Elvis is a good boy. He's loyal. You make a friend of Elvis, you got a friend for life.

"Anyhow," Vernon continued. "It's just us for dinner tonight. Is that all right?"

"Certainly, sir," Ray said.

Everyone was being so awkwardly polite that after Vernon's monologue no one could think of anything proper to say, so they said nothing. After a silent pause, Dee asked, "What do you do for a living, Ray?"

"I'm afraid I'm at the other end of the rope from Elvis," Ray said. "I've done a number of things but currently I'm driving a truck for a lumber company."

"Hell, I drove truck," Vernon said. "So did Elvis, for years. Absolutely nothing wrong in driving truck. It's got to be done."

"Are you married?" Dee asked.

"Now, don't make this a damn quiz show," Vernon Barked.

"No, ma'am. I got a 'live one' going but . . . I guess the time just hasn't been right."

"You certainly don't want to be in a hurry," Dee stressed.

"No, ma'am."

Another silent pause ensued as everybody tried to subtly study each other.

"It's awful hard for me to think that you could be Jesse," Vernon admitted after a moment.

"I know, sir. For me, too," Ray agreed.

Another silent pause was ended when Vernon asked, "Hungry?"

"Sure."

"Good," Vernon and Dee got up. Ray followed them into the sumptuous dining room.

As before, a lavish meal was laid out for them, served by the staff. Ray knew of Vernon's extremely poor existence throughout most of his life but found it interesting how comfortable he seemed in these surroundings. Ray supposed that people can get used to anything over time, even wealth.

In a mealtime punctuated with pregnant pauses, Vernon got everyone's attention by questioning rather loudly, "What could that damn fool midwife have been thinking?"

"It seems pretty awful," Ray said. "But I imagine she was doing what she thought was right."

"Well, it wasn't!" Vernon said harshly. Ray suddenly wished he'd been a little less candid.

"More like playing God, and that ain't right," Dee added quickly.

" 'Poor' don't mean you can't be good parents," Vernon topped.

"No, sir."

"And we were surely poor," Vernon said, slowing things down as he mentally relived this difficult time. "Hell, we buried you in a shoe box."

No one moved as the impact of what Vernon had said soaked in. Finally, Vernon asked, almost to himself, "I wonder, who got buried in that little box?"

A silent moment followed as each became lost in their own thoughts. Dee brought everyone back when she said, "It's a shame you couldn't have been found while Gladys was still alive. It could have made all the difference."

"She mourned for you her whole life. Never got over it," Vernon said quietly.

"I wish I could have met her."

"She was a good woman," Vernon said simply. "If you want to see a picture of her, there's one around the corner in the music room."

"I'd like that. Thank you." After another moment, Ray decided to mention something that had been bothering him. "I know Elvis wasn't real happy about me showing up and I do feel bad about that. I really don't want anything from him. I honestly don't."

"That's mostly the Colonel talking, Ray. Elvis has got to sort out in his own mind what he's going to do, and then he'll do it. Just give him some time."

"That's fine," Ray said. "I was also wondering, how's Elvis doing? He didn't seem to be feeling real good when I was here last and I heard somewhere that he was pretty sick."

"You'll hear everything about Elvis," Vernon said. "And I'll tell you right now, it's all bullshit! He's a good God-fearing boy. He don't use the Lord's name in vain, takes care of his family, don't smoke, don't drink, don't do drugs. He's a good boy."

Memories of the plate full of pills Elvis took the other night crossed through Ray's mind. Of course, perscription drugs were different from the ones you just get high on, so he supposed they were all right. Anyway, Ray wasn't about to bring it up. "I'm sure you're right, sir."

"Listen, the boy is not well," Vernon continued. Ray got the feeling this was not the first time Vernon had come to defend his son.

"He's under a doctor's care, a bunch of 'em, as a matter of fact. I sometimes wonder about it myself, but what good are a couple of crackers like us questioning the best doctors in the whole damn world? It don't make sense."

Vernon stopped, still a bit riled. "Expensive enough, I tell you."

Ray decided to let it be, which was fine. Once again, he had no idea what to say anyway.

The dinner soon wound down. After a few more minutes of small talk, the evening was over. As Ray left the dining room and entered the music room, he looked for the picture Vernon said was there. Ray soon found it on the mantel and walked over to it. It felt odd looking at this strange woman who was probably his mother.

Everyone knew she was the most important person in the world to Elvis but even so, she seemed out of place in that room. Surrounded by high-toned glitz was this little black-and-white picture of what could have been a washerwoman or a maid, a woman of good, solid peasant stock.

She seemed to have no physical characteristics of Elvis or Ray, but then neither did Vernon. Strangely unmoved by the encounter, Ray rejoined Vernon and Dee, who were waiting by the front door.

"Glad you could come over. Enjoyed it," Vernon said.

"Me, too. It was good seeing you. And, Dee, it was nice meeting you."

"And you, Ray."

Vernon reached into his back pocket and pulled out a small card, which he handed to Ray. "Put this away somewhere," he said. "It's our private number. You get in any trouble, have any problems, just give me a call. Okay?"

"Okay." Ray took it, touched by the gesture. "Thank you."

Ray put it away and started for his truck. He turned back halfway there and saw Vernon and Dee still in the doorway.

"Thanks again. 'Night."

Vernon and Dee waved as Ray climbed in his truck and started to drive off. The fans were gone as the gates opened for Ray to drive through. As he drove away, the lights of a waiting car went on as it followed Ray down the street.

Monday, May 23, 1977

The next day, Ray had just finished making himself a sandwich, which he put in his lunch pail. He grabbed a jacket and set out to work.

As Ray opened the door, a barrage of screams made him jump back. He recovered quickly and looked back out the door again at a group of teenage girls screaming and jumping up and down . . . until they got a better look at Ray. The screams started to die down. He wasn't Elvis, but. . . ?

"Who are you?" one of the girls asked.

"Who the hell are you?" Ray countered.

"We thought maybe you were Elvis," another said. "I guess you're not."

"You must be the smart one. No, I'm not Elvis."

"But you were at Graceland last night."

"Do you know how many people live at Graceland?" Ray asked.

"A lot?" one ventured.

"A lot."

"Do you know Elvis?" one of the girls asked.

"We've met."

"You look like him."

"I know," Ray said simply.

"What's your name?" a girl asked.

"Ray Johnston. Can I go to work now?"

"Yeah, sorry," one of the girls said as they all started to back away slowly, still watching him closely.

Another of the girls was looking at him quite suspiciously. She slowly, coyly came back to him and handed him a small book. "Could I have your autograph anyway?"

This surprised Ray somewhat, never having been down this particular road before. "Uh . . . sure."

He took the book and thought for a moment, since he'd never

signed anything like this. Finally, he figured out what he'd do. He signed it, *Ray Johnston* .

But just so the girl would remember who it was and when and why she'd gotten that particular autograph, he put a little *Elvis* underneath it.

Ray thanked the girl, waved to the others, got into his truck, and drove off, chuckling to himself. Him signing autographs! Who'd believe it.

22

FOR THE NEXT COUPLE of weeks, Ray's life resembled the life he used to know and love. Work was good, his times with Sheree were as pleasant and peaceful as always again, and he even found time to break out the motorcycles a couple of times with J.D.

He was able to put Elvis and all that out of his mind for a while and let himself openly enjoy being paid up on his bills for a minute.

Unfortunately, that peace of mind ended at the beginning of next month. Tomorrow. Everybody needed more payments on everything but Ray had needed a break. Break over. That old feeling of strangulation started creeping back, turning everything it touched a dull gray.

He was going to have to get creative again. Just the thought of the little farmer and his field of trees made Ray's body hurt, but he was going to have to come up with something.

As Ray drove home from work, he mulled over his possibilities. The first step had been taken that day, talking to the foreman about extra shifts again, more hours, et cetera. It was basically the same spiel he'd used before but he figured people had to be reminded of his intent just to know he was sincere.

As usual, they'd see what they could do.

Ray was tired from a full day's work and was looking forward to a beer in the lawn chair as he opened his front door, which had never been locked as long as he had owned the place. Ray went into the kitchen, put down his lunch pail, and started for the refrigerator when two men jumped out of the hallway and pounced on him, knocking him down.

They then sat on him and tried to get hold of his flailing arms to tie them behind him. After the initial shock subsided to the point that Ray could breathe again, he started yelling and fighting. The two men on top of him were holding on as tight as they could. The one trying to do the tying wasn't having too good a time.

He almost got Ray's hands tied a couple of times but Ray fought them loose. Ray was calling them every name in the book and asking them what the hell they thought they were doing but the men said nothing.

A few minutes into this altercation, a third man came in. Ray could only see his boots and noticed that he limped a little. Then he saw the man grab Ray's baseball bat, which he kept leaning up in the corner.

The man approached the tussling group and tried to take aim at Ray's head. It seemed the man didn't know exactly where he was supposed to hit. Of course, since Ray's head was about the only thing he could still move, it was all over the place.

The first swing the man took at Ray was quite tentative. It did little more than hurt like hell and make Ray even angrier. He proceeded to fight harder.

These were definitely not seasoned thugs. Actually, they had no idea of what else to do. A knock on the head always flattened someone in the movies, here it just made him madder. They didn't need that, he was hard enough to hold down anyway.

One of the men on Ray told the third man to try again harder. He did. This time it worked. Ray hardly felt the blow to the back of his head this time. It was as though someone had turned off the lights. He was out.

Wednesday, June 1, 1977

Ray woke up in the living room of a small house he'd never seen before. He was roped, tied, and duct-taped to a chair in the middle of the room. His arms and hands were secured behind him and his legs were taped together. There was also a piece of duct tape over his mouth. Obviously, they didn't want to fight him again.

As consciousness began to return to Ray, the first thing he was aware of was a splitting headache and a knot where he'd been hit. The second was that there were three men sitting on a couch in front of him, studying him like a laboratory specimen.

Ray tried to say something but the tape only permitted an unintelligible mutter to escape.

Ray quickly took in his surroundings; the room was small, cheaply and sparsely furnished with blankets and sleeping bags piled in a corner, giving the impression that a number of people might be staying there.

Two of the men seemed in their midforties and appeared to be laboring types, wearing work boots, jeans, and denim shirts, rather like how Ray looked when he went off to work. The third seemed like he didn't quite belong. He appeared to be in his late twenties, skinny, wearing a tank top T-shirt with long, dirty hair and tattoos.

"Well, he's finally coming around," one of the men said. "I was wondering if you'd killed him."

"That would have been all we need. Jesus!"

"You sure that's Elvis?" one asked.

"Looks like him . . . kinda," another said. " 'Cept maybe the hair and sideburns."

"I thought Elvis was supposed to be fat," the skinny one chimed in. "Maybe it's just how he looks in them Superman suits he wears."

Again, Ray tried to say something with no luck. He also tried to squirm loose from the ropes and tape. Nothing moved a bit.

"Hold on there, fella. You'll knock yourself over. You don't want to get hurt now, do ya?"

Ray thought of many caustic answers to that but since he couldn't talk, he reluctantly settled back down and glowered back at them.

"What do you think we should do now, Ben?" one asked.

Ben, the forty-year-old that had the limp, thought for a moment, then said, "Leonard, get Sue Ellen in here."

Leonard, the other forty-year-old, got up and disappeared down a hallway. The skinny one just sat and glowered at Ray. A couple of silent minutes later, Leonard reappeared, followed by a teenage girl. Ray looked over at her. There was something familiar about her. Then it came to him: she was the girl who had asked for his autograph at his trailer.

"You sure this is Elvis?" Ben asked Sue Ellen.

"I thought he might be," she replied uncomfortably, shyly looking over to Ray.

"*Thought* he might be!" the skinny one snapped. "Christ on a crutch, we go and steal a man because you think maybe he *might* be Elvis?"

Ray tried again to speak. Nothing.

"Del, dammit, I told you, he came out of Graceland and went to this old trailer. But look at him. Maybe Elvis wanted some time away from being a star, you know? So he died his hair, cut off his sideburns, and got himself a little place like that trailer where no one would ever dream he'd be," Sue Ellen explained. "Where he could, you know, live like a real person for a while."

"Oh yeah, like living like a real person is something that anyone would want to do," Leonard said. "Especially somebody who doesn't have to."

"And remember how he signed my book," Sue Ellen went on. "He signed this name but under it wrote 'Elvis' and sorta smiled. Why would he do that? I think he was trying to tell me something."

"Well, dammit," Ben exclaimed after a moment. "Of all the problems I tried to anticipate, knowing for sure whether or not we actually had Elvis was not one of them."

Ray started squirming around, trying to speak again. They looked over to him.

"Let's talk to him," Sue Ellen said.

"Are you crazy?" Del asked.

"Why not?" Sue Ellen asked simply.

"Well . . ."

"Hell, we might as well," Ben said as he got up, went over, and pulled the tape off Ray's mouth. "Didn't mean to hurt you there."

"Jesus Christ, what the hell are you doing?" Ray bellowed. "This is the stupidest thing I've ever heard of."

"You shut your face, asshole," Del said threateningly. "I'd just as soon punch you as look at you anyway."

"Put a sock in it, Del," Ben said firmly. "Nobody gets hurt here. This is just for the money. Remember that."

"Who the hell do you think is going to give you money for me?" Ray asked sarcastically. "I think you're beginning to notice, I'm not Elvis."

"If you ain't Elvis, who are you?" Sue Ellen asked.

"Ray Johnston. Like on my driver's license, like I signed on your picture."

"Why'd you put 'Elvis' on it?"

"Well, I sure as hell shouldn't have, I can tell you that," Ray said. "It was just so's you'd remember the conversation and why you got it. I could just see you looking at your book a year from now, wondering who this 'Ray Johnston' guy was. I thought it would remind you, that's all. Just trying to be nice."

"You do look a lot like Elvis," Leonard said.

"Well, excuse the hell out of me," Ray snapped. "I never realized that was reason to get kidnapped."

"You were at Graceland."

"Yeah, and I can go to the White House and not be the president, can't I?"

"Shit." Ben was not pleased by the direction this was taking.

"Look, I got an idea," Ray said. "Probably the best way to prove to you that I'm not Elvis would be to find out where the real Elvis is. I think he's on tour someplace." Ray turned to Sue Ellen. "Call information and ask for the Elvis Presley Fan Club. Ask them where Elvis is today. Even ask them where he was last night. They'll know."

"You don't give the orders around here," Del said menacingly as he slowly started to stand.

"Oh, sit down," Ben said as he looked over to Sue Ellen and nodded. "Might as well." She left the room.

"Listen, guys, while she's gone," Ray said quietly, "I got a problem. You got me tied up here real good but I gotta go to the bathroom bad. You think you could let me up for a minute?"

"We'd have to untie you," Ben said.

"I heard Elvis is a black belt. I don't think we should untie him," Leonard said to Ben.

"For crying out loud, if I was a black belt you think I'd be here right now? I would have whupped your sorry butts back at the trailer. Look, keep me tied up if you want, I just need to go. But quick."

The men looked at one another and seemed to silently agree that it was cruel and unusual punishment to deny a man his right to bathroom privileges. Ben got up, pulled out a pocket knife, and started cutting Ray loose from the chair.

"No funny business, all right?" Ben said. "You try anything, that's the last time you get untied. Hear me?"

"I do," Ray said.

Ben soon finished cutting him free from the chair. Ray's hands were still tied/taped behind his back and Ben said they were going to stay that way.

"Take him in there and watch him every minute," Ben said to Leonard, who armed himself with a kitchen knife on the way, just in case.

It was practically ten minutes later when they came out. Leonard's face was a bright red.

"Well, that was different," Ray said as he sat down in the chair again. Ben started retaping Ray to the chair.

"I think I'll wash my hands again," Leonard said, returning to the bathroom. Ben just chuckled and continued taping.

Sue Ellen soon came from the hallway. "I don't think he's Elvis," she said simply.

"How come?"

" 'Cause Elvis did a show in Baton Rouge, Louisiana, last night and is doing another one in Macon, Georgia, tonight," Sue Ellen said sheepishly. "Sorry."

"For Christ's sake!" Ben said. "Then who the hell is this?"

"I told you," Ray said. "Ray Johnston."

"And you're, what? A friend of Elvis?"

"Kinda. I know the family."

"What do you do?" Leonard asked.

"Drive a truck."

"Oh, that's just great. Who the hell's going to give us money for a truck driver?"

"Nobody," Ray said. "And that's the truth."

Del got up from the couch and went to the dining table where Ray saw his wallet, keys, and change laid out. Del looked at Ray's driver's license, shook his head, then continued looking for anything else that might help. Then he ran across the article.

A few minutes later, a grin spread across Del's face as he turned back into the room. "We ain't got Elvis here, guys," he said with a huge smile. "We got his brother."

23

IT WAS TWO O'CLOCK. Sheree was just about to wrap up the day shift at Rusty's when Pat Young, another Fields driver who worked with Ray, phoned. He'd been in with Ray and had met Sheree a couple of times.

"Sure, I remember you, Pat. What can I do for you?"

"Well, nothing for me," Pat said on the phone. "But you might want to help that boyfriend of yours."

"What's he done now?"

"Do you know where he is?" Pat asked.

"He should be working right next to you."

"Yeah. He should be, but he ain't. First he takes all this time off to do that other job, then he comes back asking for more hours and extra shifts and all, then today he doesn't even show up."

"He didn't call in sick or anything?" Sheree stopped cleaning the glasses she was working on as she talked. That wasn't like Ray. "Have you called him?"

"Nothing. It just rings."

"Well, I'll be damned, Pat. I haven't talked to him in a couple of days but I'm getting off here in a minute. I'll swing by out there and see if I can scare him up or find out what's going on."

"Good. Give me a call at Fields if you learn something, okay?" Pat said. "I'm trying to put in good words for him with Mr. Fields but he's not making it easy."

"I hear you. Thanks, Pat." Sheree hung up, finished with her glasses, and told Sonny she was leaving a little early. "And if Ray comes in here, have him call Pat at work, pronto. Okay?"

Sonny assured her it would be done.

A half hour or so later, Sheree was driving up to Ray's trailer. She was surprised to see his truck there. What was going on?

She got out and called for Ray. Nothing. She knocked on the door, then went in as she usually did. She called again. Still nothing, but what she saw scared her. A chair in the living room had been knocked over and Ray's baseball bat was lying in the middle of the room.

She looked around to see if she could get any idea of who might have been here but didn't find anything else. She used Ray's phone to call J.D., wondering if she could catch him at home. He was evidently at work. She'd call him later.

Then Sheree remembered that Ray had an emergency sticker on the back of the phone containing the number of the police. She called.

Del still had a big smile on his face as he walked over to Ben and handed him the article. "So we got with us the brother of 'Elvis the Pelvis.' "

"Never knew he had a brother."

"Oh, come on!" Ray said. "Do you think if I was the brother of Elvis Presley that I'd be living out in that piece of shit trailer?"

Ben finished reading the article. "So what are you saying? They just make this stuff up? Don't sound made up to me."

"Actually, you're right. That writer did think that I was his brother. Problem is, nobody else does, including Elvis. That's what I was over there talking about when you saw me come out of Graceland," Ray said, acknowledging Sue Ellen.

"By the way," Ben said to Sue Ellen, "why the hell ain't you in school?"

"You think I'm going to go to school when we have Elvis in our house?"

"He ain't Elvis."

"But we didn't know that this morning, did we?"

"This morning!" Ray said suddenly. "Oh no! What day is it?"

"Wednesday," Sue Ellen said.

"Goddamn it! You got the wrong guy, folks. Face it. And I'm missing work. I finally got a job. Oh no . . . do you know how hard it is to get a job in this town?"

"What do you supposed you're doing here, nimrod?" Del asked sarcastically.

"I would really like to know that," Ray replied just as hard.

"Shut up you two," Ben said from the couch and looked over to Leonard and Del. "As long as we got him, we gotta figure how to get some money for him."

"Good luck," Ray said.

"I wasn't talkin' to you," Ben said to Ray, then turned to the others. "Let's go outside." Ben then tried to get up out of the sofa but couldn't do it. Resigned, he held his hand up to Leonard, who pulled him to his feet. Ben slowly limped outside with the other men following.

Ray and Sue Ellen were left alone.

"How'd you ever get mixed up with this bunch?" Ray asked.

"Ben's my stepdad," she said. "He and my mom fell in love and got married when I was about ten. I came along in the bargain. Then, a couple years ago, my mom gets killed and Ben's stuck with a kid. Crummy, huh?"

"Yeah. Sorry about your mom. What happened?"

"Car wreck. Wasn't her fault. Some drunk." Sue Ellen tried to sound casual but there was a lot of pain just under the surface.

Ray squirmed a little in his chair, trying to get himself as comfortable as he could. "Listen, uh . . . what was your name again?"

"Sue Ellen."

"Sue Ellen. Okay. Look, I got to get out of here, and this is going nowhere. I mean, do these guys know how much trouble they could get into?"

"I suppose."

"With me, it's bad enough, it's still kidnapping, but what if they'd actually gotten Elvis? Can you believe how bad it could have been for them?"

"They had a pretty good plan going," Sue Ellen said.

"They did?"

"Yeah. They were going to ask a bunch of money in twenties and fifties. You know, so they'd be easy to spend. And if anyone said they'd call the cops, our guys would say that if they did, we'd shoot you up with drugs—I mean Elvis—and leave him someplace, then call the newspaper. It'd be like Elvis was a junky, that a lot of people think anyway. Out on a drug binge. Make him look real bad. His people wouldn't want that to happen."

"That was the plan?"

"Yeah. They even got the inside phone line to Graceland."

"You want me to tell you what's wrong with their plan, besides the fact that they don't have Elvis, of course?"

"Well . . . yeah."

"All right. That inside phone line will take you to Velma. She's the housekeeper and you don't want to screw with her. She also doesn't have any money. She would call the police immediately."

"What about the drug stuff?"

"She'd just tell the police and the newspapers what your guys told her, that they were going to set it up to look like he was a druggie."

Sue Ellen thought for a while. "Not so great, huh?"

"Not so great."

"They're all kinda desperate."

"Hey, I'm desperate, too, but I don't go around kidnapping people."

"Everybody here used to work for Vint's auto body shop. Problem was, Vint kept dipping into the company's funds until it went belly up. Everybody got screwed. The guys are all trying to stick together. You know, help one another. All the other shops are full."

Sue Ellen thought for a moment, wondering how much more she should say, then decided she might as well. "You know Ben? The one who's limping?"

"Yeah."

"Well, he's really sick. It's real hard for him to keep a job because sometimes he can hardly get out of bed."

"What is it?"

"He doesn't really know and he can't afford to see a doctor. Today's a pretty good day for him. Some days he just stays in bed and drools. It's really bad."

"Sue Ellen, I'm sorry about Ben. I really am. But this is really serious. You're sure as hell making my life harder because I'll probably lose my job over this, just as I'm starting to get some bills paid, but if these guys get caught, they're in *huge* trouble. They'll go to prison. You'll probably end up in an orphanage. What were they thinking?"

Sue Ellen seemed to be on the verge of crying. "Ben was just trying to do something right. He thinks this stuff he's got is killing him. He doesn't think he'll live much longer and he was worried about me, being sixteen years old and all alone in the world and broke on top of that. He figured I could take care of myself better if I had some money. That's where most of his share was going. Del's will probably just go for drugs. I don't like him very much."

"He's easy to not like." Ray just shook his head. "Well, I don't know what to say. All my friends are as broke as I am. This is not the way to solve anything."

They sat quietly for a minute. "Are you hungry?" Sue Ellen asked.

"Yeah."

"I think we have the makins for a peanut butter-and-jelly sandwich. Would that be okay with you?"

"That'd be great. Thanks."

Sue Ellen went into the little kitchen. Ray tried again to find some slack in how he was tied up but couldn't. He just tried to relax and keep his wits about him. It was hard anticipating the actions of people that have no idea themselves what they were going to do.

Sheree was not getting any satisfaction from the young officer who had driven out to Ray's trailer. He saw a chair that had been knocked over and a baseball bat on the floor. According to him, there were a million reasons why that could have happened and none of them would have anything to do with foul play.

As for missing a day of work, maybe he went fishing. Who knows? Again, it could be a million things. Besides, he'd only been gone a day. One day!

"Have you noticed anything missing?" the officer asked Sheree.

"I haven't looked that close, but no," she admitted.

"You say that's his truck outside?"

"Yes."

"Out here all alone like this? Ma'am, if there were bad guys around, that truck would have been long gone."

"What if they wanted him for something else?"

"What? His money?" the officer asked, looking around at the worn, spartan decor. "Look, if you haven't heard from him in another week or so, or if you get some more information, let me know," the young officer continued. "I'll keep my ears open but it's just too new a situation for us to really get into."

"It's just that this is so unlike Ray. If you knew him you'd know what I mean."

"I'm sure I would," the officer said condescendingly. "I hear that about twelve times a day, where a woman tells me that some man is doing something that is just not like him at all. You know what? They thought they knew him. Thought they knew everything about him. Turns out they didn't know him at all and what he was doing was exactly like who he was. They just didn't know it."

Sheree resisted the urge to punch him. "I don't think this is one of those cases," she said quietly.

"Well, we'll see," the officer said on his way out. "Give it a little time."

He left. Sheree sat down on the couch and looked at the tipped-over chair and baseball bat, wondering if she was overreacting. No, she decided. She did know Ray and this wasn't like him. She was scared.

* * *

Sue Ellen fed Ray his peanut butter-and-jelly sandwich and had one herself. After their earlier chat, conversation died down considerably. The men were still at it outside, though. Occasionally, snatches of a heated discussion would carry into the house but not enough for Ray to have an idea of what they were arguing about.

The men had probably been at it nearly an hour when they abruptly came inside. Ben, limping, led the way and plopped into the couch across from Ray.

"Okay, here's the deal," Ben started. "You're either Elvis's brother or you ain't. If you ain't, that's a whole other set of problems. But, if you are, that's worth a couple of bucks to someone. Well, who? First would be Elvis's dad, your dad. What'd you say his name was, Sue Ellen?"

"Vernon."

"Yeah, Vernon. 'Course, it's damn near impossible to get ahold of someone like that. He'd pay money to keep one of his boys safe. I just don't know how in hell we could ever reach him and we don't have all the time in the world here."

Ray was pleased that they didn't know that Vernon was temporarily living at Graceland. If they'd known, their inside number probably would have worked, though Ray had no idea if Vernon would have paid any money for him. He was glad he didn't have to find out.

Ray's wallet and its contents were still strewn out on the table. No one had any idea whose card it was that was sitting right on top next to his keys, the one with a phone number and "VP" on it.

"So we decided to go after Elvis himself," Ben continued. "We know where he is and he'd probably be anxious to help his brother out of a jam, don't you think?"

"Oh, don't do that," Ray said. "Please. It's just going to be embarrassing."

"You let us worry about that," Leonard chimed in. "We got a new plan."

"First, we call the chamber of commerce in Macon to find out where he's staying. They always have that kind of information," Ben said. "Then Sue Ellen here will act like an operator, saying this is a call from Graceland. That ought to get us past the front desk. After that, we use your name, Ray Johnston, to get to the big man himself."

"How's he going to know we've really got him?" Leonard asked.

"Who the hell would make up a story like this?"

"Maybe we ought to chop off a finger and send it to him," Del suggested.

"Del, damm it!" Ben started.

"It could be anyone's finger," Leonard interrupted. "I think you only do that when you have a really neat ring or something like that that you leave on the finger. But it was a good idea."

"It was a terrible idea," Ray objected.

"You shut up. We'll deal with that when the time comes," Ben said, taking charge. "Leonard, go get those numbers."

Everyone waited quietly while Leonard went about instigating their "new plan." Ray watched Ben, who seemed to get more tired and sink deeper into the sofa by the minute. One of his eyelids was beginning to droop and he was drooling.

24

MUCH TO RAY'S SURPRISE, everything went pretty close to how Ben had called it. The chamber of commerce did indeed know where Elvis was staying and was only too glad to give out that information.

The hotel was being besieged with calls for Elvis, none of which were being put through, but when Sue Ellen got on the phone, acting like a long-distance operator with a call from Graceland, the switchboard couldn't send it upstairs fast enough. In spite of everything, Ray was really impressed by what a good job little Sue Ellen did. She was quite the actress.

She quickly handed the phone to Ben before the connection upstairs was made.

"Hello," the phone was answered. Ben could tell that it was not Elvis.

"A call for Mr. Presley please," Ben said officially.

"Who is it?"

"For Mr. Presley *personally!*" Ben stressed.

"I asked who it is. You've got three seconds." The voice on the other end of the phone was very hard.

"Tell him it's about his brother. Very important."

"He ain't got no brother."

"You'd be surprised. Tell him we've got Ray Johnston right here and he's in a heap o' trouble. Tell him!"

Ben heard the phone receiver being covered up and a muffled conversation going on. The next voice Ben heard was unmistakably Elvis.

"You got who?"

"We've got your brother here, Mr. Presley. He's tied up like a Christmas package right now, but for the amount of one hundred thousand dollars we'll let him go unharmed," Ben said, trying his best to keep his nerves in check. "If you don't come up with it, I'd hate to think what could happen to him."

"He tell you he's my brother?"

"He didn't have to. We can read, sir."

"What are you going to do, kill him?" Elvis asked.

"Maybe. Yeah."

Elvis laughed. "Listen, buddy, do yourself a big favor and untie the poor, sorry son of a bitch and start looking for another line of work. You kidnap an impersonator and want me to give you money to set him free? I love it. You made my day."

Elvis was still laughing when he hung up.

Ben slowly put down the receiver. Everyone watched. Ben said nothing for the longest time.

"Well?" Leonard finally asked.

"Ain't going to work," Ben said flatly. "Says we got ourselves an Elvis impersonator here."

"I ain't no impersonator!"

"So there's no money?" Del asked.

"No." Ben shook his head.

"Damn it. After all that."

"Shit."

That seemed to sum up everyone's reaction. They sat in stunned silence for a while. This was definitely not the way they thought this would end up. Del got up dejectedly and walked back to the table containing the contents of Ray's pockets and started looking over them again, thinking.

"What do we do now?" Leonard asked the question they were all wondering about.

"Elvis asked if we were going to kill him," Ben said.

"What? Kill me?"

"Oh, pipe down. I didn't say we were going to do it, that's just what he asked," Ben said, then added after a moment, "What else can we do?"

"I think we should kill him," Del said flatly, his back still turned to the room.

"He does know who we are," Leonard said, getting a little afraid of the direction in which things were headed.

"Wait a minute," Ray said emphatically, realizing he'd better get involved here very quickly. "What else can you do? I'll tell you. Nothing. Lots of things. Get out of this situation before you get in any deeper. And you're wrong. I *don't* know who you are. I was unconscious when you brought me here, remember? I don't know what city we're in, let alone what street or house. I don't know any of your last names."

As Ray talked, Del casually removed Ray's driver's license from his wallet and put it and Ray's keys in his pocket. He then returned to the room and sat down.

Ray continued, hoping he was getting through. "Hell, I couldn't find you again if I wanted to, and I don't want to! Other than giving me a headache and probably losing me my job, which does piss me off, you really haven't done any harm. Blindfold me, take me home. I could never find this place again."

"We need to keep him at least until tomorrow," Del said.

"Why?" Leonard asked.

"There still might be a way to make this work. Let's don't be in too much of a hurry."

Ray leaned forward as much as his constraints would allow and softened his voice considerably. "Ben, Sue Ellen told me about your condition and I'm sorry. I really am, but this isn't the way to take care of anything."

"What is?" Ben asked, deflated. "I can't get a job. I don't need much but we still got to eat."

"Give me until tomorrow afternoon," Del said, standing. "If we haven't come up with a good plan by then, we can let him go."

"I think we should let him go now," Sue Ellen said.

"Well, I personally don't give a shit what you think, little girl," Del said, then turned to Ben and Leonard. "Look, we've already got him. Another day or two isn't going to make any difference to anybody. I got an idea. I'm going to split for a while. Promise me we'll keep him till then."

"What's your idea?" Ben asked. "We should talk about this."

"Just something I want to check on. Might be nothin'," Del said as he started to leave. He turned at the door, smiled a menacing grin at Ray, and said, "But it might also be great." He left.

The room suddenly got quiet.

"You know, I disagree with what he was saying. I think the sooner you—"

"I thought you'd disagree with that one," Ben said, trying to get out of the couch. This time he made it. "But he's got something going. It isn't going to hurt to wait a bit. Make yourself comfortable. I'm going to take a nap."

Ben left the room. Ray, Leonard, and Sue Ellen looked at one another a moment before Sue Ellen got up.

"Guess I'll go do homework," she said.

Leonard settled in, scanning through a nearby *Playboy*. Ray tried to relax as much as he could. It appeared as though he was going to be there a while.

25

DEL DIDN'T RETURN THAT evening or night, which aggravated Ben and Leonard. They were all supposed to be in this together and what the hell was this plan he'd been working on?

Ray found himself alone with Sue Ellen many times and they chatted casually about most everything. When Ray wondered where Del could have gone, she told him about this married woman he'd been fooling around with. "She's really trashy. Her husband's in the service overseas. Del stays with her a lot. I think that's really crummy."

Ray agreed. Pregnant pauses stretched into hours. It was a long night.

Thursday, June 2, 1977

The next morning, Del still hadn't shown up and Ben and Leonard were upset. They also didn't know what to do. They'd promised Del they'd keep Ray a while longer but then with Del gone, how long should they wait? The whole fiasco was over as far as either one of them was concerned. The sooner they could get Ray out of there, the better.

It was early afternoon when Ray and Ben started discussing his health, the job market, and the problems he was facing. After a while, knowing that Ben had stooped to extortion rather than face the situation head-on and deal with it, Ray blew.

"Ben, damn it! I know you've got some physical problems but so do a lot of people. There are all sorts of things you could do. Hell,

I work nights at Nedermeyer elementary school as a janitor, for Christ's sake. You could do that. Look around. Get creative!"

Ray had just finished his diatribe and Ben was thinking about it when Del came bursting through the door.

"Where the hell have you been?" Leonard asked.

"Doesn't matter," Del said. "I thought I had a handle on what we should do here but it didn't work out. We can let him go anytime now as far as I'm concerned."

Del walked off to the bathroom, leaving everyone wondering what Ray was still doing there.

"Cut him loose," Ben said to Leonard, who quickly got a knife and started cutting the tape away from Ray's feet.

Just as Del came out of the bathroom, Leonard asked Ben, "We should still keep his hands tied, shouldn't we?"

"You're damn right you should," Del answered for him. "We have no idea what this guy's going to do."

"Are you going to call the police?" Sue Ellen asked.

"I been thinking about that," Ray said. "You know, it was just a big stupid mistake. You let me go now and, no, I won't call the police."

"What do you think about that, Sue Ellen?" Del asked. "Think we should believe him?"

"Listen, I'm as broke as you are," Ray said. "When you don't have nothing, the only thing you do have is your word, and I'm giving you that. No police. Just take me home and drive away. Nobody got rich but also nobody's a criminal. It's over."

Sue Ellen was studying him. "I think we can trust him. I really do."

"Remember what I said, I couldn't find you guys if I wanted to."

"Well, all right," Ben agreed after a moment. "But keep his hands tied just in case. We'll untie him at his place."

Leonard continued freeing Ray from the chair while Sue Ellen helped haul Ben out of the couch.

They were ready to leave in a few minutes. Ben paused before taking Ray outside to the car. "You really think I could do that school job?"

"Of course you could, but don't stop there," Ray said. "Look at kinda out-of-the-way places. There are people who'll work with you. There really are. You just have to get after 'em."

The "thanks" that Ben mumbled was minimized by the fact that right then Leonard put a paper bag over Ray's head as a blindfold. Del helped guide Ray into the car, then stepped back. "Well, I don't think you need me anymore here. I think I'll take off."

"What you talking about?" Ben asked. "We're in this together. What if he starts acting up?"

"Hey, you're the one trusting his word. I would have shot him yesterday," Del said, laughing. "Have fun, guys. We'll see you around."

Ray, with the sack over his head, couldn't see Del wave as he walked over to his dirty white pickup.

"Well, that son of a bitch," Ben said.

"You're better off without him, Ben," Sue Ellen said.

Ben grumbled that she was probably right as he struggled into the driver's seat.

Both vehicles drove off at the same time in opposite directions.

It was about a half hour drive before Ray felt the familiar bumps and ruts of his road. When the car stopped, Leonard voiced his concerns.

"Now look, all that stuff you said about 'your word' and everything, the same goes here, okay? I mean, when I cut you free, you ain't going to fight us again or anything like that. Right?"

"Relax. It's okay."

Sue Ellen and Leonard helped Ray out of the car and took the paper sack off his head. Leonard went to work on the mounds of duct tape he'd used to secure Ray's hands.

"Sorry about all this," Ben said from the car. "Hope we didn't muck things up for you too bad."

"I hope not, either," Ray said, getting circulation back in his hands as Leonard neared completing his task. "My job is going to be the problem."

"You've been a really good sport," Sue Ellen said.

"Just don't try anything like this again . . . with *anyone*. Please."

Ben silently nodded as Leonard finished with the duct tape and backed away quickly from Ray, just in case.

"You take care of yourself, you hear?" Ray said to Ben after Leonard was safely back in the car.

"You, too. Thank you." Ben looked at him a moment, then quickly drove off. Ray looked at the license plate and quickly memorized it. He started to run inside and write it down, then stopped. He looked out at the car disappearing in a cloud of dust and decided to let it go. Ben had even more problems than Ray and there weren't many people in that category. The number was immediately forgotten.

Ray could hardly believe how good it felt to be home. He allowed himself about fifteen seconds to appreciate it all, then got on the phone.

26

SHEREE'S REACTION CAUGHT RAY off guard. He had barely said, "Hey, babe. I'm home" before she said, "Oh, thank God. We'll be right over." And hung up.

Ray was standing there looking at the phone wondering who *they* were. He had no sooner put down the receiver than the phone rang. It was Sheree with an out-of-breath afterthought. "Call Pat at Fields. I love you," she said. *Click.* Very strange.

Ray did call but then hung up quickly before Pat had a chance to answer. Ray had to think for a minute. What was he going to tell them down there? The truth? He couldn't be sure they'd even believe he'd been kidnapped, especially if he wasn't going to the police. That wouldn't make any sense to them. But what would?

A few minutes later he tried again, telling Pat that he'd been called away suddenly for a "family emergency." He'd explain later (when he thought of something to tell them). As to the status of his job, Pat had tried everything he could but Mr. Fields said he'd had enough.

Not showing up after they'd bent over backwards for him while he took that other job with the farmer that paid him more, then trying to accommodate him when he wanted extra hours . . . well, Mr. Fields felt like he'd been taken advantage of and didn't want any more of it. Pat was sorry.

So was Ray. He'd try to talk to the man in person but he wasn't holding out any great hopes.

★ ★ ★

It was about twenty minutes after their phone call that Sheree and J.D. sped up and dug to a dusty stop in front of the trailer. As Ray opened the door, Sheree ran into his arms, hugging him.

"Thank God, you're okay."

"Yeah. I second that," J.D. said, giving Ray a cuff on the shoulder. "What happened?"

"It started out scary and ended up kinda funny, actually. A bunch of girls saw me come out of Graceland and thought I was Elvis. Some people they knew then kidnapped me for ransom. Can you believe that? When they realized they got the wrong guy, they tried to get some money for me out of Elvis. Needless to say, that didn't work so they let me go. Basically, that's it."

Sheree and J.D. sat while Ray was explaining. When he finished, they just stared at him. They then exchanged looks and turned back to Ray. After a moment, Sheree asked Ray, "Do you have your driver's license?"

"Sure," Ray said, feeling to make sure he had his wallet. He did.

"Take a look," Sheree said.

Puzzled, Ray opened the wallet. His driver's license was gone. "I'll be damned."

"How about your keys?" she then asked.

Ray felt in his front pockets . . . then looked at his friends. "No. I don't have them, either. What's going on?"

By way of an answer, Sheree reached into her purse and handed Ray his keys and driver's license.

"How'd you get these?"

Sheree looked over at J.D. "He doesn't know any of it."

"Know what?" Ray asked. "Talk to me."

"Okay, but don't go all crazy about the money," J.D. said. "We'll work something out. In fact, we ought to probably call the police and get—"

"Wait! Wait! What money?"

Sheree took a big breath and started. "Things have been rather exciting around here the last couple of days, too," she began. "I got a call yesterday from a man telling me that you'd been taken and were being held by a bunch of guys who didn't like you very much. If I didn't get together twenty thousand dollars by this morning, they were going to kill you."

"What?"

"That's what he said. As proof, he said he had your driver's license and keys. He described that little scrimshaw boat you always have on your keys and described how you were dressed. I guess the kicker was when he said, 'You know . . . the guy that looks like Elvis?' "

"Twenty thousand dollars!"

"Eight of it's mine. Your pal here came up with the other twelve."

"You're getting that money back. I promise," Ray stated firmly. "Did you see who it was?"

"Sorta," J.D. said. "Sheree was told to drop off the money on your stairs. The keys and license were left there, again for proof, I guess. This guy said he'd be watching and if there was any police or funny business—that's what he said, 'funny business'—he wouldn't show and you would be a goner."

"So J.D., being the smart guy that he is," Sheree continued, too excited to let J.D. tell the whole tale, "figured that this guy probably didn't know there's really only one way in and out of your place. So he waited behind the trees down by that lower ditch."

"Sure enough," J.D. took over again, "an hour or so later, this guy drives past me and directly up to your place."

"What'd he look like?" Ray asked.

"Young guy. Long black hair."

"Yeah," Ray said. "I know exactly who it is. Did you get a license number?"

"I did."

"Let's get it checked."

"Way ahead of you," J.D. said. "The brother of a girl I used to see sometimes is a cop. Owed me a favor. It was a rent-a-car. Guess who rented it?"

"Who?"

"You."

"Excuse me?"

"Rented to Raymond Johnston. Probably used your driver's license as ID."

"The son of a bitch." Then something occurred to Ray. He turned to Sheree. "How'd he know about you?"

"I wondered that, too. I'll bet he roamed around your place some, probably saw that picture of me on your bedroom cabinet, signed 'Love Sheree,' and looked me up in the address book by the phone. I checked. I'm the only Sheree in there." She smiled. "Something like that maybe."

"Now that you're here, we'd better get the police in on it before this guy gets too far gone," J.D. said

"Wait a minute." Ray got up and paced. "I got a problem here. Damn it! I am so sorry, guys. Give me a minute."

Ray walked outside and continued pacing there. He just had to think a minute.

He knew he didn't have to honor his word about not calling the police after all this but wasn't sure it was still the right thing to do. The main thing was to get Sheree's and J.D.'s money back. The idea of a scumbag like Del taking advantage of his two best friends, two decent people who came up with more money than they'd ever even seen to keep Ray safe, infuriated him.

But the main thing was to get the money. He had to concentrate on that. If he called the police, he was sure they'd catch Ben and Leonard, who probably didn't know anything about this at all. Del would be in another state by now with the money and Sue Ellen would end up in a foster home. And Sheree and J.D. would still be out their twenty thousand. No. There had to be a better way.

Ray went back inside the trailer and explained his rationale. Sheree and J.D. didn't know whether to agree or not but there was no mistaking the fire in Ray's eyes. If things didn't work out, the police would be called but he was sure as hell going to try his way first.

27

THE FIRST THING WAS to clear his mind. Ray asked Sheree and J.D. to bear with him for a few minutes. He got everybody a beer, went back to his bathroom, threw more water on his face, changed clothes, and realized he'd better check to see if the elementary school was expecting him that night. He hoped they were.

They weren't. The school didn't even seem all that upset. They realized that what they paid was not going to get them the highest-class person (that wasn't what they said but Ray felt it was what they meant), so they knew people were going to come and go.

Fine. But they still needed to keep positions filled. Since he hadn't called, they had no idea how long Ray would be gone, so they'd moved other people into his time slot.

The secretary told Ray that the night foreman was on vacation for a week. She suggested he call back next Thursday or so. He thanked her and hung up.

That gray feeling of dread was starting to come back but Ray fought it off. No. No feeling sorry for himself, no depression. Focus! Get back the money first, then he could mope all he wanted.

Ray sat back down with Sheree and J.D. and started trying to figure out a plan of action. He remembered telling his kidnappers how he couldn't find their place again if he'd wanted to. He wondered if that was exactly true.

Ray explained how Sue Ellen had seen him coming out of Graceland and had unwittingly started off the whole debacle. She might be the key to finding them. He recalled that it took about half an hour to get to Ray's place from where he was being held. He went to the map in the front of the phone book and drew a circle with his place in the middle. The circle represented what he knew to be about how far he could go in town in half an hour.

"What do you think, guys? Would a teenage girl in this area go to Central or Jefferson?"

"Most of it would be Jefferson, I think," Sheree said.

"Yeah," J.D. agreed. "Except for that little section down at the bottom. That would start to bleed into Central."

"Good," Ray said. "Do either of you know where I could get a Jefferson yearbook? I'll bet that girl would be in there."

"I got a cousin who goes there," J.D. offered.

"Think she'd let me borrow it?"

"Sure. I'll stop by on the way home."

"You look tired," Sheree observed. "It was quite an ordeal, wasn't it?"

"Yeah. I guess so. I haven't really had time to think about it. I *am* kinda beat."

"We ought to leave and let you get some sleep. Is there anything you need before I go?" Sheree asked, coming into Ray's arms.

"Oh, baby, you've done so much already. Both of you. I think sleep's definitely the ticket. I'll be raring to go in the morning. Hopefully, I can get that bastard before he gets too far away."

Ray walked his friends to the door, thanked them profusely again, and got ready for bed. Two semisleepless nights duct-taped to a chair was taking its toll. As an afterthought, for the first time since he'd owned his trailer, Ray locked his door.

Friday, June 3, 1977

That morning, on his way to work, J.D. dropped off the Jefferson High School yearbook he'd borrowed from his cousin. Over his morning coffee Ray perused the book, finding her less than an hour later. There she was. No mistaking. Sue Ellen Houtchen, a junior.

Ray looked for Ben Houtchen in the phone book but there wasn't one. He then called information and got a phone number for a Ben Houtchen but not an address. He wasn't planing on calling Ben but he wrote it down just in case.

Ray was in the process of figuring out how to get in touch with Sue Ellen when Sheree stopped by to see how he was faring. She was glad to see him up and around and looking much more rested than the day before.

He told her what he'd found and his dilemma. If he went down to the school and started asking questions about Sue Ellen, like trying to find out what room she was in, they'd probably call the cops on him.

They both thought for a minute before Sheree came up with an answer. "How about if I call pretending to be this girl's mother?"

"Her mother's dead."

"Do you think whoever's going to answer the phone would know that? There's a lot of kids in that school."

"Want to give it a try?"

"Sure. What's her name?" Sheree said, getting comfortable by the phone.

"Sue Ellen Houtchen. She's a junior," Ray said, pointing out the school's number in the phone book. Sheree thought for a minute, then dialed. She held the phone out a bit from her ear so Ray could hear, too.

"Jefferson High," a rather nasal-sounding voice answered.

"Hello. This is Mary Beth Houtchen, mother of Sue Ellen Houtchen," Sheree started, trying to sound as casual as she could. "Well, my girl, bless her heart, did all her homework last night and left it here. I just found it. I'd like to drop it off for her, if you don't mind. I wonder if you could tell me what room she would be in about an hour from now?"

"Oh, don't worry about that," the nasal voice said. "Just leave it with us at the office. We'll see that she gets it."

Sheree and Ray exchanged a quick look before Sheree continued. "Well, you see . . . actually, it's kind of embarrassing and I really don't want to go into it, but I do need to speak with her for a minute. Girl stuff, you know? Won't take but a minute."

"Of course, let's see what we have here . . ." Ray and Sheree relaxed a minute as the woman looked up the information. "At eleven, Sue Ellen would be in Mr. Pefly's math class. That would be in room two-oh-three, right at the top of the stairs."

"That's great. Thanks very much," Sheree said, then hung up.

"Way to go," Ray said. " 'Girl stuff.' I like that."

"Always works. No woman's ever going to question that."

"I didn't know you were that good a liar."

"Comes from working in a bar for half my life. Do you guys really think you're as clever as I let on?"

"Well, yeah."

Sheree laughed. "Fortunately, you are, but *you* are the exception, believe me."

"Thank you for that. I think I'll put on some presentable clothes and go pay Miss Houtchen a visit."

"Do you think she's a part of this?"

"I'd be willing to bet she isn't. I know who did this and she doesn't like him very much."

"Neither do I," Sheree added.

"He'll get his," Ray said. "I don't know exactly how yet, but . . . it'll happen."

Sheree kissed Ray good-bye and took off for work. Ray climbed into a shower, trying to decide what in his closet made him look the most like a respected member of society.

28

JEFFERSON HIGH SCHOOL WAS a three-story brick building built like a huge cube. The rather ornate façade around the front door wasn't enough to make up for the uninspired drabness of the design.

As Ray stepped inside, he could see by the beige and mint green walls that the spirit of dreariness was continued. Ray incorporated his one pair of slacks with his too-small sport coat again, which seemed to work just fine, lending him an air of economical respectability.

He walked right by the front office and received only a casual glance from the woman there. Since Ray seemed to know where he was going, he evidentially didn't need her services so she went back to what she was doing.

Ray went to the second floor and found room 203 right where he was told. He composed himself for a moment, then opened the door and stepped halfway into the room. Mr. Pefly and the entire class turned to look at him.

Very quickly, Ray picked out the panic-stricken face of Sue Ellen.

"Excuse me, sir," Ray said to Mr. Pefly, the tall, white-haired teacher. "May I speak with Miss Houtchen in the hall? It will just take a moment."

Not being used to or anticipating any sort of underhandedness on an ordinary school day, the teacher saw no need not to comply.

"Certainly," Mr. Pefly said. "Sue Ellen."

Sue Ellen got up tentatively. Ray could see the distress in her face and hoped the teacher didn't.

"Is everything all right?" Mr. Pefly asked, just as Ray was hoping he wouldn't.

"I'm a friend of her father's," Ray said. "I just have to pass on a message. It's important but quick."

"All right then."

Sue Ellen stepped out into the hall. Ray closed the door behind her.

"You promised you wouldn't come after us," Sue Ellen attacked in a loud whisper.

"Relax. I'm not after you and I don't think I'm after Ben, either," Ray explained. "Did you know Del ransomed me to my friends for twenty thousand dollars?"

"What?"

"I'll take that as a no. Do you know where Del is now?"

"Twenty thousand!"

"Yes. From really good people who can't afford it any more than you or I could. Do you know where he is?"

"He was moving out this morning. Leaving, just like that. The other guys are a little pissed at him, I think."

"Do you know where he went?"

"He said he was leaving town but I heard him talking to that trashy girl on the phone, said he was coming over with a surprise."

"You wouldn't know where I could find her, would you?"

"Yeah. Her name's Dolores Watt. She lives in a trailer park on thirteenth . . . around Fullton."

"How would you know all that?"

"We used to live next door to her. That's how Del met her. It's a pit. I'm really glad we got out of there."

"What's Del drive?"

"A dirty white pickup."

"Good, Sue Ellen. Thanks. I'm sure Ben and Leonard aren't involved with this. If they're not, I'll keep them out of it but I am going after Del. All right?"

"Sure. I'd better get back inside."

"You've helped a lot. Thanks again."

Sue Ellen started to open the door but stopped just short. "Ray?" she said just as he was starting to leave. "You get Del good, okay?"

"Okay," Ray said quietly but firmly.

Sue Ellen returned to her class. Ray left the school with a new determination. He was a man on a mission.

Ray sped up his dirt road and was surprised to see a car he didn't recognize parked in front of his trailer. A middle-aged couple were wandering around his property.

Ray parked and walked over to them. "Can I help you folks?"

"Oh, not really," the man replied. "We're just looking. Can that trailer be moved easily?"

"What are you looking for?" Ray asked.

"We're just looking at the lot, actually," the woman clarified. "We understand it may be on the market soon."

"Who told you that?"

"I think it was that man at Tennessee Federal, wasn't it, Boo?" the lady asked her husband.

"I'm paid up," Ray said, not liking this at all.

"That's what they told us but they also expected that situation to change. I assume you're the owner. Are you going to be moving?"

"Yes, I am the owner and I'm going to stay the owner. I ain't going nowhere. Now, get off my property."

"Now, we were just looking. There's no need to—"

"You're trespassing!" Ray said menacingly, staring at them, almost daring them to say something else.

The two looked at each other and decided there was no point in lingering around there any longer. They quickly got in their car and drove off.

Ray was so angry he was shaking. When he was sure they had gone, he went inside, popped a beer, and after storming around for a few minutes got on the phone to J.D., telling him to get his butt over there right now and bring a gun. He then hung up before J.D. could even ask why.

Ray was in his bedroom changing out of his monkey suit when the phone rang. Ray answered.

"I guess they didn't kill you," the recognizable voice asked.

"No, I guess not."

"What the hell was going on?" Elvis asked.

"They kidnapped me. Thought I was you. Probably would have tried to get a couple million to set you free. When they found out they had the wrong guy, they kinda panicked. They saw that article and figured they still might be able to make some money off of me."

"I thought not taking them seriously would be the best way to handle it."

"It was."

"They rough you up any?"

"Hit me over the head with my baseball bat, which hurt like hell, and kept me duct-taped to a chair for a couple of days, which wasn't my idea of a good time."

"You get the cops on them?"

"I don't know if I could even find them again but, no. They weren't really bad folks. Just desperate."

"I'd sure as hell go after them," Elvis said. "Someone saw you leave Graceland, didn't they?"

"Yeah."

"Damn it. I don't want stuff like this happening! Why do you think I'm never alone? There's crazies out there. Half the friggin' world is nuts!" Elvis paused a moment. "I can't keep you safe, too, you know?"

"Don't worry about it. I can take care of myself."

"You sure about that?"

Ray almost laughed. "Actually, that's exactly what came into my head. This little stunt cost me my job, both of them, in fact . . . my head still hurts, and now somebody wants to buy my land right out from underneath me and I'm not sure I can stop them." Ray caught himself before telling about his friends being bilked out of their money. Elvis didn't need to know everything. "Oh yeah," Ray continued. "I take care of myself real good."

"Can't help you with none of that. Got a shitload of troubles of my own. We'll both just have to change a few things, I guess. Well, glad you're all right."

"Thanks."

"Good luck to you," Elvis said and hung up.

Ray slowly put the receiver down, already regretting confessing to Elvis how incompetent he was. Evidently, Elvis still didn't want to have Ray in his life. Why did he have to make himself seem even worse?

What great twins they were; one became the most famous person in the world and the other got his friends ripped off for every penny they had and couldn't quite keep up his house trailer payments. Great. Just great.

29

RAY QUICKLY SAW WHY Sue Ellen was glad to have moved away from the trailer park. "A pit" was a good way to describe it. Ray felt it was people and places like this that gave trailers a bad name.

The mailboxes told Ray that the Watts were in space 32. He was glad he had been able to talk J.D. into taking the afternoon off. Ray felt better having J.D. beside him, complete with his thirty-ought-six and shotgun, driving slowly down the narrow drive between trailers until they saw number 32 ahead . . . with a dirty white pickup parked in front. An equally dirty pink '56 Ford was parked next to it.

Ray's heart was beating a mile a minute as he parked a couple trailers away. They thought sneaking up on the trailer carrying a couple of rifles was probably not the best way to go about not being noticed, so they left their weapons behind and tried to act casual as they walked up to the Watt trailer.

The peeling, crusted pink paint, the trash, and the smell emanating from the totally neglected, dilapidated trailer made Ray's look like the Taj Mahal. So far it seemed that they hadn't garnered any interest from the neighbors so Ray went up to the pickup and looked in. A suitcase was on the passenger seat and the door was unlocked. A trusting soul.

Ray quietly opened the door, then popped open the suitcase as J.D. stood guard. Clothes had not been packed with care. Wads of wrinkled clothes, a stack of papers, and a pair of old shoes filled the suitcase. Ray was looking for a bank pouch like the one Sheree had described to him. The one containing the money she gave Del. It wasn't in the suitcase.

As Ray put things back, he tried to anticipate what Del would have done. He didn't think he'd put the money in the bank. That would leave too easy a trail, and a safety deposit box wouldn't do him any good if he was leaving town. No, Ray thought, Del would have it with him somehow.

Even before they got close to the trailer, sounds of bedroom activity were heard, leaving no doubt what was going on inside. It seemed safe to look in the living room window, which it was. It was empty.

J.D. whispered to Ray, "She's a screamer."

Ray agreed. "Good."

They turned back to the window, where they both saw the pouch at the same time. There it was on the coffee table. Del clearly had wanted to show off some.

J.D. thought he was crazy but went along as Ray tried the front door. It, also, was open. That didn't surprise Ray. Most people don't lock their doors after company arrives. As the door opened, the sounds of amorous gymnastics were even louder. She was a screamer indeed. They didn't have to worry about being heard.

After checking to make sure they couldn't be seen, J.D. crept slowly but steadily over toward the pouch. Ray stood guard, surprised at how nervous he was. His knees were physically shaking.

In the mess that was the living room, Ray could see the scene that must have played out. Men's and women's clothing were strewn across the room and down the hall to the bedroom. The money was evidentially quite a turn-on. On the floor by Ray was a dirty pair of men's Levi's. Ray reached down and took Del's wallet from them and pocketed it.

As soon as J.D. picked up the pouch the sounds from the bedroom stopped. Ray and J.D. froze and exchanged panicked looks, looks that seemed to say "Why didn't we bring the rifles in?" Suddenly a blood-curdling scream, that could easily have been heard throughout the trailer park, cut through the silence.

That was enough. Before the reverberations of the scream died down, Ray and J.D. were out of the house and halfway to Ray's truck.

As an afterthought, Ray decided to make one more quick stop. He opened the hood on Del's pickup and took the rotor from the distrib-utor. Del wasn't going to be going anywhere in that truck for a while. Setting the hood back down quietly, Ray then took off for his pickup. Moments later, they were speeding happily toward Ray's trailer. They'd done it!

They were a thousand dollars short. J.D. was still thrilled and kept telling Ray not to worry about it. They got back nineteen thousand! That was fine. J.D. would gladly eat the missing thousand. But Ray wouldn't hear of it. Nobody was going to lose anything on his account.

Ray checked the wallet he had lifted from Del's pants and found one hundred seventy-three dollars. A nice little present but far short of the mark.

Damn! It appeared that his adventure wasn't over quite yet.

Ray and J.D. were having a creative session in the lawn chairs with a couple of beers, trying to come up with a way to make Del responsi-ble for that last thousand, when the phone rang. Ray went inside and answered, "Hello?"

"Mr. Johnston?" a male voice asked.

"Yes."

"This is Bob down at Bluebird Rent-a-Car and we're not real happy right now. I thought I explained to you real good about how we had to check over the car when you brought it back. Good Lord, man, what were you doing, playing bumpercars with it? We've got over eight hun-dred dollars' worth of damage to that left front fender."

"I'm sorry," Ray said. "But I'm not the guy that rented the car. I don't—"

"You Ray Johnston?"

"Yes. Look, a guy took my driver's license. I don't know anything about—"

"I don't care about that. Your name's on this form and you're re-sponsible. You owe me eight hundred dollars, at *least*! I'll have the full amount here in—"

"Guess what, pal? I don't care about *that*!" Ray hung up.

As he walked back outside, the phone started ringing again. To hell with him, Ray thought. Even though he wasn't answering the phone, Ray knew he was going to have to deal with it somehow. His credit rating couldn't stand another big negative hit. That son of a bitch Del. Ray really didn't need this.

Ray explained the call to J.D. and kicked their plan making up a couple of notches. It wasn't just the thousand anymore. He needed another eight hundred or so . . . the sooner the better.

A half hour later, they had a plan: "When the going gets tough, the tough get going." Ray was proud of how well they worked under pressure. If they could pull this off without getting shot, it just might work.

Around six that evening, they returned to the run-down trailer park. They took J.D.'s truck this time in case someone might recognize Ray's from earlier. Ray sunk down in the seat as J.D. (who Del didn't know) drove slowly past the trailer.

Del's truck was still there, as they knew it would be, but the pink Ford was gone. All the lights in the house were out. It appeared as though no one was at home. Perfect.

Much more nervous this time than before, Ray got out and checked to see if Del might have left the keys in the truck. He hadn't. Ray could kick himself for not thinking of grabbing them when he took the wallet. They had probably been in the front pocket of Del's pants.

J.D. said he still remembered how to hot-wire a truck, though, so while he got a small piece of wire out of his tool kit, which seemed to contain every tool known to man, Ray proceeded to replace the rotor in Del's engine.

There was still just enough light that they didn't need a flashlight but hopefully dark enough that no one would notice them. They were both outrageously skittish and practically dove under the truck when some headlights started down the lane toward them. They started breathing again when the car turned into a space down the block.

Both men finished about the same time. No sooner had Ray gotten the rotor back in than the beefy V-8 kicked over and sprang to life. J.D. got back in his truck, pleased to be back next to the rifles. Ray started to jump in Del's when something got his attention.

"When the flag is up on a mailbox . . ." Ray started talking to J.D. through his open window. "That means there's a letter going out to be picked up by the mailman. Right?"

"I think so."

Ray quickly went to the mailbox that had the little red flag up and opened it. Sure enough, there was a letter Mrs. Watt was sending to her husband, Corporal Edwin Watt, and his post address in Germany. Ray pocketed it and dove into Del's idling car. They both quickly drove off, watching closely to see if they had aroused any attention. It didn't appear that they had.

Since Ray didn't have a garage, they drove over to J.D.'s and hid Del's truck inside.

J.D. wondered what Ray wanted with the letter but Ray didn't know for sure. He was going to mail the letter as soon as he copied the address. You never know when something like that might come in handy.

Del's suitcase was still in the cab. Ray remembered seeing a stack of papers there when he'd checked it the first time. He looked through them and found the title to the truck. Yes! That's what he was hoping for.

Ray knew that Del was not going to take this lying down and also knew that Del knew where Ray lived. The ramifications of their acts were yet to play out but for now, it was kick back on J.D.'s porch with a beer and laugh about how brave (and scared) they had been.

Saturday, June 4, 1977

The next morning, Sheree followed Ray as he drove Del's truck along back side streets to the other side of town, to a small locksmith shop. A story about losing his keys out fishing, the title, and Del's driver's license did the trick. Half an hour and two dollars and fifty cents later, Ray had a set of keys to Del's truck.

Ray had heard that some states were starting to put pictures of people on their driver's licenses. He was glad Tennessee hadn't gotten around to that. He thought they probably never would.

They then drove over to the nearby Memphis Auto Mart where it plainly stated on a large sign: $ 4 YOR CAR!

After much deliberation, the salesman offered Ray eight thousand dollars for Del's truck. Ray knew that it was worth at least fifteen thousand, but said, "Fine."

He had seen Del's signature on some of the other papers in his pouch and had practiced it for a while at J.D.'s house before he had signed the back of the title. The salesman took the driver's license information and didn't look twice at the signature.

Very soon it was a done deal. Ray went straight to the bank and was relieved when the check went through. He had been trying to decide how to divide it. He came up with the following;

One thousand dollars to make up the full twenty thousand Del had extorted.

Two thousand dollars, a thousand to both J.D. and Sheree as interest and also to compensate them for coming to Ray's rescue.

One thousand dollars to Ray to pay some bills. He felt justified because Del was primarily responsible for Ray losing his jobs. Without Del, the other kidnappers had been willing to let him go that next day. He might have been able to salvage his job with just one day out. But Del had needed the time to get the money from Sheree and J.D. so Ray lost out. Yeah, another payment on his mom and an extra trailer payment just in case: seemed appropriate.

Eight hundred fifty dollars was going to Bluebird Rent-a-Car. Ray didn't much care for the guy there but he was damned if Del was going to hurt Ray's much-maligned credit rating anymore.

Although there were still many bills that the remaining thirty-one hundred bucks (roughly) could go to, Ray decided to wait. It was important to him that he didn't become a bad guy himself in the process of dealing out justice and retribution. He'd know the right thing when the time came, he was sure. For now, though, he was just going to slow down a bit.

30

OPENING TIME FOUND RAY waiting by Mr. Fields's door. When the man arrived Ray apologized, mentioned the family emergency, knew he should have called but was upset, et cetera. Mr. Fields sat down at his desk and let Ray talk himself out. When Ray couldn't think of anything else to say, Mr. Fields responded in a calm, easy manner.

"Ray, I like you. I always have, but I don't feel you've made Fields Construction a part of your life. You take time off at the drop of a hat, don't show up for weeks because you're making more money somewhere else. I want people who want to be here, Ray. Part of the team, the family, that will make us a priority, not just be around when you don't have anything better to do."

Ray launched into another speech about how he was exactly that guy, how much he loved and enjoyed Fields Construction and felt honored to be part of the—

Mr. Fields got up in the middle of Ray's retort and started to leave. "If you'll excuse me, Ray, I've got a meeting." He left. Ray stood in the middle of the quiet office for a couple minutes before leaving, also. Well, that had been pretty clear. Damn.

The rest of the day was spent pounding the pavement. It was like "déjà vu all over again." Everyone was sorry Ray was out of work but nobody needed anybody right at the moment.

Ray took another good look at his finances and realized they were starting to get scary. Much against his will, but seeing no other way, Ray did something that nearly made him cry. He sold his truck. Good ol' truck. It was only four years old and had been Ray's only extravagance in an otherwise bargain-basement life. He got a good price for it, though (he definitely did *not* go to good ol' Memphis Auto Mart), and, coupled with Del's thousand, was able to pay off LifeCare and pay for his mom's funeral. Two major loads off his back. He was even able to put an extra payment on his land and trailer, which should keep away anyone thinking of buying.

He was hoping to get some ahead but that didn't work out.

There was no cushion. He was closer, though, to being caught up, which felt pretty darn good. He still had to keep working at it but the hole he had to dig himself out of was now considerably smaller.

He also bought another truck. An old one. An ugly one. He hated it . . . but the price was right and the engine looked like it had a few more years in it, so it would do just fine for now. It aggravated him that the truck he bought was older and crummier than the one he'd sold out from under Del.

Driving his new/old truck home, Ray realized how many people, like him, lived and worked strictly for survival. Sure, every once in a while they'd shoot pool or go fishing, but ninety-eight percent of everything they did or made went to keeping a roof over their heads and food on the table. Period.

In his wildest dreams Ray couldn't imagine him taking a week off and going someplace like Hawaii, or on a cruise. Those were for other people.

Ray cast a quick glance skyward. "How come I got put in this group? I'd be a really good rich person. I really would. You'd be proud of me."

His reverie was broken by a rattle coming from the left front bumper. Gee, and he'd almost made it all the way home. He'd have to look into that . . . or was that God letting him know he should hang on, don't get too comfortable just yet.

Actually, it was just a screw under the fender that had come loose. A few minutes later, he was under the truck, tightening it, when a car drove in. Ray scooted out from under the truck and found himself looking at the pink '56 Ford. Del climbed out of the passenger side.

"Did you really think you'd get away with that?" Del asked threateningly.

"That's what I was going to ask you," Ray said, just as hard.

"All right. Taking back the money. That was good. That's what I get for being careless. But where's my truck?"

"I sold it."

"You what?" Del asked incredulously.

"You had some outstanding debts, Del. I had to satisfy them. My friends needed their money back. All of it. I did think that rent-a-car business was real cute, though."

Del just stood glaring at Ray. Ray could tell he wanted to hit him so bad it hurt but Ray was considerably taller, bigger, and in better shape than Del.

"Want to take a swing at me?" Ray asked, taunting, his arms hanging loosely by his sides. He would love nothing more than for Del to come after him but he also knew he wouldn't do it. Del had been real brave while Ray was tied up but this was different.

"You haven't heard the end of this, asshole," Del said as he started back to the Ford.

"You decide," Ray called out to him. "But realize, just like now, anything you do to me, I'll do back at you, only worse."

Del flipped him the bird and got in the car. Ray didn't get a good look at the woman driving but could just imagine what a piece of work she must be.

He finished tightening the bolt under the fender and retired back to the lawn chair and the guitar. Del had left him a bit riled. Music always helped.

He was still at it an hour later when Morgan Bates drove up to the trailer, parked his yellow Chevy, and walked over to Ray.

"Thought I was looking at Elvis for a minute there."

"Hey, Morgan," Ray said as he leaned the guitar up against the trailer.

"Haven't heard anything for a while," Morgan said, sitting in the other chair. "How are things going? You thought about it?"

"Actually, things have been pretty strange but I have thought about it," Ray said, and he had. He'd had a lot to think about these last few days and Morgan, with his promise of big bucks, flitted through Ray's consciousness a couple of times.

"Have you had any luck with Elvis?"

"Some." Ray couldn't help but think how Morgan would love his kidnapping story. That would definitely be worth a few bucks but, strangely, even for the money, Ray didn't feel like telling Morgan much of anything. He'd keep him on the string for a while, though. Just in case.

"What's that mean?" Morgan asked. "Have you been to Graceland?"

"Some." Ray also decided that it probably wouldn't be a good idea to tell Morgan that Elvis really didn't want to have anything more to do with him.

"Great. Have you met Vernon?"

"Yeah."

"Is he your dad?"

"Might be."

"But you did meet him?"

"Yeah."

Morgan got very excited, quickly dove into his car, and came out with a tape recorder. "This is excellent. Let's get some of this down."

"Hold on a minute."

"What?"

"Like I said, I've been thinking about it," Ray said. "I don't care what you say, I don't think Elvis would like me selling out to you. Besides, if I start giving you little bits and pieces right now, ain't nobody ever going to be impressed enough to give me the whole million."

"We can do it in payments, starting right now," Morgan offered anxiously.

"I don't think so." Ray wondered what he would have done if this conversation had taken place before he sold his truck but since he didn't need the money right this minute and didn't like this Bates character all that much anyway, it wasn't too hard to turn down.

"Don't go getting too cute here, Johnston. People aren't exactly lined up out there to believe you, you know?"

"Mr. Bates, you just might be getting more than you bargained for. Regardless of what happens, there's a pretty darn good chance that I really am Jesse Presley. I haven't decided exactly what I'm going to do about it, but what I've got could be a gold mine and we both know it.

"Hell, it may be worth more than a million," Ray continued. "But I also know as well as you do that the minute this stuff starts to get printed, that's the last time I'll ever set foot in Graceland. I think I'll just keep building memories. If the time is ever right, we'll talk real serious and do it all in one big shot."

Morgan thought about it a moment, then put his tape recorder away. "All right, but know that a 'pretty darn good chance' doesn't mean a damn thing. The only thing that will make your case solid is if you can *prove*, and I mean without a shadow of a doubt, that you are this Jesse Garon Presley. You prove that, then you are home free. As long as you can't, you are pretty much stuck with me because I seem to be the only one willing to take a chance on you."

"I'll risk it."

"As long as you realize that that's exactly what you are doing. Use your head. Don't draw it out too long. There's interest in this story now. I can't promise that it'll always be on the table."

Morgan wished Ray luck as he got in his car and drove off. Ray watched him go, then went into the trailer with mixed thoughts. Even though he didn't like Morgan or his rag, he had to ask himself, Why not? He didn't know if Elvis was still trying to get any more information about their birth situation or not, but Ray doubted it. It sure seemed to be over as far as Elvis was concerned. He was definitely distancing himself from Ray.

But that didn't make them any the less brothers. Just because Elvis didn't want to have anything to do with it, why couldn't Ray? It really didn't matter if one twin was famous and one wasn't. They should both have equal rights to deal with their circumstances as they saw fit. Right? Nobody said they had to believe and act the same way.

Just what Ray needed. More to think about.

31

Tuesday, June 7, 1977

IT WAS FOUR O'CLOCK in the morning when Ray was blasted awake by the sound of gunshots. He rolled out of bed, fleetingly glad that Sheree had not stayed over that night, and laid low. Four gunshots were fired very close to the trailer. Ray didn't see any holes or telltale signs that any of the shots had been into his bedroom, but it was still pretty dark. He couldn't be sure.

A few moments later, he heard a car dig out of his place and drive down the road. He stood up in time to see taillights, already too far away to identify.

Ray cautiously put on a bathrobe and slippers, grabbed his shotgun, and crept to the front door, keeping the lights off. Seeing no activity outside, he opened the door and stepped out, shotgun at the ready.

Not only was no one there, Ray couldn't even find what had been shot. Of course, he felt that it was Del's doing but he certainly must have hit something. He wouldn't have been happy with just scaring Ray like that.

Well, he seemed to have left for now. Ray went back in, being careful to lock his door again. He never did get back to sleep but he gave it a good try.

The next morning, in the full light of day, it was quickly obvious what Del had shot. There were four large bullet holes in the hood of his new/old truck. The engine would be a goner. Ray had to laugh. Boy, would he have been mad if Del had done that to his good ol' truck!

Now it was just an imposition. Sheree wasn't working until evening so she could take him around truck hunting. Suddenly, a cause had been found for the rest of Del's money.

The best affordable truck Ray could find at the moment was for twenty-five hundred dollars. Ray told the sales guy about the pickup with the bullet holes in the engine. The fellow figured that the tires and parts would be worth something so Ray got him down to an even two thousand. He'd even come out and tow it off Ray's property.

Ray felt pretty good about the whole thing except for the fact that the quality of his trucks kept getting worse and worse. Now he had to come up with some way to end this back and forth with Del. This could not go unavenged but Ray also wanted it to stop.

A couple hours with the guitar and the blues did the trick. At first, Ray thought he'd use the address of Corporal Watt to tell him what a slut his wife was and with whom, but that would just punish and upset the poor guy. He hadn't done anything. That didn't seem right. Ray decided to throw away his address.

But a variation on the theme came to him. That night he called the police saying that he also lived in the trailer park and wanted to report what sounded like a woman being raped in space number 32. As a good neighbor he knew that the woman's husband was stationed overseas, which made her even more vulnerable. An unsavory-looking fellow had been seen lurking around the premises. He'd been hearing screams. Ray suggested they check it out soon.

As Ray hung up, he wondered if he'd ever know what happened out there. All he could hope was that she was in the middle of one of her more vocal outbursts as the police arrived. Wouldn't that be nice?

She was married. What was she going to say? Ray gave her an out, if she'd take it, but maybe she'd stand up for Del. Who knew? In any case, they may deserve each other. Bottom line, Del would be given a good scare.

Ray didn't really expect to hear from him anymore. Even so, he did feel that locking his door was a good habit to get into.

Ray even determined what to do with the remaining money. He was going to take Sheree and J.D. out to the best dinner either had ever had. Just 'cause. That left a thousand dollars. He decided to give it to Sue Ellen. Her lot in life got to Ray and she seemed like a good kid. Her help made it possible for him to get everyone paid back, so Ray figured it was only right that she benefit some from it all.

Wednesday, June 8, 1977

The next day he had a money order made out to Sue Ellen Houtchen and wrote a brief note.

> Sue Ellen,
>> *This is for your college fund. Put it*
> *somewhere safe and keep it.*
>> Ray

> P.S. We got Del good.

He put them in an envelope with her name on the front and dropped it off at the front desk of Jefferson High School. They assured him Sue Ellen would be given the envelope that afternoon.

Ray went job hunting for most of the day, then went home and took a nap. That night he'd go see the night man at his school. Perhaps he could at least salvage that job.

When Ray hunted him up, the head janitor told him basically the same things the secretary had. When Ray missed nights before, he'd always called and told them. When he just didn't show up, they had no idea if they'd ever see him again. And no one answered when they tried calling him. So they moved some people around and even hired another guy.

The head janitor said he'd put Ray back on the list but he had to go to the bottom of it and work his way up again. There was nothing for him at the moment but they'd let him know when something opened up.

Dejected, Ray walked toward the front of the school, trying to figure out what to do next. He turned the corner and ran into . . . Ben . . . using a buffer on the linoleum floors. Ray's linoleum floors! The two men saw each other at the same time and froze.

Ben had the guiltiest expression on his face that Ray had ever seen and looked prepared to bolt. Options immediately flooded over Ray; he could punch him out, he could turn him in, explain, and perhaps get his job back. Maybe he should call the police after all, he knew exactly where Ben was. The son of a bitch! He had probably come down to the school immediately after dropping Ray off and untying him.

But in the seconds that the men were looking at each other, it also occurred to Ray that he really hadn't done anything except what Ray and his big mouth had suggested. Why hadn't Ray just said "Check out the school system"? Why did he have to mention Nedermeyer? Ben had just done the responsible thing and had acted on the tip immediately. Not exactly creative, but effective.

Fear and failure were also imprinted on Ben's face. Hell, Ray couldn't even be mad at him. Ray just nodded to Ben and walked on by. Knowing Ben took his job, however, Ray might not have been so quick to give that thousand to Sue Ellen.

Outside, Ray shook his head and laughed as a phrase occurred to him: "No good deed goes unpunished." Perhaps it was about time for him to have another little chat with God. Obviously, they still hadn't gotten themselves on the same page.

Thursday, June 9, 1977

Ray read the want ads over and over, circling jobs that might be possibilities. (Ray wondered exactly what "animal husbandry" was? It sounded a little odd.) When Thursday morning arrived, he was ready for another assault on the Memphis job market. He'd showered, shaved, was wearing clothes he thought he looked pretty spiffy in, and he had a handful of places to go. He knew today was going to be a good one.

He had just left the trailer, closed the door, and locked it (he was remembering) when he heard the phone ringing inside. For a minute he thought he'd forget it and let it go, but at the last minute, he decided to unlock the door as quickly as he could and answer it.

Good thing. It was Mr. Fields. It seemed they could use another worker after all. Ray could have his old job back if he wanted it . . . and if he tried to be a team player and do all the other things they talked about. Ray promised that he would indeed do all those things, and more! He'd be right down.

He threw the pile of contacts into the air, looked up to the ceiling, and opened his arms out wide. "Yes! See how easy it is? Thank you, thank you, thank you." He ran back to the bedroom to change out of his looking-for-work clothes and get into his going-to-work clothes.

Friday, June 10, 1977
It felt so good to be back working again. Ray was, once again, going to be the first one there and the last to leave. He was bound and determined to be the perfect employee.

Friday afternoon, when Ray went into Mr. Fields's office to pick up his check (for two days' work), he was surprised to see an autographed picture of Elvis on the wall. It hadn't been there before. It startled Ray a bit but he managed to say, "Nice picture." He read the inscription, which said:

> *Marv,*
> > *To a good man.*
> > > *Best,*
> > > > *Elvis*

Mr. Fields looked questioningly at Ray. "Yes, it is. I understand you . . . know Mr. Presley yourself."

"Yeah, I do, sort of."

Mr. Fields was obviously burning with about a hundred questions but it was as if someone had asked him not to pursue that particular line. Finally, Mr. Fields just nodded and said, "Good to have you back. Have a nice weekend."

Ray nodded in acknowledgment, let him know he was glad to be back, and left, realizing he might have been premature in thanking God for getting his job back. Perhaps he should have thanked the King, but he also thought God had his hand in there, too.

Elvis may have felt a little responsible about Ray being taken, since he had been mistaken for Elvis. It occurred to Ray that even though Elvis didn't seem too thrilled to have him around, so far he had never let him down. In a way, that seemed almost . . . brotherly.

Ray found it hard not to smile as he drove home that afternoon.

32

RAY WAS IN HIS trailer, loading dirty clothes into a bag, when Sheree came in carrying a newspaper.

"Hey, babe."

"Hey, yourself," Ray said as they kissed hello. "You got here just in time. How about a laundry run?"

"You are a hopeless romantic, aren't you?" Sheree said, still in his arms.

"Do hopeless romantics run around in dirty clothes?"

"You've got a point," Sheree said as she backed away and let Ray finish loading his laundry bag. She then changed the subject with a more serious tone in her voice. "When is the last time you talked to the 'big guy'?"

"It's been a while," Ray said. "How come?"

By way of answer, Sheree opened the paper she was carrying and showed him the headlines:

ELVIS NEAR DEATH

SOURCES CITE MENTAL & PHYSICAL EXHAUSTION

Ray read it and was stunned. "Jesus."

"Do you think you should do anything?" Sheree wondered.

Ray read some of the accompanying article before saying, "Maybe I should."

He got out his wallet from his back pocket and pulled out the little card Vernon had given him.

"What's that?" Sheree wanted to know.

"Vernon gave me their private number in case I ever needed it."

Sheree had a tough time believing this. "You mean, you have the private number into Graceland?"

"Into Vernon and Dee's house, yeah."

Sheree was amazed.

"They just had it painted," Ray added for no reason at all.

She had to sit down to assimilate what this actually meant. It was one thing for them to hypothesize about Ray being Elvis's twin, but if the Presleys themselves were believing it, too? That was something else again. Ray saw her confusion and asked about it.

"Ray, what this means is that . . . you are actually his brother!"

"Nobody seems to want to do anything about it but . . . yeah, I probably am." Ray smiled and looked at her questioningly. "This isn't exactly new news, you know?"

"Well, yeah, sure, it's been great . . . pretending, you know, 'what if?'" she stammered. "But . . . I don't know, it just hit me. I guess I never *really* thought . . . wow!"

Sheree still sat, overwhelmed by her realization, while Ray dialed Vernon's number. Vernon answered.

They exchanged formalities, asked after each other, et cetera, before Ray got down to the reason for the call.

"I know what you said about all the stuff that gets written about Elvis but there are some pretty scary headlines out there right now. Is he okay?"

Vernon reiterated what he thought of most of the stuff written about Elvis. He said, yeah, he'd been under the weather a bit but that happens to everyone once in a while, doesn't it? Headlines don't appear when most people get a cold or something. He thought it was all a crock.

But after he'd railed against the press for a while, Vernon said that he thought Elvis would love to see Ray if he'd like to come over there one of these days . . . like, maybe . . . right now?

"Are you sure?" Ray asked, surprised. "The last couple of times we talked, he—"

"Listen," Vernon interrupted, "I know him better than anyone, I think he needs you right now. You can help him. Come by."

"Well, if I could help . . . I sure owe him a big one. Well, okay." Ray hung up, concerned.

"Is everything all right?" Sheree asked.

"He said Elvis is fine, just not feeling too great right now, but would probably love it if I came over to visit."

"You didn't seem sure."

"No, and I'm still not.

"But you're going over there?"

"Vernon seems to think I could help Elvis in some way. Imagine that. Me helping Elvis. I hope he knows what he's talking about."

"Looks like you're going to find out."

"Looks like," Ray agreed.

Just then the phone rang. Ray answered, and it was Vernon. Ray listened for a while, laughed, and said, "Good idea." Ray thanked him again and hung up.

"They'd obviously talked about the kidnapping and didn't want it to happen again. A car's being sent for me. Tinted windows."

"Now?"

"Yeah."

"So you're bailing on our romantic trip to the Laundromat?"

Ray took her in his arms. "I'll have to make it up to you."

"Oh, yes you will," she said as they kissed and held each other very close. They were becoming more aware that they had become a part of something much bigger, something which neither had the faintest idea where it was headed.

Sheree was the first to leave that day. Ray changed out of his T-shirt into something more suitable for Graceland and was ready to go when Ned and the limo arrived.

As they drove past his lions and turned out into the main road, neither paid attention to a dark man in a light blue Buick that was parked a ways down the road. Nor did they notice him start up and follow them as they left.

33

VELMA, ONCE AGAIN, GREETED Ray and led the way upstairs. Ray knew that now he was truly going where few had gone before. Many people had seen the main floor of Graceland. Elvis even conducted tours himself every once in a while like he had for Ray, but never upstairs. That was private. Yet here he was, walking up the famous mirror-lined staircase that he'd seen a million pictures of, to the sumptuously elegant room of the King himself.

Elvis looked bloated and tired, Ray thought, as he entered the bedroom. Elvis was propped up by pillows, surrounded by books, magazines, and fan mail with a pitcher and glass of orange juice on the table beside his massive bed.

"Let me feel your bump" was the first thing that Elvis said, putting down the magazine he had been looking through.

Ray went over to him and bent over. Elvis felt the good-size knot on the back of his head.

"Yeah. That's a good one."

"Didn't feel so good the other day," Ray said. "How are you doing?"

"Not worth a damn," Elvis replied simply. "Sit down. Sorry you had to go through that. You sure you're all right? I'm pretty well connected in the law enforcement world, you know. We could get these guys. I have no doubt about it."

"Actually, I already took care of it," Ray said. "Things should be all right."

"Okay. Then I'll let it go." It got quiet for a moment before Elvis said, "I don't think I've been real nice to you, Ray. Sorry about that.

I ain't used to having a brother. I always kinda prided myself on the fact that there wasn't nobody else like me in the world. Now there is— you. Maybe it bothered me that I wasn't quite so unique anymore."

"Are you kidding? What we have in common goes back to the first five minutes we were born, and the way we look. You grew into one of the most unique people in the world . . . and what you've done! My God, nobody else has even come close.

"I just turned into a regular kinda guy," Ray continued. "And I don't even do that so well."

"You're doing just fine," Elvis said. "When you're not being kidnapped, of course."

Both men started laughing. Elvis laughed so hard he started to cough. Ray wondered if there was anything he should do but Elvis quickly got it under control and stopped.

"Just look at you," Elvis said, after he caught his breath. "Damn, if you don't show me the way I oughta look. Like looking in one of them skinny mirrors."

"Hey, you're sick."

"Shouldn't be. I'm takin' a blamed pharmacy for everything." Elvis leaned back and sighed. "Oh, I get this shit every once in a while. I'll be back kickin' butt in a couple of days."

Elvis threw back the covers. "I'll tell you one thing, though, I surely am getting tired of this room. Let's take a walk."

Elvis, weakly, got out of bed in his white silk monogrammed pajamas and put on a maroon velvet robe. Ray followed him from the room.

"By the way, I want to thank you for getting me my job back," Ray said on the way downstairs. "I saw your picture magically appear on the wall the other day."

"Hell, I thought it was a good trade. Glad he did, too." Elvis laughed and walked on, subject forgotten. "By the way, I appreciate what you said upstairs. Those were nice words."

"I meant them."

"I know you did."

Elvis led the way out the back of the house to a walkway leading to a nearby pasture. Four horses and a pony were peacefully grazing there.

"That there palomino is my guy. Rising Sun. He's a good one."

Elvis seemed to get progressively weaker walking in the warm summer sun. Whenever they ran into shade, he would stop a moment, panting, before starting out again as though nothing had happened.

They were walking toward the swimming pool when Ray noticed Elvis's necklace, which hung outside his pajamas. "That's quite a chain you got."

"Yeah." Elvis fingered each item as he named it. "Got a cross, a Star of David, and a *chai*—Hebrew symbol for the life force."

"Got your bases covered, eh?"

"Don't want to miss out on heaven 'cause of some technicality."

Ray laughed as they continued walking.

"You a religious man, Ray?" Elvis asked after a moment.

"Sort of. I don't go to church much but I've always felt . . ." Ray paused, searching for the right words. He found them just as Elvis chose to finish the sentence for him. At exactly the same time, they both said "a special relationship with God."

They both looked at each other and laughed. Then Ray continued. "It's like I know he's there. I don't pray much but . . . sometimes I just talk to him. I got to admit, though," Ray continued, "that I also yell at him sometimes, too."

Elvis laughed, put his arm on Ray's shoulder for a moment. "Me, too, Ray. Me, too."

Elvis led Ray to a lovely area with a pool and fountain that Elvis called his meditation garden. They sat on two of the benches. Elvis obviously felt better by sitting down but seemed like he wanted to say something. It took a while before he could actually get it out.

"You know you hold your fork weird?" Elvis asked.

"Yeah. I noticed you do, too."

"Imagine that."

"I think Vernon did, too."

Elvis nodded his head. "Yeah." Everything got quiet for a minute.

"You know," Elvis began, haltingly, "the more I look into it, and I've gone about as far as there is, the more it seems that . . . you are Jesse. How do you feel about that?"

"I don't know," Ray admitted. "I feel that, too, but it's so big, it just hit my girlfriend this morning, after all this time. I don't know if it's really fully soaked into me yet."

Elvis looked off, seemed to take in the beauty of it all while he thought. "All these years, for you, Elvis was just this singing star, out there someplace. But 'Jesse' has been a painful, very real presence for me my whole life. I cried for you, prayed for you, Mama even kept a little coffin in the living room so we'd never forget you. Hell, I even tried psychics!

"The thing is . . . what we've got to realize," Elvis continued, "is that we're never going to know for positive. Someday there'll probably be tests for this, but now, there's no way we can ever know for sure. However, I really do feel you're my twin brother. I do . . . and, in spite of everything, I'm glad you're here, but I can't think of you as Jesse. That's something else. You're Ray. You'll always be Ray. Understand?"

Ray nodded. "I think Vernon feels the same way."

"He does," Elvis said, looking off, thoughtful again. Then he turned, looked over at Ray, and smiled. "Damn it all. Whether I like it or not, I got me a brother, and I think I'm going to like it. We got to celebrate . . . do something. Let's go for a drive. Get me outta here. Let me breathe some. C'mon."

Elvis, determined, slowly led the way back into the house.

After he changed into street clothes, Elvis led the way to the garage area and his impressive collection of exotic cars. He walked over to his well-known black 1973 Stutz Blackhawk with gold-plated trim and threw Ray the keys. "You drive."

"I ain't driven one of these before," Ray admitted.

"Hardly anyone in the world has," Elvis said as he got in the passenger side.

Ray found himself glad Elvis had sent the limo and that he hadn't driven his new/old beat-up truck to Graceland. That would have been too embarrassing.

Ray gingerly, reverently climbed into the impressive cockpit of the car, with its red leather interior, realizing that there were only about three other cars like this in the world.

The engine started the millisecond he turned the key and purred like no engine Ray had ever heard. He was in heaven. Before he pulled out, Elvis reached in the backseat and grabbed a bag, handing it to Ray.

"I got something a little weird here for you. It's the Colonel's idea but I got to listen to him. He ain't often wrong."

Ray opened the bag and pulled out a fishing-type hat, black-rimmed sunglasses (very un-Elvis-like), and a mustache that fit into Ray's nostrils.

Elvis continued. "The Colonel doesn't want the world to know about you just yet. We're talkin' about it. For now, though, you better put them on."

Ray did, feeling a little silly, but soon the thrill of driving this marvelous machine made him forget all about it.

As they drove, Ray decided to bring up a question that he'd wondered about ever since this "twin" stuff started.

"How come we don't have the same color hair?"

"We do. I've been dying it since I was fifteen," Elvis answered casually. On seeing Ray's curious look, he continued, "Looks better on stage, you know? Photographs better."

Having his answer, Ray drove in silence for a while, until Elvis said, "So you like motorcycles?"

"Mostly scrambles," Ray said.

"Got me some cruisers, couple of three-wheelers," Elvis said. "Never got into bouncing around on those little guys."

"Oh, it's great fun. We should do it. Really, you'd like it a lot."

"Well, we might have to see," Elvis said. "You'll also have to come for a ride with me on the Harleys. Let's see what the neighbors think when they run into the two Presley boys, eh?"

Elvis laughed. It was out before he knew it; a concept he'd never even considered. The laugh faded quickly, followed by a thoughtful moment. "Yeah," Elvis said quietly. "This'll take some getting used to."

After driving along in silence for a while, Elvis looked over at Ray and laughed.

"What?" Ray wanted to know.

"Have you looked in the mirror?" Elvis asked, still chuckling.

Ray hadn't but turned the rearview mirror toward himself so he could see his disguise.

"Hell, I look like Groucho," Ray said as he started laughing. That started Elvis off again. Elvis seemed to be feeling better as the two drove off down the street, laughing and enjoying the moment immensely.

The lighthearted feeling they both felt shattered quickly as a car full of rowdy teenage boys pulled up alongside them at a red light. The Stutz was definitely not for traveling incognito. Even though the windows were tinted, the occupants could still be seen a little. Besides, everyone knew whose car it was.

The teens were obviously out to hassle, leaning out the window, yelling at them and giving them the finger. "Hey, Elvis, eat me!" "Screw you, Pelvis!" "If my girl could see you now, she'd puke!" "Nice pimpmobile."

All the noise the teens were making got the attention of a car full of girls on the other side of the Stutz. They looked over, also recognized the car, and went crazy. These were obviously fans. They rolled down their windows and were asking for autographs between their screams. The street had turned into a cacophony of sound.

Elvis sunk down in his seat, the fun suddenly having gone out of it all. He suddenly looked much older than Ray, and quite ill. "Lose them."

When the light turned green, Ray gunned it. The Stutz sped off but the two other cars were in mad pursuit. Ray felt that this great car could lose them eventually, but also knew how dangerous speeding through the streets of Memphis could be and the King was, after all, in his care right then. Whatever he did had better be done right. He told Elvis, "Hang on."

Ray eased up a little to let the cars catch up with them. After making sure there wasn't anybody else they would run into, he suddenly slammed on the brakes. As the two other cars sped by, Ray quickly turned behind one of them and headed down a residential street. A couple more turns and they were alone and quiet.

Elvis looked over at Ray, impressed. "Now, that was nice."

"Thank you, sir," Ray said. "A little scrambles move."

"I'm definitely going to have to give that a try," Elvis said. "Let's get out of here before they come back. It'd be too easy for me to shoot somebody today."

They drove off, pleased that they had lost the teens but unaware that there was one car they hadn't shaken. The light blue Buick slowly followed, unnoticed, from about a block in back of them where it had been during their whole ride.

Safely behind the gates of Graceland, Ray parked the Stutz by the back door. Both men got out.

"Well, that was fun . . . for a while," Elvis muttered.

"Guess you get that a lot."

"Why do you think the damn walls are so high?" Elvis said, still looking weak and tired. "I'm going to hit it. I'll send Ned up for you."

Ray thanked him and, rather unconsciously, looked over toward Vernon's house. Elvis saw him. "Heard you had a good time the other night."

"Sure did. Met Dee. They were both real nice."

"Don't get me started on her," Elvis said, starting to walk off. "Going out on tour for a couple weeks. You take care." Then he turned back as if he had an afterthought. "Oh, and Ray . . . you can take that stuff off now."

Ray had forgotten all about it. Both men laughed as Ray got out of his disguise. Still smiling, Elvis gave a final wave and entered the house.

Ray enjoyed the few quiet moments alone, just soaking up the rarified ambience before Ned arrived with the limo. Ray had just been accepted by his most famous brother and had also gotten his first glimpse into the downside of that magical world. He couldn't believe he ever considered selling him out.

Ray had an enjoyable ride back to his place with Ned, who he was actually getting to know well from these trips. He seemed like a good guy. Neither had any reason to notice the light blue Buick that followed them, then parked alongside the road just outside Ray's property line.

34

Wednesday, June 29, 1977

WITH ELVIS OUT OF town, Ray's life returned to a much more familiar pattern. Lots of work, many quiet evenings with Sheree, and, of
course, the trusted camaraderie of J.D.

That afternoon was typical in that after work both men would
meet at Ray's, pop beers, commandeer the lawn chairs, and discuss the
great problems known to man.

Ray had arrived home first and had already assumed the position
when J.D. pulled in. "Yo" was the day's greeting as he went straight
inside, grabbed a beer, and settled into the lawn chair adjacent to Ray.

"I am so excited," J.D. said in his usual flat, nonexcited drawl.

"Speak."

"Well." J.D. arranged himself in the chair so he could look at Ray.
J.D. didn't get much more excited than this. "You know how they're
trying to get an expansion football team or even a semipro bunch up
here?"

"Yeah."

"I know what to call it. I got the perfect name. You're going to
love it."

"What?" Ray asked.

"Are you ready?" J.D. was milking this as much as he could.

"What's the damn name?"

"The Kings!" J.D. announced with a flourish.

"The Kings?"

"Yeah, but not 'kings' like royalty. It would be 'kings' like in 'the
King,' like Elvis. Think about it, the helmets could be painted like

black hair with sideburns down by the ear holes and the uniforms could look like white jumpsuits. It would be so cool."

Ray thought the best way to handle this would be to not say anything. He did smile, though.

"The cheerleaders could be real sexy babes in skimpy Elvis outfits, like lady impersonators."

"Would the players have blue suede cleats?" Ray couldn't resist asking.

"You know, that's a good question. I hadn't thought of that," J.D. said seriously as he took a minute to do just that. "I don't think it would work. The blue suede shoes came before the jumpsuits and I don't think they'd go that well together, but it was a good shot. Creative."

Things got quiet as they each visualized the Kings taking the field for the first time. Ray had to laugh out loud.

"What?"

"You might be on to something, J.D. Let me know what happens," Ray said, still chuckling.

"I thought you, of all people, would have the sensitivity and vision to appreciate this."

"Oh, I appreciate it a lot," Ray said. "I just think you might have a hard time selling it. It would be memorable, though. I'll give you that."

The men sat on in silence, Ray, visualizing a white-suited team of helmet-haired Elvises in jumpsuits and shoulder pads, J. D., disappointed that his friend didn't share his enthusiasm. Ah well, they were still best of friends even though their intellectual leanings might differ now and then.

Sunday, July 3, 1977
Ray and Sheree finally made it to the Laundromat. They scooted the plastic chairs together and snuggled while watching the clothes go around in the dryer. Ray had added just that little extra touch by stealing a daisy from a planter next door and putting it in a glass jar half-filled with water.

Sheree thought it was very romantic. It rested on the Formica table next to her. As what usually happened when conversations between them went on for a while, eventually, they lead back to Elvis.

"It's like he's a prisoner in this really fancy cell," Sheree said.

"Yeah, and he's sick as a dog and still has most of the year booked with concerts. He's got a different life going, all right, but he works hard for it."

After a moment, Sheree said, "So everyone agrees you're Elvis's twin brother. What happens now? You move into Graceland, or something?"

"Not quite. I'm still a secret, remember?" Ray reminded her. "Think about it, I'm not involved in Elvis's life at all, his music, his friends. They don't even know I'm here."

"But he seems to like you," Sheree said.

Yeah, Ray had to admit that it was getting better all the time. Her question prompted him to actually put into words what he felt was happening, something that he hadn't tried to do before.

"I think I'm kind of a break for him," Ray started hesitantly. "All his friends are on the payroll in one form or another. There are jealousies, politics, all sorts of things that he doesn't have to worry about with me.

"I know he's having trouble with some of the guys around him," Ray continued. "Investments, his health . . . I'm not a part of any of that and I think he likes it that way."

"Well, I think it's pretty neat," Sheree said. "Do you think I'll ever meet him?"

"I sure hope so, honey. I really do."

One of the dryers stopped so both of them walked over to it and started pulling hot clothes out, stacking them on the nearby table. Sheree immediately started sorting.

"So what are you going to do, Ray?" she asked.

"It all depends upon how he wants to play it. I mean, I can't—"

"Wait, wait, wait!" Sheree said, topping him. "Sorry. Elvis can only go so far in our lives. I mean what do *you* want to do? Do you want to drive Fields's trucks forever? Want to stay here? Want to be a fireman? What?"

"Actually, I don't really know," Ray began slowly. "I been thinking about it, too. It kinda comes down to what *can* I do. All I know is driving and the lumber business. Guess I'll do them as long as I can." Ray thought a moment more. Morgan Bates and his big bucks came fleeting across Ray's mind. He felt embarrassed every time he thought that way, but the thoughts kept coming anyway.

"Hey, where'd you go?" Sheree asked, waving her hands in front of his face. "I could just see you tune out and go somewhere."

"Just possibilities. Lots of different roads."

"Does one of those roads lead to Paris?" Sheree kidded.

"Don't know about that. I think one leads to Bartlett . . . another might go to Collierville."

They laughed.

"Hell, it doesn't matter. I like hanging out with you right here," Sheree said much more seriously.

"Me, too, with you, kid," Ray said softly.

Their soft moment was soon shattered by the second dryer buzzer announcing that the towels were dry. Sheree jumped up but told Ray to stay seated.

"Why?" he asked. "What are you doing?"

"This!" she said playfully as she grabbed an armload of hot towels and smothered his face in them.

"Hey, wait a minute!" Ray said as he tried to fight his way out from under them.

"No, no. Relax," Sheree said, getting him to calm down as she arraigned the towels just so on his face. "There's nothing better than hot towels right out of the dryer."

Ray relaxed. "You're right. This feels pretty good," Ray said, his voice muffled by the towels.

"*Pretty* good?" Sheree asked as she sat down next to him and plopped a bunch on her own face. "It's the best, that's all . . ."

And there they sat, happy as can be, not thinking of jobs or money or the future . . . just fully experiencing the simple delight of hot, fresh towels straight from the Laundromat dryer.

"It really is a wonderful life, you know?" They both chuckled but Ray had to agree with her. It sure did have its moments.

Sitting there with their faces covered by hot towels, neither noticed the dark man at the window taking pictures of their silliness.

35

RAY WAS JUST ARRIVING home from work when he heard the phone ringing inside. He hurried to get it in time.

"Hello . . . wait, honey! What's wrong? . . . What? Grant? . . . That son of a bitch! Did you call the police? . . . Honey, there's not going to be anything for you to be afraid of. Hang on, I'm leaving right now."

Ray hung up, thoroughly pissed. He went back into the bedroom and was looking for a clean shirt when the phone rang again.

"Yeah? . . . Oh, Elvis. Hi." Ray stood a little straighter as he always did talking to Elvis. "I'm glad you're feeling . . . you know, I can't. I just got a bit of an emergency and I'm just leaving . . . the guy who lives next door to my girlfriend just killed her dog. . . . Yeah, poisoned it . . . she said it had been sick, you know, whining, barking. Anyway, I guess it bothered him. I'm on my way over to 'bother' him some . . . no, Elvis you can't . . . look, I can . . . really, you shouldn't get—"

Elvis hung up. Damn it. Here was a case when Ray actually said no to Elvis and even that didn't work. He was definitely a man used to getting his own way. Ray thought briefly about leaving quickly before Elvis got over there but couldn't quite bring himself to do that.

He got dressed and was sitting on the trailer stairs when Elvis sped up in the Stutz fifteen minutes later.

Elvis, obviously feeling better, was half out of the car before it came to a complete stop, already in the act of strapping on a shoulder holster.

"You better drive," Elvis said, grabbing a jacket and starting over toward Ray's truck. "The Stutz isn't exactly undercover."

Ray just stared at the holster and the gun it now held. Elvis noticed and misinterpreted the look. "Oh yeah." He went back to the Stutz, opened the glove compartment, and pulled out a .38 and offered it to Ray. "Want a gun?"

"No." That would be the last thing Ray would want. That wasn't why he was staring. Why in hell did Elvis want one? What was he going to do, shoot this guy?

"Suit yourself," Elvis said while casually throwing the gun in the backseat and going over to the truck. "Let's hit it," he said as he climbed in. As embarrassed as Ray was about having Elvis in this old truck, he was thankful, at least, that it started the first time and actually drove off under its own power.

Ray started to ask about the disguise but figured the fury of the moment made it not quite so necessary. Neither one of them wanted to deal with it, so he let it go.

When they reached the end of Ray's drive, by the lions, Ray noticed a man in a light blue Buick quickly turn his head as they approached. He wondered why someone would do that.

As they drove off the hill, Ray couldn't help but be aware of Elvis's energy. He could hardly contain himself.

"How'd he do it?" Elvis asked.

"Poisoned a pound of raw hamburger and threw it over her fence to the dog. The vet said it was arsenic, rat poison. It looks like he put too much in it. The dog only ate half of it before it killed him."

"Did she see him?"

"No, but he'd been complaining about the noise. The meat was found in a corner of her yard that butts up against Grant's. That's the guy's name. She's real sure it was him."

"Man, stuff like this really pisses me off. I love animals. You can drive faster, you know?"

"Elvis, you shouldn't be getting yourself mixed up in—"

"You don't know who you're talking to, do you?" Elvis interrupted. He pulled out his wallet and flashed an FBI badge to Ray.

"Card-carrying member of the FBI, and also member of the

Memphis Police. I'll have to show you my badges back at the house. Got more than anybody . . . I'm talking *real*! Not this honorary crap, so don't worry about it. I got you covered."

Since Elvis was going to be involved whether Ray liked it or not, he stepped on it a bit more. As they raced through the city streets, Elvis slipped on the light jacket that effectively covered his shoulder holster. He was ready for action and could hardly wait. Ray didn't even want to think about what was going to happen.

Ray pulled over and parked by a group of small bungalows in a lower-middle-class suburb of Memphis. They were close together but each building stood apart.

"My girl lives there," Ray said, pointing to a bungalow next door. "And this one is his," he said, indicating the one they were parked in front of.

"Does he live alone?" Elvis asked.

"I think so."

"Let's get him."

As they climbed out of the truck, Elvis felt something heavy in a pocket. He pulled out . . . another gun. He showed it to Ray.

"Sure you don't want a gun?"

"Really. No."

Elvis shrugged and put it back in his pocket as they walked quietly to the front door.

"See if the door's unlocked," Elvis whispered to Ray.

Ray carefully grabbed the knob and tried to turn it. It turned! He nodded to Elvis, who stood next to the door, drew his gun, looked over at Ray, and said, "This is my favorite part."

Elvis took a big breath, blew it out, opened the door, and burst into the room, gun drawn, and yelled, "Freeze!"

Inside the modest bungalow, Grant Ferris, a man in his early thirties, was working at a card table. Papers were everywhere. His initial reaction to this intrusion was to jump up and run. The only escape route, however, took him past Ray, who doubled him over with a fist to the stomach as he tried to run by.

Elvis then grabbed Grant by the collar, threw him on the couch, and straddled him with his gun in Grant's mouth.

"I thought I said 'freeze'!" Elvis said menacingly, as he took off his dark glasses to better glare at his prey. "You have trouble hearing?"

A petrified Grant shook his head no, his eyes big with fright and confusion. The last thing Grant expected to see that day was a very large Elvis Presley in his living room, sitting on top of him holding a gun in his mouth.

"Ray, see if you can find some arsenic laying around here."

Ray went to the kitchen and started looking.

"I understand you had some business with a small dog this morning?" Elvis said quietly.

Grant shook his head like he didn't know what Elvis was talking about.

"Perhaps I should remind you that there's a gun in your mouth. If I were you, I'd quickly become the most honest man on the planet." Elvis's manner was calm, quiet, and outrageously intense.

"Got it," Ray said, holding up a box he'd found in a utility closet.

"Let's try that again," Elvis said a little harder.

Grant tried to speak but couldn't do it with the gun in his mouth. Elvis realized that and took it out but kept it trained about three inches from his face.

"Talk to me."

"Look, I work at home," Grant said, trying to catch his breath. "I've got a lot of book work to do and have to concentrate. The dog was whining and barking for two days. It was driving me crazy."

Elvis put the gun back into Grant's mouth, pissed. "He was sick! Is that how you treat sick animals? Kill them?"

Grant, very quickly, shook his head no. Elvis thought for a moment about what to do with this problem. Ray watched from a few feet away, wondering what was going to happen next.

Ray could tell Elvis really wanted to pistol-whip the guy for what he'd done but forced himself to be calm. Finally, Elvis seemed to come up with a plan. "Are you very, very sorry about the mistake you made?" he asked softly.

Grant again nodded.

"Then you'd probably like to do something about it, wouldn't you?" More nodding. "What do you suppose that would be?"

Elvis took the gun out of Grant's mouth to allow him to answer.

"Uh . . . buy her a new one?" Grant proposed.

"Nice idea," Elvis agreed. "And if this dog shits in your bed and barks all night, what are you going to do about it?"

"Uh . . . nothing?"

"Good answer," Elvis said. "What else?"

Grant thought for a moment but didn't come up with anything.

"How about apologizing?" Elvis suggested. "Let this little girl know just how sorry you are."

Grant nodded quickly. Yes, he could do that. Elvis took a look around Grant's small bungalow.

"How much money do you make a month?" Elvis asked, once again removing the gun.

"About eight hundred."

"Give her half of it. Give her four hundred bucks."

"But I don't have—"

The gun went back in Grant's mouth and Elvis's intensity level went up four notches. "But you'll get it, won't you? This week."

Grant nodded. Elvis removed the gun. "If any of these agreements are not met, I will know," Elvis said quietly. "And we will talk again."

Elvis got off Grant, stretched a bit, put the gun back in his holster, and started for the door. Grant didn't move. At the door, Elvis turned.

"Oh, and if you tell anyone about what happened here today," Elvis paused, smiling, "they won't believe you."

Elvis walked out, leaving Grant and Ray looking at each other, each sighing a bit of relief. Figuring anything he would say now would just be anticlimactic, Ray simply cocked his head toward Grant as he started for the door, and said, "Grant."

Grant, still not moving, acknowledged, "Ray."

Ray left. Grant didn't move for some time.

Ray found Elvis leaning up against his truck, out of breath but laughing.

"Oh, that was fun," Elvis said. "I love that. I'm sorry for your girl's little dog, but I liked that."

Elvis seemed to be having a hard time catching his breath. Ray started to worry about him when Elvis turned, opened the door to the cab, and hauled himself up. Ray also got in.

Elvis still fought for his breath. He then reached into his pocket and pulled out two small pills. He also saw Ray's look of concern.

"Don't worry about it. Happens. I'll be fine in a minute," Elvis said, taking the pills. "Let's get out of here."

Ray checked the rearview mirror before pulling out into the street. He was surprised to see the light blue Buick parked about a block away. He wondered if it was the same one he'd seen earlier. Sure looked the same. Ah well, Elvis is probably used to people following him around by now.

Elvis was back to his old self by the time they reached Ray's trailer.

"It has just been too long," Elvis said as he climbed out of the truck. "I haven't had that much fun in . . . hell, I can't even remember. Thanks, Ray. Good man."

"Thank you. That was great. I couldn't have done that."

"Sure you could have," Elvis said as he opened the door to the Stutz and threw his gun on the passenger seat. "You just ain't crazy enough." Elvis waved and laughed as he drove away down Ray's road.

Ray watched him go, feeling as though a whirlwind had just left. Ray had to smile, reliving it all already. It was pretty impressive the way Elvis handled the situation. Yep, quite a guy, that brother of mine, Ray thought as he went back into his trailer.

36

Monday, July 11, 1977

RAY GOT HOME ABOUT half an hour earlier from an exceptionally dirty day on the truck. He had just climbed out of the shower and was finishing getting dressed when he saw Sheree's white Chevy pull up outside. He went outside to meet her.

"Hey, babe. What's up?"

"I guess I can't say I just happened to be in the neighborhood, can I?"

"Not if you want me to believe you," Ray agreed.

"Ray, what did you say to Grant?"

"Why? Is he still giving you a bad time?"

"God, no," Sheree said. "He's been sickly sweet. He apologized, he gave me money. What did you do?"

"Honey, there are some things I can't talk about right now. This is one of them. You'll get the whole story later, I promise."

"I was afraid it might be something like that," Sheree said.

"It'll be all right. It really will," Ray assured her.

"Actually, I believe you. I have something to show you," Sheree said as she started walking back to her little car. "Nothing can take the place of Rags . . ." She reached into the backseat and pulled out the cutest little beagle puppy in the world. "But this little guy is sure going to help."

Ray laughed, took the dog, and held it to him. He got smothered in licks for his effort. "This is great. What a cutie. Have you got a name for . . ." Ray held him up at arm's length so he could check. "Him?"

"Yeah. I hope you like it," Sheree said coyly. "I'm thinking of calling him Jesse."

Ray held the dog a little closer and smiled. "Jesse the beagle. I like that. I like that a lot."

Sheree came over to him and gave her two guys a hug. "He's something else, isn't he," Sheree said, grinning.

"He's great."

"Well, I gotta run but I wanted you to meet this little guy."

"I'm glad you did," Ray said.

Sheree put young Jesse in the car and started to get in herself when Ray remembered something.

"Oh, babe, could you do me a favor?"

"Sure."

"On your way out, could you look and see if there's a light blue Buick parked anywhere around the turnoff to the property?"

"What's going on?"

"Don't know for sure. Just wondered."

"I got to tell you, Ray, I'm not crazy about all this secrecy stuff. I'll check for you but I'm going to want to know what's going on around here pretty quick."

"I promise."

"I'll hold you to it. 'Bye, honey." Sheree left.

Although he half expected it, Ray was still surprised when Sheree called a couple hours later to tell him that, yes, a blue Buick had been parked out there.

"You're not in any trouble, are you?

"No, not at all. I'll clear everything up real soon."

"You'd better!"

Ray hung up and sat down, his mind whirring. What this meant was that Elvis wasn't being followed, Ray was. What was that all about?

Saturday, July 16, 1977

A major negative in being the most famous person in the world, Ray was learning, was that Elvis couldn't do many simple little things that people take for granted; he couldn't take a simple ride in his car without the risk of having it become an incident, couldn't go to a restaurant, couldn't walk down the street, couldn't go to a football game, see a parade, go shopping. He couldn't even see a movie without renting out the whole theater.

Elvis confided to Ray that that's exactly what he had had to do on many occasions, like when Lisa Marie wanted to see a movie, or even just he and his buds. He'd often rent the whole theater for the night. Actually, he had one coming up as a surprise for Lisa Marie. He was going to rent the entire Libertyland amusement park. He wished Ray could come join them but the Colonel wasn't quite ready for that yet.

"You understand?" Elvis asked Ray as though the answer was "of course, yes."

Ray just nodded although, no, he didn't understand at all. He was definitely learning, though, that some things just had to be put away and dealt with in their own time. This, evidently, was one of those things.

Another of life's little pleasures that Elvis couldn't openly partake in was trying his skill at the scrambles track. But, when in doubt, buy it! Or in this case, rent it. Which is exactly what Elvis did.

That was how Ray found himself at the lighted scrambles track at twelve midnight alone except for Elvis and Ned. Elvis rented the place for the night to engage in this simple pleasure. Ray didn't even want to guess how much it cost.

Elvis looked awful that night. Ray realized that the floodlights made everyone look pale but Elvis looked a pasty white that didn't even seem real. He didn't appear to feel much better than he looked but was determined not to miss this opportunity.

Ray was setting up the bikes while Ned watched and Elvis talked about the meaning of life. He was in a philosophical mood and was concerned that so many people just didn't "get it."

"How can people possibly think that 'making it' in our society is what it's all about? Can you believe that? This is the God that created galaxies and atoms and quantum physics. Where does 'making a lot of money' fit in with that scene?

"I'm worried about my people," Elvis continued. "I even devoted a couple concerts to just trying to help them. I think I·pissed them off but it's for their own good, you know? They've got to start thinking about the big picture and get out of their own tiny little selves."

Nobody said anything for a few minutes.

"Yeah, life can be rough for people in a lot of different ways," Ray said. "But, you know, sometimes just getting away from all that and listening to some good ol' rock 'n' roll by probably the best person on the planet to sing it means something, too."

"Well . . . yeah," Elvis admitted quietly.

Ned looked over to Ray and nodded approvingly. It seemed that Ray already could say things to Elvis that even his closest friends couldn't.

Finally, the bikes were ready to go. Ray took one out just to show them what the point was. Ray sped around the track, taking the jumps high and having a great time. He hadn't ridden for a while and had missed it. Every muscle in his body was activated as he maneuvered the relatively small motorcycle around the track and over the jumps. Ray always found it exhilarating and this night was no exception.

After a few laps, Ray turned off the track and rode over to where Elvis and Ned had been watching. He switched off the bike, removed his helmet, and walked over to the cooler they'd brought and got himself some water.

"Hell, you do know how to ride that thing," Elvis said, impressed.

"It's a little easier without someone trying to knock you out of the way. Don't often get the track to myself," Ray said.

"Comes with the territory."

"Want to give it a try?" Ray asked Elvis.

"Damn straight. What do I do?"

Ray took him over to a nearby bike and started it for him. As it warmed up, Ray explained.

"You're a rider. You won't have a problem. This will be lighter and easier to handle than your big guys. Start out slow, ride the track like it was a bumpy road. When you get the feel of that and want to go faster, take some of the jumps, just stand up in the seat a bit and keep your weight forward. Let your legs act as shock absorbers. That's all there is to it."

"So you say," Elvis said as he laboriously got on the motorcycle. "This sucker seems small."

"You're used to your hogs," Ray said. "These guys are light but you'll be amazed how they can scat. C'mon."

Ray got on his bike and eased out into the track, Elvis following alongside. Ray let Elvis set the speed he was comfortable with and Ray trailed a little behind. Elvis took it slowly for one lap, then was ready for more action.

He cranked it open a bit more, stood on the peddles as Ray had instructed, and started taking the jumps. He certainly didn't go as high as Ray did or look as graceful in the air, but he did it. Even though he was sick, the natural competitor in Elvis couldn't help but show through.

After a few laps, they both pulled into their staging area. They dismounted and took off their helmets. Elvis was wet with sweat and out of breath, but excited.

"Great! You're a natural," Ray said.

"Oh, that's fun." Elvis panted. "I may have to build me one of these suckers out back." He turned to Ned. "You know where the perfect place for one of these would be? The ranch."

"It'd scare the hell out of the horses," Ned pointed out with a laugh.

Elvis chuckled as he went over to the cooler, still out of breath, popped himself a Pepsi, and grabbed a sack of beef jerky.

"Your turn," he said to Ned. "Show us what you got."

"I don't know," Ned said apprehensively, then turned to Ray. "I think I'm the only person Elvis knows who doesn't ride."

"What are you talking about? I bought you a Harley," Elvis said with a mouthful of jerky.

"Yeah, and it's great, but I don't really ride it very much," Ned confessed.

"Well, it's about time," Elvis said, throwing him a helmet. "It'll come back to you . . . like falling off a bicycle. Just do like Ray said, slow and easy at first. Gear shift's on this side."

"One up . . . three down," Ray said as he started it for him.

Ned got on the bike and hesitantly let out the clutch so slow that he hardly moved. He then tried to do it faster and accidentally popped the clutch, which caused the bike to shoot out from underneath him, leaving Ned flat on his back, fortunately unhurt . . . and laughing.

Elvis and Ray also cracked up. As Ray went to help Ned up, they both noticed that Elvis's laughter had turned to choking. Ned quickly got to his feet and peeled his helmet off. He said, "Oh, shit!" as he ran to Elvis, who was doubled over, gagging.

"Keep trying to cough!" Ned cried forcefully to Elvis as he stepped in back of him and put his arms around his waist in preparation for the Heimlich maneuver. Elvis was large and Ned was not; his arms barely reached around Elvis's midsection. He made a fist with one hand and as soon as the other hand touched it, gave a hard, fast, upward thrust-pull.

Elvis continued to cough. Ned gave another more powerful jerk. Nothing came up. Elvis was starting to turn blue and he collapsed to his knees. Ned stayed on his knees behind him, encouraging him to cough as he repeated the upward thrusts to his midsection.

Then Elvis stopped coughing and fell over, unconscious.

"Damn it!" Ned said, as he rolled Elvis over on his back, tipping his head back, his neck in an arch.

"What can I do?" Ray asked, in a near panic.

"Nothing!" Ned replied sharply. He was too busy to elaborate. Once he got Elvis in position, he gave him three big mouth-to-mouth breaths, then put one hand on top of the other and pushed down strongly three times on Elvis's breastbone.

Ned then opened Elvis's mouth and did a finger sweep inside his mouth, feeling back into his throat. He pulled his fingers back out holding a piece of beef jerky. That cleared Elvis's windpipe.

After a couple more thrusts, Elvis started coughing and breathing again. Soon, he was sitting up on the ground, panting, conscious and alert, but still fighting for breath. It all happened so quickly.

Ray was concerned for Elvis but equally impressed with how swiftly and efficiently Ned had gotten into action.

"Are you going to be all right?" Ray asked Elvis.

Elvis was still too out of breath to answer but nodded and reached up and patted Ned in thanks.

"That was great," Ray said to Ned. "How'd you learn that?"

"We all know how," Ned said simply. "It happens every once in a while." Then he turned to Elvis. "Take it easy for a minute. Pain gone?"

Elvis nodded, already starting to breathe a little better. Elvis smiled and pointed over at Ned's crashed motorcycle.

"Try again," he said in a gravelly whisper, still smiling.

"Thank you so very much anyway, but I don't think so." Ned was through playing.

"Got the kit?" Elvis roughly whispered.

"Yeah, but I think we'd better get you home," Ned said, helping Elvis to his feet. "Get you in a steam. That always helps."

Elvis turned to Ray and made a helpless, open-armed gesture like, "What can I do?"

"Hey, don't worry about it. Get out of here. Take care of yourself."

As Ned helped Elvis to the Stutz, Elvis motioned back for Ray to enjoy the track. Ray smiled and nodded.

After getting Elvis into the car, Ned said, "Nice riding, Ray. See you soon."

"Yeah, thanks. Good work."

Ned got behind the wheel and quickly sped away, leaving Ray alone at 12:30 at night, with three motorcycles and an empty scrambles track. Ray just sat down and looked around. Suddenly everything seemed quite lonely. Somehow the fun had gone out of it.

37

RAY WAS MANAGING TO work himself back into the good graces with the folks at Fields and had even managed to get an extra time-and-a-half day for coming in on Saturday. Sheree and puppy Jesse had come over to help clean up Ray's place in exchange for a promised dinner out.

That's why Sheree was there and Ray wasn't when a short, balding, older man knocked on the door. Sheree answered. The man asked if this was where Ray Johnston lived.

"Yes, it is," Sheree said.

"Is he here?"

"No. He got offered an extra day of work today and took it. Can I tell him who called?"

"You must be the girlfriend he told us about. I'm Vernon Presley."

Sheree practically froze but managed to reach out her hand to shake with him. "I'm Sheree Norton. It's a pleasure, sir."

"Likewise," Vernon said. "Could I come in for a minute?"

"Of course," Sheree said. "Please excuse the mess. I'm in the middle of cleaning."

Vernon stepped inside, did a visual sweep of the room. Little Jesse had been sleeping but woke as Vernon came into the trailer. He bound into the room and was all over Vernon's ankles, smelling, licking, jumping up.

Sheree picked him up. "Now, Je—" She caught herself. Vernon might not appreciate Jesse the beagle like she and Ray did. "Jethro, you cut that out," she said, thinking as quickly as she could.

She put Jesse in another room and closed the door. "Excuse him," she said, coming back.

"That's fine. Love pups," Vernon said. "I wonder if you could help me. Ray told us about these journals . . . the ones that got this whole thing going. Do you think Ray would mind if I took a look at them?"

"I'm sure it would be fine, especially for you." She got them out of the cupboard where Ray kept them. "Sit down, please. The pages that deal with all this are marked. Would you like coffee or a soft drink or anything?"

"I'm fine," Vernon said, sitting down and taking the journals from Sheree.

"Any of this true, do you think?" Vernon asked.

"Actually, I think it's all true, Mr. Presley," Sheree said, surprised at the question. "I am sorry. I'm sure this is painful for you."

"Yeah," was all Vernon said as he started reading.

Sheree went out to the kitchen and tried to continue cleaning without making any noise. She could hardly believe that this was the real Vernon Presley, Elvis's dad and maybe Ray's dad sitting there. She watched Vernon read. Watched emotions pass across his face, watched his lips move as he read. When he finished, he silently stared straight ahead. Sheree said nothing, waiting for Vernon.

"She was a terrible woman," he said finally.

"I think she probably was just trying to do what—"

"Yes, I know!" Vernon interrupted. "Trying to do what she thought was right. Well, she was wrong! If this is true, then she stole my baby. My wife cried her whole life for that baby." Vernon paused. Sheree was reluctant to say anything.

"Do you think this . . . Ray . . . is the one?" Vernon asked.

"Yes, I do," Sheree said with a conviction she didn't know she had.

"Seems like a good man." Vernon stared off again. "He could have been my son."

"Actually, doesn't this show that . . . he *is* your son? I mean, it's terrible that you never—"

"And another thing!" Vernon interrupted loudly. "I weren't a drunk. Never! I was worried. Hell, going to a bar is what a man did in those days while their wives had babies. I didn't have a job right then and knew that I was going to have twin 'something or others' to take care of. I was pretty scared.

"Way she wrote it made me sound like a drunk," Vernon continued. "Weren't a drunk. Just poor, that's all. Just poor. She had no right."

"I agree, sir. It was not right for her to—"

"It was horrible! A horrible thing she did." Vernon sat still for a moment. "The other day in conversation the question came up, what would I do if something happened to Elvis?" Vernon paused a moment, feeling emotional. "You know I'd never even thought about that? What would life be like? What would I *want* it to be like? Gets one thinking."

After a moment, Vernon abruptly got up. "I'll go now," he said, heading for the front door.

Sheree followed. "As awful as this must be for you, at least you may have found your other boy."

Vernon stepped out of the trailer, turned, and looked back at Sheree. "I think I'm going to forget I ever came here." He then walked away toward his waiting car.

Sheree waited until Ray had had a beer and a chance to unwind after the day before telling him the tale. At first he couldn't believe Vernon had come out there and he'd missed him, damn! By the time she finished, the room was very quiet.

"He said he wanted to forget about all this?"

"I'm sorry, Ray, but yes. I know it's hard not to take it personally," Sheree began. "But I don't really think he meant it. Vernon's an old man. Many people deal with things they don't know what to do about by not dealing with them at all. I think that's what he's doing . . . for now, at least."

"I thought reading the journals would make him more sure. I guess not."

"For now," Sheree stressed. "This is a big shock. He likes you. He said so. I'll bet he just needs some time."

Ray felt like he was on an emotional roller coaster. He had never felt more like he was actually Jesse Garon Presley, but that would make Vernon his father . . . and his father wanted to forget all about it.

38

DURING THE COUPLE OF weeks following the scrambles track incident and Sheree's experience with Vernon, Ray had had no contact with the Presley side of his life except when Elvis called to thank Ray for the motorcycle experience and apologized again for messing it up. They were both looking forward to giving it another go. Elvis seemed to recover well enough to have been out of town most of that time.

Ray decided to take Sheree's advice concerning Vernon and "give it some time" since there wasn't much else that he could do anyway.

All was well with Sheree and they doted unmercifully on young Jesse. (Sheree told Ray about her close call with Vernon. Ray thought she had done right. Vernon might not appreciate a beagle named Jesse.) She and Ray seemed to be getting closer, testified by the fact that she was spending more time lately at Ray's than at her own place.

That, too, was just fine with Ray. Even little Jesse seemed to like it there and became "trailer broken" very quickly. Everyone was proud.

Ray was showering before going to bed that evening when the phone rang. Sheree, in her bathrobe, answered.

"Hello . . . Well, he's . . . could I say who's calling, please?" Sheree immediately straightened up. "Oh, Mr. Presley. Yes, just a minute."

She put the phone down and ran to the bathroom door, opened it, and yelled above the shower noise, "Ray, it's Vernon Presley. He says it's important!"

Ray turned off the water, wrapped a towel around him, thanked

Sheree, and went quickly, still wet, to the phone, a cold feeling already starting in his stomach.

"Yes, Vernon. Is everything all right? . . . Well, sure, if you think I . . . he did? . . . All right . . . okay, I'll see you in a bit. 'Bye."

Ray hung up, concerned. He started drying himself off as he explained to Sheree. "Says Elvis is real upset. Guess he's asking for me. Vernon wants me to come by his place first."

"It's ten o'clock at night," Sheree pointed out.

"That's when Elvis starts living. You know that."

"What do you think is happening?"

"No idea, but I'd better hustle," Ray said as he went back into the bedroom and started getting dressed. Halfway through, something occurred to Ray. He went back to Sheree, held her face in his hands.

"Honey, I'm sorry but I really do have to do this. You do understand, don't you?"

"Sorta," she said softly. "I can say that I don't want our lives to revolve around Elvis forever but I do know you have to do this now. I hope it's nothing too serious."

"Thank you, babe," Ray said as he kissed her gently, held her a moment, then returned to the bedroom and quickly finished getting dressed.

There was little traffic at that time of night so Ray made good time driving to Graceland. Just in case, Ray put on the disguise as he approached the gates. He removed it enough for the guards to recognize him and wave him through. He took it the rest of the way off as soon as he got inside, parked in what was becoming his usual spot, and walked back to Vernon's house, wondering when, if ever, he should say anything about the journals.

Vernon met Ray at the door and invited him into his nicely decorated living room. Vernon paced for a while before sitting opposite Ray and telling him what was on his mind.

"Elvis has always hated confrontation when it came to his friends or money. We had to deal with a situation that was both. He was having a little trouble with some of the guys and we also had to cut back financially. Elvis had me do it. The guys involved didn't take it so good."

Vernon paused, not wanting to go on but knew he had to. "They wrote a book, a terrible book, accusing Elvis of all sorts of horrible things. I think these boys broke Elvis's heart. He's having a tough time with it."

"What can I do?" Ray asked.

"I don't know, but you are the one he's asking for. I just wanted to let you know what you're walking into. I think the back door's open."

They both stood. Vernon walked Ray to the door.

"Thanks, Vernon. I appreciate it."

Vernon nodded. "I think it's real important you came."

Having no idea what to expect, Ray walked across the drive to the back door of Graceland.

Velma again met him but Ray remembered the way to Elvis's bedroom and went upstairs alone. Through the partially opened door, Ray could see Elvis sitting on top of his large bed surrounded by a couple of hundred galley sheets. He was reading and hadn't heard Ray.

Ray took a deep breath and walked into the room. "Hey, Elvis."

Elvis looked up with a tear-stained face. He had been crying while he was reading. Ray could not remember a more sad, vulnerable sight.

"Why did they do this to me, Ray?" Elvis was crushed. "These were my guys. I loved these guys. I've known them all my life." Elvis paused a moment, the lump in his throat making it hard for him to talk.

"What'd they write?"

"Private moments. Trusted moments. Things friends do that nobody else could understand or should ever even know about," Elvis said sadly. "You know, this could be it? I could be ruined right here. Everything. It could all be over right here."

"No way," Ray said positively. "You're stronger than anything they could do. The world loves you."

"Do you have any idea how hard it is to get on top and stay there as long as I have? Of course you don't. Nobody does. Nobody can." Elvis looked very tired. "I don't want to fight anymore, Ray. I'm damn sick of fighting."

"Did they just make this stuff up?"

"What difference does that make, damn it? These were my friends!" Elvis got up off the bed, seeming suddenly to have much more energy than a moment before. "We trusted each other! Goddamn it, we grew up together!"

Elvis continued ranting as he went down the stairs. It seemed to Ray that he was strung out on something. His motions were big, loose, his speech was slurred. He walked in a lumbering manner. Everything seemed just a little off. Ray followed him downstairs.

Elvis walked to the living room, where he paced angrily, looking for an outlet for his energy. "Those sons of bitches. They'll never work again in this town, I'll tell you that for damn sure. Shit!"

"They shouldn't have done that to you."

Elvis stood, looking around wildly. Suddenly he changed his demeanor, becoming more suspicious, paranoid.

"This is a lesson, Ray," Elvis said quietly. "God is showing me that I can't trust nobody. None of them. I'm going to fire them all. Every last one of them. But I need you, Ray. I need you by me."

"I'm here for you."

"I know you are. I don't have to pay you to be my friend. Everybody wants something; money, clothes, cars, girls, whatever . . . stop that coming and they turn against you."

Elvis went to Ray and held Ray's face in his hands like Ray had earlier held Sheree's.

"But you . . . I can trust you because . . . you are me . . . and I am you. The same blood courses through our veins. We're different from anybody in the world. That's another reason for me to keep you secret. If they find out who you are, they'll try to get you, too. They know we're special. They won't let you rest."

Elvis's attention suddenly shifted to one of the ever-present television sets. The one in the living room showed the three guys who wrote the book. The sound was off but it was obvious an interview was under way. Elvis blew.

"Damn it! There they are, the bastards!" He ran over to the couch, reached under a seat cushion, and pulled out a .38 pistol. He quickly put three bullets into the picture tube, quite effectively knocking out the TV and scaring Ray half to death.

Elvis then threw the pistol down on the couch and walked into the kitchen like nothing happened. "Assholes!" he was muttering under his breath.

Elvis went to the refrigerator, pulled out a Pepsi. "Want one?" he asked Ray casually.

"No, thanks," Ray said, still in shock.

Elvis opened his, took a drink, thought a moment, then looked back to Ray with tears starting to form in his eyes again. Once more, he was a broken man. He crossed to Ray, put his arms around him, his head on his shoulders, and cried.

Ray had no idea what to do so he just held him. Elvis bouncing back and forth between all these emotions set the tone for the night.

Tuesday, August 2, 1977

Even though it was past three o'clock in the morning when he got home, Ray still had to go to work the next morning. Sheree had stayed over, got up with him, and made him eggs and toast before he left. Ray was still tired but not so much that he couldn't relate the occurrences of the night before.

"Then Velma, the maid, comes in. I start to explain to her about the TV when she shuts me up. She just wheeled the TV away, said it happens all the time. I swear, ten minutes later there's another one sitting there and putty in the wall's bullet holes. Damnedest thing I ever saw."

Ray struggled to his feet. "Well, thanks for breakfast, babe. I'd better hit it."

"You going to be all right?"

"Nothing wrong with me that a couple of days' sleep wouldn't cure."

"Tell you what, I'll give you a rest tonight. I've got to work late anyway."

It made Ray feel like a hundred years old to admit that that was probably a good idea. He kissed her good-bye, promised to call later, and went off to work.

What really woke Ray up that morning was seeing the light blue Buick parked off by the side of the road as he drove out of his property. Damn it! He felt sure that whoever it was had to have something to do with Morgan Bates. Even if he didn't, Ray was tired of it. He didn't quite know what yet, but he did know it was time to do something.

He continued on to work, his mind churning.

39

WHEN RAY GOT HOME from work that evening, the phone was ringing. It was Elvis, saying that it seemed he was always regretting one thing or another. He had taken a couple of pills the night before that were supposed to make him feel better but ended up turning him into a blithering idiot. He was sorry Ray had to see that.

Anyway, he was feeling better now, still pissed and revengeful as hell, but at least the fountain had been turned off. He called to see if Ray would be up for taking the Harleys out on Saturday. Ray realized that Elvis had to plan things like this in advance because of all the people that depended on Elvis for their social life.

To the people in his group, Elvis was the top priority, so if he was going to make plans to do something without them, Elvis had to let them know. Otherwise, they'd be coming over or be waiting by the phone for someone to call and tell them what they were all going to be doing that weekend.

Ray said that that would be great. They agreed to meet at Graceland at two in the afternoon (Elvis generally got up about then).

Ray was doubly pleased about this. He'd been looking forward to going riding with Elvis but this also worked into a plan he'd been concocting in his mind about what to do about the light blue Buick. This should work out perfectly.

As soon as Ray hung up from Elvis, he called J.D. to make sure he'd be available on Saturday. He was, but of course Ray had to tell him everything. This time he could, and did.

Saturday, August 6, 1977

That Saturday Ray and J.D. got together at the trailer about noon and went over the details of the plan. Even though they laughed like crazy, they thought it was a good plan. After lunch, J.D. left a few minutes before Ray to get in position. At the appointed time, Ray also left.

Sure enough, the light blue Buick was parked off a ways from Ray's access road, hoping he wouldn't be seen. Ray drove slow enough that the guy had no trouble following him. As Ray drove up to the Graceland gates, he saw the Buick pass him and park across the street. Ray knew it would be somewhere close enough for the driver to see everything. Ray saw that J.D. had not parked far away and was already getting into position.

The guard, who recognized Ray by now, started to open the gates. As quickly but calmly as possible, Ray told him not to do it yet and that he would explain later. Ray then got out of the truck and paced around the gates, looking at his watch as though he was waiting for someone.

Ray hoped the Colonel didn't show up about now. He'd been real good about putting the disguise on whenever he was around Elvis or Graceland, but it was important at this moment that the man in the Buick not be confused about who he was watching. Ray was sure the Colonel would understand just this once.

Ray made himself very obvious as he paced, knowing the man in the Buick would be keeping his eyes on him, watching and wondering about his every move. Ray also realized that the guard must think he was crazy, but he'd just have to deal with that for now.

Knowing the man in the Buick's attention would be elsewhere, J.D. set about putting their plan into action. He had crept out from behind some nearby trees and was on his hands and knees, sneaking up behind the Buick.

As the dark man watched and took pictures of Ray, J.D. quietly crawled to each of the Buick's four tires and wedged three-penny nails between the asphalt and the tires, leaning them on both sides so that a nail would enter the tire no matter which direction the car went once it started moving.

Once all eight nails were in place, J.D. crept back to the trees, then casually walked over to where he had parked his truck and drove away. When, out of the corner of his eye, Ray saw J.D. drive off, he knew the job had been done.

He then told the guard he could let him in, which the confused guard did.

Ray parked his truck in the usual spot and entered the mansion from the back door. He heard music and singing and headed for the music room. Elvis was dressed in his motorcycle leathers but was sitting at the piano playing and singing a gospel. It seemed that whenever Elvis wanted to relax, he fell back on the spirituals.

Ray just stood, silently watching, knocked out as ever at this man's ability to bring such depth and richness to whatever he sang. Elvis had noticed Ray come in and, once he'd finished, asked Ray, "You about ready?"

"You bet. I been looking forward to this," Ray said.

"Well, then let's do it." Elvis got up from the piano and started toward the back door.

"Glad to have you back kickin'," Ray said as they walked to the garage.

"Hell yes," Elvis said. "They can knock me down but I'll be damned if I'll let them keep me there."

Ray was thoroughly impressed by Elvis's garage and the number of "toys" he had. They considered taking Elvis's two three-wheelers but finally settled on the regular Harleys. Ray was riding Joe Espisito's bike that was kept in the garage with Elvis's.

Both men wore helmets that covered their faces so it wasn't necessary for Ray to be in his disguise, but he had it in his pocket just in case.

The gates opened and the two men rode through. After a moment,

Ray openly laughed when he heard four loud *bangs* behind them. Elvis turned to Ray. "What was that?" he yelled above the roar of the bikes.

"Sounded like a blowout," Ray yelled back.

Elvis just nodded as the two of them rode down the street. The light blue Buick didn't follow.

Elvis led them on a pretty drive through some nice parts of Memphis and into the surrounding countryside. Both seemed to enjoy riding side by side over the picturesque country roads.

After a while, Elvis pulled over at the end of a cul-de-sac with great views. A few houses were nearby but most of the panorama was open. Elvis seemed weak as he dismounted, took his helmet off, and walked haltingly over to a bench. He peeled off his jacket and sat down, breathing hard. Ray was struck by Elvis's sickly pallor, which seemed to have come on quickly. He hadn't noticed it at all back at Graceland.

"How do you like that baby?" Elvis asked between breaths.

"Oh God, it's the smoothest bike I've ever ridden," Ray said, sitting down next to Elvis. He also had taken off his leather jacket. "You doing okay?" Ray asked.

"I might have pushed it a bit," Elvis said, still panting. "But hell, I was going stir-crazy. This is just a warm-up. Tomorrow I've rented Libertyland for Lisa Marie and a few friends. She'll love it but it always wipes me out."

"That should be fun."

"Yeah." Elvis paused for a moment and looked around. "I feel naked."

"Naked?"

"I never go riding without at least four or five of my boys. I can't remember the last time I rode like this. Feels good. Weird, but good."

Ray watched Elvis as he looked around, openly reveling in each moment when he could act like a regular person and enjoy the little things that weren't so little to him.

"Sure glad you're doing better than the other night," Ray said. "You had me worried."

"Yeah, I was pretty screwed up. Still can't get it out of my mind," Elvis admitted.

"Getting out like this has to help, though, doesn't it?" Ray asked.

Elvis looked over at him and smiled wryly. "You still think things happen by accident, don't you?" Elvis asked, then pointed to the house nearest them. "One of those sons of bitches lives right there."

Ray didn't know what to say, but he was beginning to realize that Elvis was right. There were no coincidences, at least not where Elvis was concerned. Ray had heard it said that he paid an extraordinary amount of attention to minor details. Of course, Ray surmised that Elvis would probably also say that there were no "minor details."

"Besides coming out here to scare the hell out of my old friend, I wanted to talk to you. This seemed as good a place as any," Elvis began. "One thing I've learned from all the shit that's been happening is that life is too short not to do what you think is important. So, screw the Colonel! We don't have to do nothing public, but private . . . I'd like you more in my life, Ray. And I'd like to be more in yours."

Ray could hardly believe what he was hearing.

"I'd like to meet your girl, your friends," Elvis continued. "Have you meet Ginger, Joe Espisito and his wife, Joan, and Ned's wife, Caroline, and Billy and Al. What do you think about that?"

Ray was beaming. "Elvis, I think that would be terrific."

"Good. It'll be done then. I have no idea what my schedule is for the next week or two but let me check on it and we'll work something out. Sound good?"

"Sounds great," Ray confirmed.

Elvis seemed pleased, too, then he looked off and seemed to soften a bit. "Wish you could have met Priscilla. She was a peach. I kinda messed up there. Might have to wait a bit for Lisa Marie, too. You'd confuse the hell out of her right now."

Elvis stood quietly for a moment, looking off. His whole demeanor seemed to change. "Most important was Mama. What would she have done if she'd known you were alive?" he asked, mostly to himself.

"Our mama was a wonderful woman, Ray. I'm truly sorry you never got to meet her."

"Me, too."

Elvis stood a moment more, then came back to the moment, shaking off his reverie. "Well, guess we'd better get on with it." He looked over at his ex-friend's house. "Looks like the bastard isn't going to show himself. Probably watching us through the curtains, wondering if I'm going to go down there and shoot him."

"Which is exactly what you want him to think, right?" Ray asked with a twinkle.

"You're starting to get the idea," Elvis said, smiling back. He then stood and stretched, the mood of a moment ago already past. "Well, I've had all the fun I can stand. This daytime living will kill you. Let's limp these hawgs back home."

As they started putting their gear back on, Ray asked, "You aren't doing this just so you can steal my girl, are you?"

Elvis laughed so hard Ray was afraid he was going to choke again. Fortunately, he didn't. "Damn, if you ain't got me figured out already."

They were both laughing as they mounted up and rode off.

When they approached the gates of Graceland, Ray was pleased to see that a AAA truck was still helping the dark man, who was openly furious. It seemed no one was quite prepared for four flat tires at one time. The man glowered at them as they rode in. Elvis hardly noticed.

40

AS ELVIS AND RAY were taking off their leathers and putting the bikes away, Elvis asked a question that he'd been wondering about ever since he first knew of Ray's existence.

"I was drawn to music at such an early age and it's been so important to me, I'm surprised you never felt anything like that."

"Who said I didn't?"

"Well, damn. I guess I never asked. Did you?"

"Yeah. I've been pickin' a little guitar since I've been about fifteen," Ray said. "Mostly blues. I left the rock 'n' roll to you."

"Well, thank you for that." Elvis laughed. "I'll be damned. You got a minute? Come play something for me."

Ray tried to talk him out of it but lost. Elvis led him downstairs to the TV room, where he had about ten guitars. While Ray was looking over the acoustical ones, trying to find the one that was just right, Elvis said, "I was pretty shy as a kid. I fought it off by performing. That's what got me into all this in the first place."

"I was a shy kid, too," Ray said, sitting down with the guitar he'd chosen. "But I stayed one. I just honkered around at the back of the room and watched guys like you fight it off."

They both laughed. Ray made all the usual excuses about not playing much lately, not really remembering any songs, but when he absolutely couldn't procrastinate anymore he played his riff. It got the desired reaction.

"I'll be damned," Elvis said. "You can play that thing. Sing me something."

Ray stumbled around for a minute before he broke down and sang a Muddy Waters tune called "Catfish Blues." Elvis knew it and sang along with him every once in a while.

Ray felt embarrassed, singing to the most famous singer in the world, but Elvis loved it. He kept after Ray to sing another, which he finally did; a Freddie King song, "Have You Ever Loved a Woman?"

Elvis was moved by the song and speechless at the fact that he was sitting there listening to his brother sing to him. When Ray got up to leave, Elvis gave him a hug, complete with brotherly pats. It seemed to feel right to both of them.

They talked a while longer, each having enjoyed the day immensely. Elvis would get in touch with Ray as soon as he knew what his schedule was going to be. A new chapter was beginning. They could both tell it and both were looking forward to it.

Ray had made a very cryptic invitation to Sheree and J.D. to come out to his place at seven o'clock sharp. He wouldn't tell them why. The only thing he did say was that it would change their lives. Needless to say, they were both there on time.

After letting the suspense build up as high as it could go, Ray finally told them.

"Elvis would like to meet you two and have us meet some of his friends. How would you like to come to a little get-together at Graceland?"

The electric silence was eventually broken by a stunned Sheree. "At Graceland?"

"Us?" The reaction of disbelief was also shared by J.D.

"You got it. Sometime in the next couple of weeks. Or is that a bad time for you?" Ray kidded.

Sheree jumped up and ran over to hug Ray. "Oh, baby, I can't believe this. Thank you, thank you, thank you."

"Hey, it was his idea. All I said was 'you bet.'"

J.D. was still off in his own world, talking to himself. "I'm going to Graceland. I'm going to meet Elvis. Me. In person. Me. Graceland."

"Oh my God," Sheree said, suddenly turning serious. "What am I going to wear?"

Ray laughed. "Easy, honey. You've got at least a couple of weeks."

She jumped off Ray's lap. "That's not enough time." She grabbed her purse and started to run out of the trailer, turned, came back, and kissed Ray. "I love you." Then she turned and ran out the door.

Ray and J.D. looked at each other and laughed. Yeah, it was going to be great.

Sunday, August 7, 1977

The next morning, Ray was awakened by Morgan Bates pounding on his trailer door. Ray was in his underwear, half-asleep, when he opened the door. Morgan was furious.

"It's time, Johnston," Morgan said angrily. "It's shit-or-get-off-the-pot time."

"What?"

"It's time to talk," Morgan clarified, elbowing his way past Ray into the trailer. He sat down on the sofa and pulled out his tape recorder. "We've dicked around long enough. If we're going to do this, we do it now. Talk to me."

"Jesus Christ!" Ray said, turning a burner on under some water. "All this before coffee. Wait a minute."

Ray went back to the bedroom and put on a T-shirt, glad that Sheree had left so early last night. She wouldn't have liked Morgan Bates at all.

Ray came back and started preparing his coffee while waiting for the water to get hot. He didn't ask Morgan if he wanted any.

"I wasn't particularly amused by that flat-tire stunt," Morgan said dryly.

"Oh, was that one of your guys?"

"You know damn well it was."

"Maybe I don't like being followed," Ray said, pouring the water into his instant coffee.

"I'm in the information business. You may tell me what you want me to know, but how am I to learn what you don't want me to know?"

"You don't."

"Well, see, I don't accept that," Morgan said, settling into the sofa. "Let's get on with it. The amount of payment will, quite frankly, depend on the quality of your information and the degree of your cooperation. You still haven't been able to prove that you're his brother, have you?"

Ray sat down with his coffee, savoring it in front of Morgan. "Actually, I'm glad you came by. I'm kinda sorry about wasting your time but not really. There's not going to be any story, Morgan. Elvis turned out to be a pretty good guy. I'm not going to do anything to hurt him. I'm ashamed to think that I even considered it."

Morgan looked at Ray for a long moment, then smiled. "Do you suppose this comes as a surprise? Listen, my naive friend, there is already a story. Many of them, in fact. The only question is whether or not you are going to participate in the rewards."

"What do you mean?" Ray asked.

"Why do you suppose you were being followed? We've got pictures chronicling everything. If you are with us, we'll use the pictures to add credence to your story. If you're not, we'll just run the story without you."

"Elvis will sue your ass! Hell, so will I!"

"Of course you will. And our lawyers will drag out the case as long as they possibly can, and they're good at that, by the way. That's their main job. Of course, we'll be publishing sensational articles every week for a couple of years . . . and then you'll probably win."

"And cost you a bundle."

"Sure. Probably a million, maybe more, but it will be worth it. We've got great stuff already that will probably bring in two to three times whatever we'd lose. Not a bad return."

Ray sat fuming for a moment.

"I'll tell you what I will do, though," Morgan said. "I'll be true to my word. This 'brother' angle is a great one, whether it's true or not. I'll still get you your million in exchange for your signature on a contract guaranteeing us a couple of years' worth of interviews. Far and away the easiest money you've ever made and you'll never have to worry about anything again. Or, we can give the money to the lawyers. We win either way."

Morgan sat back, quite pleased with himself, and threw a manila folder onto the coffee table between them.

"What's this?" Ray asked.

"Incentive."

Ray opened the folder and took out about ten eight-by-ten black-and-white pictures. These were shots taken through a telephoto lens by the man who had been following him.

There were shots of Ray driving his truck into Graceland before the disguise was given to him. Their similarities were obvious. There were also shots of Ray and Elvis, in his bathrobe, walking in back of the mansion, riding motorcycles in the streets, riding in the Stutz and being hassled by teenagers, there was even one of Vernon talking to Sheree at Ray's trailer.

The most damaging ones, though, were the ones showing Elvis choking and falling down at the scrambles track and the one showing Ray and Elvis, gun drawn, about to burst into Grant's bungalow.

"Just a small sampling," Morgan said simply. "Without you, we'll just supply the captions ourselves. It's always more fun like that anyway."

A cold feeling passed through Ray. When Morgan started to laugh, Ray blew and started tearing up the pictures.

"Help yourself," Morgan said, laughing harder. "Those are your copies. I have plenty more, believe me."

Morgan stood and pocketed his tape recorder. "I've been looking forward to this. Most of the people in the office don't even know what I've been up to. They are going to go crazy," Morgan said proudly. "I'm going to be a hero."

Morgan moved toward the door. "You've got one last chance, pal. Having you aboard would be great but, as you can see, it's certainly not necessary. Think about it. I'll call you tomorrow. It's time to rock 'n' roll."

"Save your dime!" Ray yelled after him. He couldn't tell if Morgan heard or not. Ray could hear Morgan, though, laughing all the way to his car.

Ray tried to piece together the torn pictures as he spread them out on his coffee table. What he saw saddened him greatly. Here were private moments, little moments that had formed his relationship with Elvis, Vernon, and Dee. The thought of having them think Ray sold them out or had been using them the whole time did more than bother Ray, it made him feel so bad it scared him.

No! They couldn't think that! It wasn't the truth. But it didn't take much imagination to figure out what kinds of stories Morgan could build around these pictures.

He couldn't let that happen, he really couldn't. But how? It was with desperation and fear that he called J.D. that night and asked him to come over, now! He didn't know what to do and needed help. Hurry!

*41

Sunday, August 7, 1977

J.D. WASN'T A WHOLE lot of help at first. Ray had a tough time getting him to seriously consider the problem. J.D. was too knocked out by the pictures.

"My God!" he kept saying. The shots of Ray and Elvis together, his old buddy and the King, overwhelmed him. Like Sheree, hearing about all this was one thing. Actually seeing the proof, the pictures right in front of him, surprisingly, was something else.

The one that really got J.D.'s attention was the one where Elvis had his gun drawn and was ready to confront Grant. Ray had told the story but J.D. still seemed shocked to see that it was actually true. Ray had to go through the whole tale again before J.D. could begin to get back to dealing with the problem at hand.

While J.D. was getting used to what Ray had known for a while, Ray was beating himself up inside. How could he have been such a greedy fool? Maybe Ray hadn't been any big success at anything but he'd always had his integrity.

People knew where they stood with him. Friends didn't come and go with whims. His word was as good as a contract and never, never had he been a person that could be bought. And even though it had been hard for him, he took care of his mom. He was a good guy!

Usually. But, he thought, when he decided to blow it and become a scumbag, he didn't mess around. Not only was he just about ready to hurt some people who had been very nice to him, he was also ruining what could be a most wonderful addition to his life.

Ray was brought back to the present by J.D. pointing out a picture that showed Ray's and Elvis's faces side by side.

"This is amazing," J.D. said. "Check it out. Take the shoe polish out of his hair and have him lose forty pounds, you guys would be impossible to tell apart."

Ray tried to gently remind J.D. that that's what the big deal had been for the last few months; they were twins! Get it? Now, what can they do about this muckup? Everything was going to go to hell tomorrow. They had to think of some way to stop it. Now!

Ray finally got through to J.D. and the two spent the next hour working at it, but they failed. Ray was starting to panic when J.D. came up with a suggestion that changed everything.

"Maybe we've been looking at this all wrong," J.D. said. "Like in that deal with Grant, you said Elvis had more balls than sense. He also said you 'weren't crazy enough.' Maybe we ought to be. What do you think Elvis would do?"

Well, that did it. Actually, J.D. turned out to be a big help. Ray was trying to figure out how Ray would solve this problem. Couldn't do it. Ray didn't know how to solve it, but to look at it from a whole different point of view . . . Elvis didn't have the limitations Ray did. Elvis could do anything and he knew it. As a result, he did.

No sooner had J.D. gotten Ray to think like Elvis than a plan started to materialize. It was bizarre, but what the hell, it just might work. Besides, this was the only plan that came to him. Even trying to think like Elvis, it wasn't as though he had a lot of choices.

As Ray explained it to J.D., there was a lot of nodding and grinning. They were going to go for it.

Later that night, they were in J.D.'s pickup heading for the address of *Dish* magazine as stated on Morgan Bates's business card. Ray was trying to get comfortable in his "costume." He was in yet another "Elvis garb," the very best he could create from his and J.D.'s closet.

That translated as casual pants, a semiwild shirt, light jacket, baseball hat, and mirrored glasses that he could hardly see through in the dark. Ray was also hyperventilating and scared because it just occurred to him that if this didn't work, not only would he be a traitor in the eyes of the Presleys, he'd be in jail. He could probably also get shot.

The address led them to the outskirts of Memphis to an area where warehouses and factories were predominant. Both were pleased it was a Sunday night. Everything seemed locked-up and deserted.

J.D. parked around the side of the building, out of sight from the street. He thought it was real nice of this Mr. Bates to tell them where the pictures were. He was also going to show Ray a little trick he'd learned from James Bond. By way of evidence, he held up an arrow with a suction cup on the end that he'd borrowed from his five-year-old nephew.

Ray asked if James Bond also had an arrow. J.D., not missing a beat, said, "Absolutely. It won't work without the arrow, and—" he held it up for Ray to see "—Mama's ring."

They both walked over to a secluded ground-floor window that led to a darkened office. They could see that lights in the hallways were always kept on. So far so good.

J.D. hooked the suction cup to the middle of the window and, using his mama's real diamond ring, cut a large hole in the glass. He then used the suction cup arrow to stop the window from falling inside and breaking. Instead, he was able to make it fall outward, gently and silently, into his outstretched hands.

After giving Ray a leg up and helping him through the hole in the window, J.D.'s job, other than getaway driver, was over. Ray's, however, was just beginning.

Once inside, Ray tried to calm down his heartbeat, which could probably be heard three doors away. He peeked out into the hall and, seeing no one, started checking the name plaques on the offices, looking for Morgan Bates.

After checking half that floor, Ray found it. He also found that it was locked. As he was trying to figure out how to get inside, a voice behind him made him jump.

"Freeze!"

Ray had tried to prepare for this moment but was still petrified as he turned around and faced the young security guard shakily holding the gun. The boy seemed as nervous as Ray was . . . then the guard realized who he was looking at.

"Holy shit!"

Ray lowered his voice about half an octave and tried to strike a good Elvis pose as he talked to the guard.

"You came along just in time," Ray said in his very best Elvis voice. "Please open this door for me, if you would be so kind."

"I can't do that," the young guard stammered. "You're not supposed to—"

"Excuse me, but I am in a bit of a hurry here," Ray said, knowing he had to get and keep the upper hand. "C'mon, now. Don't worry about it. I'll show you what I'm doing and I promise you'll be glad to help me."

The guard hesitated.

"Open this door, son," Ray said louder, stronger. "For Christ's sake, you know who I am. If you can't trust me, who can you trust?"

That seemed to make sense to the boy, who balked for a moment, then pulled out a master key and opened the door to the office. Ray thanked him and quickly crossed the room to a filing cabinet and started looking through the drawers and folders.

"What are you going to do?" the boy asked. "I don't think you should be doing that."

"One minute," Ray said as he continued to search as fast as he could.

It was in the third drawer that he found the folder marked "Johnston." He could hardly believe the relief he felt. Inside were copies of the pictures Morgan had shown him, along with many more, including . . . the negatives!

There was also page after page of handwritten notes, as well as some audiotapes. Ray figured they were from the tape recorder Morgan had had running while they talked.

Ray tucked the folder under his arm and started to leave the office. "All right. We're out of here."

"You can't take that file," the guard said.

"C'mere, let me show you something," Ray said, slurring his words a little more, really getting into his Elvis. He opened the folder and spread some of the pictures out on Morgan's desk.

"I think you'll have to agree that these pictures are of me, therefore, they are mine," Ray said matter-of-factly. "Now, if I don't want this person to have them, and I don't, and if he has them anyway, against my will, then it's actually my duty to get them back. Right?"

The guard thought on that for a moment. It seemed to sort of make sense, but . . .

"Tell you what I'll do, son," Ray said, not wanting him to think about the logic of this too much. "You give me your name and address and I'll send you an autographed picture. I want you also to know that you will always have my respect and gratitude. Would you like that?"

Ray had hit a home run. The guards eyes widened, he quickly put his gun away, and searched for a paper to write on. Ray found one in Morgan's center drawer.

"This will be good," Ray said, pocketing the paper and walking back toward the office he'd entered by. "Now, listen here. Let me show you where someone broke in here today. I'd wait about ten minutes after I go to report it. Looks like it was done before you came on duty. Good thing you caught it. Who knows what kinds of bad guys could have gotten in here?"

After showing him the office with the window removed, the guard thanked Ray and unlocked the front door for him. As Ray left, he shook hands with the boy and gave him his very best "thankyou-verymuch."

Needless to say, J.D. was a bit confused seeing Ray, folder in hand, being politely helped out by a guard via the front door, but sped off as soon as Ray got in anyway. Questions would follow.

Ray soon started breathing again. He still could hardly believe it. He didn't know if he was more scared or excited. What a rush! It was overwhelming the power that Elvis had. Hell, he could do anything and get away with it. No wonder he had more balls than sense. He didn't have to worry about the same things regular people worried about. Wow!

It had already been too long for J.D. to wait.

"All right! C'mon, what happened? The guard catches you and ends up helping you out the front door? Jesus! Talk to me."

Ray asked him to hang on for a couple minutes more. All would be told. Right then, Ray still needed to breathe a little longer.

42

ALL THE PICTURES WERE laid out. Every surface in Ray's trailer was covered. Ray and J.D. pored over and commented on them for over an hour. There were literally hundreds of pictures.

Knowing now the way these rag magazines worked, Ray realized there were more than enough pictures to keep headlines going for at least a year, perhaps longer if they got creative, and he knew they would.

Ray was still trying to get his nerves back under control from his evening's escapade. He even traded in his nightly beer for a scotch and tried not to think of the damage he barely avoided by stealing these pictures.

The most troubling to him were the many different story angles Morgan had been trying out. God only knew how many he actually would have used. Maybe all! Probably more!

Presley Twin Found Alive!! Shunned by Family All These Years
Jesse Garon Presley LIVES; Elvis Does Not Share Him with the World.
Presley Twin Sells Out for One Million $$!!
Presley Twins Break and Enter!! Assault Charges Pending
Elvis Near Death, Collapses After Motorcycle Jaunt
Is Elvis's Twin Doing Shows for Him?
FLASH!! Vernon Presley Knew All Along!!

. . . and on and on.

Ray started physically shaking when he realized the hurt and devastation he nearly caused. How close it had come! But thankfulness came on the heels of fright. He had to be pleased that he had avoided all that. It was over.

Well, almost. Ray realized that as long as these pictures, notes, and negatives existed, there was always a chance of them surfacing. That wouldn't do.

He and J.D. went outside to an old oil drum Ray had used for burning garbage over the years. They dumped the whole works inside, everything. Ray started to light it but before he did, saw the picture J.D. had commented on earlier; the close-up on his and Elvis's face, showing so clearly the identical features of these two men.

Ray didn't think that that one picture could cause much harm. No one would believe it anyway. It was so easy to doctor pictures these days, people would just think this was another one. It wasn't for public display anyway. Ray just wanted a memento, a picture of the two of them together. Brothers. Twins. Who knew where all this was going to go? Besides, it was a damn nice picture.

He smiled with relief as he lit the pile and saw the pictures and tapes burning, curling black and crumbling to ash, taking all the hateful words and ideas with them.

It was about three in the morning when Ray said good night to his best buddy and thanked him for his help that night. J.D. was glad he'd been a part of it and was very impressed with Ray's cool under pressure.

They would have celebrated longer but tomorrow was a workday. They both had to be up in a few hours. Going to bed that night was rather a waste of time for Ray. He was still much too keyed-up from his adventure to sleep. He also knew he had dodged a major bullet. Oh well, at least he rested.

Monday, August 8, 1977

The next morning Ray was at Fields Construction loading his truck for the second time. Four or five cups of coffee had finally woken him up.

It was about eleven o'clock when he looked up and saw a car careening around a corner, speeding down on him. Any surprise he may have felt left as soon as he recognized the car. Morgan Bates skidded the car to a stop and flew out of the driver's side.

"One of your fellow glandular cases told me you'd be back here, you son of a bitch!"

"Good morning, Morgan," Ray said pleasantly.

"Where are they? They're mine and you know it."

"Where is what?"

"Don't screw with me, Johnston!" Morgan threatened. "I'll have your ass for this. I really will."

"I'm sure I don't know what you are talking about," Ray said, working hard to keep a straight face.

"You stole them. Breaking and entering! That's against the law."

"I still don't know what you are talking about but if a theft was involved, I'd call the police. Get them right on it. I'm certainly not one to let people get away with breaking the law."

Morgan panted with rage, getting even angrier as he realized there was nothing he could do. "So that's the way you're going to play it?"

"Play what?"

"This isn't over, Johnston," Morgan said menacingly as he headed back to his car. "You pissed off the wrong person."

"Gee, I'm sorry," Ray said innocently.

Morgan got in his car, slammed the door as hard as he could, and sped out of the lot, sending gravel flying everywhere as he went. Ray smiled. Oh, that felt good.

When he got home from work that afternoon, Ray was displeased but not particularly surprised to see that his trailer had been ransacked.

Ray had anticipated this happening and had.hidden the one remaining picture where he felt pretty sure it would be safe. He checked to see if it had survived the search and was pleased to see that it had.

It occurred to him a long time ago that whenever he saw people in movies search houses, one place they always missed was under the refrigerator. They'd check everywhere—open drawers, throw them on the floor, go through the closets, all that—but no one ever moved the refrigerator. Guess it was just too heavy to bother with.

So there it was, the two Presley boys, in a folder under the refrigerator. The satisfied smile on Ray's lips soon left as his focus shifted to the job ahead. His home had to be put back together.

Tuesday, August 9, 1977

Ray was at work the morning of the next day. He'd delivered a load to a remote area of the yard and went into the small office to check in. Nobody was there. Ray thought for a minute about what he should do while he waited, then he got an idea.

He took out Morgan Bates's card and called the work number on it. He was in.

"Morgan, Ray Johnston," Ray said as Morgan answered the phone.

"You son of a bitch!" was Morgan's reply.

"I'm not particularly pleased with you either right now so I'd watch it. I hope you and your stooges had fun at my place yesterday. I'm going to let it go this time because, by now, you know that whatever you are looking for isn't there."

"We haven't even started," Morgan threatened.

"Then you might be in big trouble," Ray countered just as strongly. "Next time I call the police. Unlike some people I know, I don't have nothing to hide."

"If you think you're going to just—"

"One last thing, Morgan," Ray interrupted. "Knowing what a sensitive and caring person you are, I sure wish you could have been with my buddy and me the other night. We had such a great fire out at my place. You would have loved it, the way it lit up the night sky. Flames dancing, really, it was something."

"You bastard! If you think this is—"

Ray hung up.

Friday, August 12, 1977

After work that day, Ray was trying to get his trailer put back together again when he was surprised by Elvis driving up in his Stutz. Elvis laboriously heaved himself out of the car and met Ray at the door.

"Hey, partner," Elvis said.

"Elvis! Good to see you. What are you doing out here?"

"I might ask you the same question," Elvis said, seeing the rubble inside. "Tornado come through here?"

"Something like."

"You're not in any trouble, are you? Anybody giving you a bad time?"

"Nothing I can't handle, but thanks," Ray said.

"You sure now? You know how I love to help."

"My God, no," Ray said, laughing. "It's all right, really."

They both laughed as they remembered the last time Elvis helped.

"How'd that work out, by the way?" Elvis asked. "That scumbag make good?"

"Yeah, he did. He did everything you said and got Sheree a great little beagle puppy. She's real happy."

"Good. That's what my spies told me but I just wanted to make sure," Elvis said. "Listen, I'm out here 'cause I got a house full of people and wanted to get away for a minute. Remember our talk about all of us getting together sometime? How about next Saturday? I'm runnin' around tomorrow but next Saturday is the twentieth, I think. Would that be good?"

"You bet," Ray said, trying not to sound as overwhelmingly happy as he felt. "That would be great."

"Good. We can control the situation better from Graceland so how about if we all meet there? Say, two . . . three o'clock?"

"Perfect. How are you feeling?"

"Not worth a damn, but I'll be all right," Elvis said, dismissing it. "Well, listen, you take care." Elvis started back for his car when Ray remembered something.

"Oh, Elvis, hang on just a minute," Ray said as he quickly went inside the trailer, soon coming out with a piece of paper. "I hate to do this, but could I ask you a favor?"

"Shoot."

Ray handed him the paper. "I was wondering if you could send an autographed picture to this kid. He helped me out and, well, it would just mean a lot if you could."

"Sure." Elvis read the paper, which consisted of the young guard's name and address, as well as how Ray would like the picture signed;

> *To Billy,*
> *You're a good man. I won't forget*
> *if you won't.*
>
> *Elvis*

Elvis read it, then looked at Ray questioningly. "Something I should know here?"

"I know it looks suspicious but I'd rather not go into it right now, if you don't mind. Maybe later?" A small smile came across Ray's face. "Everything really is all right, I promise you."

Elvis held his look a moment longer, then nodded. "All right. I trust you. This'll go out today," he said as he pocketed the paper.

"But this is for 'now,' all right?" Elvis continued. "I'm going to want to know. Sounds like there's a story here and I love stories. I don't forget things like this."

"Promise," Ray said.

"All right, then. Next Saturday." Elvis got in the car and drove off. Ray could hardly wait to tell Sheree and J.D., but first he looked up, held out his arms, and grinned. "Thank you! Thank you! Yes! This is much more like it. Boy, when you do it, you do it good, don't you? See? It's stuff like this that gets people's attention. This is great. Thank you. Thank you. Thank you."

Ray blew a kiss skyward and went inside. It was time to spread the news.

Ray invited Sheree and J.D. to come over later that evening. They knew about the ransacking and weren't surprised that he asked if they could come over and help him clean up. Actually, they thought he would have called before this.

They were puzzled when they arrived at the trailer to see that he had already taken care of it himself. Ray sat them down, got them each a beer, and explained the situation. No more maybes, they were going to Graceland.

The outcry could be heard half a mile away, calming down only when the reality of it hit them both. J.D. became catatonic again ("God, I'm going to Graceland."), while Sheree turned white when she realized she only had a week to prepare and that it was definite.

Sheree and J.D. left that night, leaving Ray feeling about as good as he remembered feeling. This was his girl and his best friend. Who wouldn't want to do something special for them? Especially something as special as this.

He still didn't have any idea where this was all leading but what the hell, he didn't need to. He and Elvis both wanted to be a part of each other's world, and now it was actually going to happen. Ray went to sleep that night a happy, contented man.

43

RAY WAS HELPING TWO other men remove the fourth load of the day from the dump truck he had been driving. The afternoon was a hot one but it felt good to work. He loved being outside and active. How people could spend their lives inside in offices he didn't know.

About half the load had been stacked when one of the secretaries leaned out a window in the trailer/office and called Ray to the phone.

"Be back in a minute, guys. 'Course, I imagine you'll have this baby finished by then."

Comments on his low birth were bantered back and forth as Ray smiled and went to the trailer. The secretary handed the phone with a long cord to Ray through the window.

"This is Ray," he said into the phone, listened a while, then turned white. "What? . . . when? . . . oh my God." Ray leaned up against the trailer for support. "Yeah. Thanks, honey."

Ray silently handed the phone back through the window to the secretary, staring off in total shock. After a moment, he walked over to Mr. Fields's office. He knocked and entered.

Mr. Fields was behind his desk, eyes moist, watching the news on TV. "Elvis Presley has been found dead in his home this morning," the announcer was saying.

"Mr. Fields . . . ?" Ray began tentatively. "I just heard. May I have the rest of the day off, sir?"

Mr. Fields looked from Ray to the TV to the picture of Elvis on the wall. A thousand unasked questions were flashing behind his eyes, but they remained unasked. He simply nodded.

"I appreciate it, sir," Ray said. He left the office and walked slowly to his pickup, thoroughly dazed. He stood there a few moments before having the strength to climb in it. The two men he'd been working with watched him. Where the hell was he going?

As Ray drove away, he turned on the radio.

"It's official now," the announcer on the radio was saying, "the King of Rock 'n' Roll is dead. An autopsy will be performed but the preliminary cause of death is listed as 'heart failure.'"

Tears came to Ray's eyes as he drove.

"Police have already been summoned to control the crowds that are forming at Graceland, legendary home of the King.

"Elvis was found collapsed in his bathroom by his girlfriend, Ginger Alden. There currently is no suspicion of foul play. As the world has witnessed, Elvis had been in declining health for some time.

"Again, if you're just joining us," the announcer went on, "Elvis Presley, the King of Rock 'n' Roll, dead at age forty-two."

Ray had to keep wiping his eyes to see. He didn't know exactly where to go. He just knew he couldn't stay at work. He drove aimlessly for a while. The truck seemed to have a mind of its own, which was fine with Ray. His mind was a million miles away.

It soon became apparent where the truck was driving. When Ray came back to reality, he found himself a few blocks away from Graceland. The streets were already filling with crazed, weeping fans. As he got closer, he found himself in the middle of a huge traffic jam.

No one was going anywhere. People were leaving their cars in the street and walked the block or two to Graceland, just to see it.

Even though Ray stayed in his truck, he started seeing people noticing him. He took the Colonel's disguise from the glove compartment where he always kept it, and put it on. As silly as it was, no one seemed to pay attention anymore.

Not feeling like being surrounded by people, Ray managed to back out of the gridlock and began driving again. Soon he found himself at the top of the scenic cul-de-sac where he and Elvis had come on their motorcycles. This was also where Elvis had asked for them to become more involved in each other's lives. A happy time.

"One wonders if Elvis suspected something was wrong," the announcer on the radio was saying. "It has just come to our attention that at two o'clock this morning, Elvis asked a friend of his to return his daughter, Lisa Marie, to her mother, Priscilla Presley, who lives in California. That was at two o'clock this morning!"

"The world is stunned by this death. Elvis Presley, perhaps the most well-known, most recognized person in the world, seemed to touch everyone's life in a special way.

"He will always be Memphis's favorite son, and will be missed and mourned here perhaps more than anywhere.

"Oh, what?" The announcer paused, evidently receiving more information. He then continued, "We have just received word that the mayor has ordered all flags in the city to be lowered to half-mast.

"Our beloved king is dead, and there is no one who will ever take his place."

Ray just sat in his pickup, looking out over the city, still in the silly disguise with tears working their way down his face from behind the fake plastic glasses.

Ray sped up to his place, took off his disguise, left it in the passenger seat of his truck, and went quickly into his trailer. He headed straight for his little bathroom, washed his hands, and threw water in his face. After he dried off, he went to his living room and sat down by his phone, looking at it.

After a few moments he got Vernon's card out of his wallet and, hesitatingly, called it. He didn't know if Vernon would want to hear from him or not, but he had to give it a try. It was busy. Ray then turned on the TV but turned the sound all the way down and tried Vernon's number again. Still busy.

This time he had to hunt but finally found Ned's business card. His call was answered on the second ring by a woman.

"Excuse me, ma'am," Ray said to the voice on the phone, "is Ned there? . . . This is Ray Johnston . . . yes, I'm sure everyone over there is pretty busy right now . . . you do? . . . You are one of a handful of people in the world who know . . . yes, it is tough . . ."

As they talked, Ray watched the soundless TV showing a collage of the ambulance leaving Graceland, shots of the hospital, film clips of Elvis in better days, crying fans, et cetera.

"Actually, we were all supposed to meet this next Saturday . . . yeah, well, that's what it was going to be about. Elvis wanted us to get our worlds together some . . . yes, it would have . . . please do. I know he's busy and probably will be for a while. No hurry . . . I hope we will, too. Thank you . . . 'bye."

Ray hung up and looked helplessly at the very busy, silent TV.

After work that evening, Sheree and J.D. joined Ray at his place. It was a somber group, the three of them, sipping their beers, staring at the TV.

They seemed to rotate shots of Elvis, Graceland, his life, ambulances, and hysterical crowds. The sound was turned back on.

"A private funeral will be held Thursday at Graceland," the TV anchor was saying. "Elvis's lifelong friend, Joe Espisito, is overseeing the funeral, which is only fitting since he was directly responsible for maintaining much of Elvis's busy, complicated life."

"Did you meet him?" J.D. asked Ray.

"No. He was one we were going to meet Saturday."

"Shit."

"Yeah."

The TV anchor continued, "Flowers and cards are already coming in from around the world as news spreads, the King is dead! Crowds continue to grow around Graceland and the Baptist Memorial Hospital, current resting place of Elvis Presley."

Ray got up, threw some more water on his face, dried off, and came back. For some reason it felt good. Woke him up. When he got back he turned the sound down again on the TV, which had now started to show commercials.

"How are you feeling?" Sheree asked when he came back.

"Numb."

"I mean, does it feel like you've lost a brother? Or are you sad like us, that we lost Elvis Presley?"

Ray had to think about that for a moment. "No matter what we were doing or talking about, I could never quite get past the idea that I was talking to Elvis. There he was, in front of me . . ."

Ray thought for another minute. "But the brother thing, I don't know . . . I mean, it was there, no doubt about it. There just wasn't time. We hadn't . . ." Ray was having trouble finding words, or maybe he really didn't know how he felt or what to say. He decided to himself that it was probably all those things.

"Damn it! We just liked each other, you know? We were going to be good friends. And he would have liked you guys, too. I know it."

"Shit," J.D. repeated.

"Have you talked to anyone in the family? Vernon?" Sheree asked.

"Line's busy."

"Probably will be for a week."

"Soon."

J.D. noticed that another Elvis overview was starting on the TV. "Want to turn it up?" he asked Ray, who was closest.

Ray did and joined them on the couch.

"The top story of the hour and probably of the year is the death of Elvis Presley. Found collapsed in his home, he was pronounced dead at two thirty this afternoon. Best wishes and regrets are flooding in from literally every country in the world. The influence this man had on the world is only beginning to be felt. At this hour, family members are . . ."

Family members. Ray wondered what would happen now after his brief moments of "family." It would really mean something to him if he could go to the funeral but he was sure that would never happen. He wondered what would.

The TV blared on, as did the commentators. Ray, Sheree, and J.D. watched and daydreamed their own quite different dreams of what could have been.

Thursday, August 18, 1977

Ray was sound asleep when the phone rang. Vowing for the hundredth time that he would get an extension in the bedroom, or at least a really long cord, he ran out to the living room in his underwear and answered the phone.

"Hello . . . Vernon, good morning." That cold feeling in the pit of Ray's stomach started coming back. "No, sir . . . I'm so sorry. I understand . . . yes. I know that . . . I didn't really expect to, but thank you . . . me, too . . . I'd like that . . . thank you . . . 'bye."

Ray stood straighter, digesting their chat for a moment. The funeral part wasn't much of a surpise but Vernon had said they should get together later. What did that mean? Ray didn't want to put too much stock in it, but Vernon hadn't needed to say it . . . yet, he had.

In spite of trying not to get too optimistic, the feeling in his stomach started to ease. He took a deep breath and called J.D. "Take a sick day, J.D. . . . look, you wanted to meet Elvis and he wanted to meet you. Today may be the closest we ever come to that. Just get your butt over here."

Ray hung up and called Sheree.

44

LATER THAT MORNING, RAY, Sheree, and J.D. were at a local cafe having a late breakfast.

"He calls you at six o'clock in the morning to tell you that you weren't invited to the funeral! Did you thank him very much?" Sheree asked, not particularly pleased.

"He just didn't think this was the time to direct attention away from Elvis."

"They seem worried about that," J.D. said.

"Yeah, but come on, he also said that he wants to get together later," Ray said, strangely finding himself defending Vernon. "He said he wishes things were different but they're not . . . and all that. It was a nice call."

"If you say so," Sheree said, not convinced.

Later, the three were in Ray's pickup. Crowds started getting thick as they neared Graceland.

"I don't know how much closer we're going to get. I may have to pull over around here somewhere," Ray said.

Then he noticed some people walking by, doing double takes as they saw him. He reached under his seat.

"Now, look, this may seem strange but I have to do something." Ray put on the hat, glasses, and mustache. Sheree and J.D. thought he'd gone crazy.

"Uh . . . why do you suppose we would think this was strange?" Sheree asked ironically, wondering what could possibly be prompting him to put on that silly disguise.

"Until he said it was all right, we were never to be seen together in public without this," Ray explained.

"Ray, he's dead," J.D. said.

"We had a deal."

Ray noticed a parking spot up ahead and quickly took it, knowing it was probably as close as they were going to get. He was starting to get irritated at his totally silent partners. When he finished parking, he said, "Look, if you want to laugh, laugh. Do it now." Then he waited.

Normally, they would have, he was quite a silly sight, but given the solemnity of the moment and how obviously important this was to Ray, even though they wanted to they knew they wouldn't.

"We're okay," J.D. said for them both. They climbed out of the pickup and joined the throng.

There were hundreds of people lining the streets around Graceland, the mood decidedly somber. The only sounds were of gentle sobs and soft inner crying. Ray (in his disguise), Sheree, and J.D. worked their way into a large crowd directly across from the gates.

Everyone's eyes were across the street. No one took a second look at this foolish-looking fellow in the bad hat.

Suddenly, the crowd gasped. The gates had started to open. Uniformed patrolmen stood by in case it was necessary to keep the crowds back. No one moved.

Motorcycle patrolmen were the first of the procession to be seen. They entered the street and stopped near the crowd to make way for what was to follow. Then the motorcade began.

The hearse led the way, followed slowly by a procession of fifteen white Cadillacs. They just kept coming. Everyone knew that they contained the family, Vernon, Dee, various aunts and uncles (many of whom also lived at Graceland), as well as Elvis's last girlfriend, Ginger Alden, Joe Espisito, Elvis's "boys" and their wives, and, of course, Priscilla and Lisa Marie.

It was a very impressive sight. Many were moved to tears by the sheer spectacle of it all. Then the gates closed. The Cadillacs drove out of sight . . . and the people just stood. This was what they had come for, and it was over. What do they do now?

Many had never known a world without Elvis Presley and didn't want to know such a world, but suddenly found themselves living in one.

People cried and hugged one another, and finally realizing there was nothing more to do, they started to wander off in various directions. No one seemed to have a destination. They just had to leave. The King didn't live there anymore.

Later that night, out at Ray's trailer, the three friends were drunk. They'd lost count of how many beers had come and gone, the TV was off, and Elvis sang from the record player. They'd laughed, they'd cried, they'd fallen down.

Presently they were in a semistoic state where the next act of movement was something that needed to be considered deeply. J.D. was on the couch, where he'd been most of the evening. Suddenly, he looked at it with a new awareness. "Hey, you said Elvis had been out here. Did he, like, come in? I mean, am I sitting in the exact spot, maybe, where Elvis sat?"

"No. He never came inside. But, follow me," Ray said as he laboriously got out of his chair, turned on the light over the door, and led them outside. He then went to the exact places Elvis had stood and marked them with an X in the gravel.

There was the place Elvis stood when he first met Ray. The time he came up before they went over to Grant's house and the last time Ray saw Elvis, when he came by and asked them all to come share his world.

When he had marked all three of these places, each of them silently went to an X and stood on it, feeling various degrees of reverie.

After a respectful moment of silence, Ray raised his bottle and said in his best oratory manner, "Friends, Memphis folks, countrymen . . . give me your ears. I have come to bury Elvis, not to praise him." Then he thought. "Why can't we praise him?"

" 'Cause it's written that way," Sheree said. "Kinda."

"Bullshit. I think we should praise him," Ray said, getting into it. "Yes, absolutely we should. If anybody deserves getting a little praise right now, it should be Elvis."

Ray walked over to J.D., who was having trouble staying on his X. Ray held out his hand in front of him as if he were holding a microphone. "J.D., what's something about Elvis that you will never forget?"

Even J.D. didn't realize how wasted he was until he tried to put together a coherent sentence. "Uh, he was really good."

Ray took his hand back. "Thank you, we'll keep that in the mix for 'most original.'" He walked over to Sheree. "I've got one," Ray said as he looked at her seriously. "I guess you know by now that Elvis went with me to Grant's house."

"I know," Sheree said.

"One of the things that was so neat about Elvis was the way he thought about things. I was just going to go over to Grant's and beat the shit out of him, which, basically, would have accomplished nothing. Jesse the beagle was because of Elvis. He made sure something good came out of it all. He didn't plan it, it was just the way he looked at things."

"Thank you," Sheree said. She was glad he'd told her that. It somehow made little Jesse all the more special. "Still, Ray, remember how you handled that whole kidnapping deal? The guy got a job and the girl got a thousand bucks. I'd say that was making some good come out of it all, too. Must be a Presley trait."

Ray just smiled. After a moment, Sheree added, "I have one. Elvis Presley was probably the only person in the world who could captivate a ten-year-old girl, her mother, and her grandmother all at the same time."

After a respectful moment, J.D. said, "That's deep."

Ray and Sheree started to laugh.

"Wha . . . ?" J.D. asked.

That kicked the laughter level up a notch. Ray and Sheree laughed so hard they almost fell off their Xs, too.

45

A GUARD RAY HAD never seen before was on duty at the gates when he drove up. He came to the passenger-side window and asked, "Do you have business here?"

"Yes. I'm Ray Johnston. I have an appointment with Vernon."

The guard took a step back when he actually noticed who Ray looked like. "Relative?" he asked.

"Something like that."

"Go right ahead, sir. Mr. Presley is expecting you," the guard said as he pushed the button that made the gates open. "Do you know which house is his?" he asked before Ray drove in.

"Yes. Thank you," Ray said and drove through the gates, not noticing the guard staring after him as though he'd seen a ghost.

Ray parked in his usual spot and nervously walked back to Vernon's house. He had no idea what was going to happen. Vernon had just called and asked him to stop by. Again, Ray tried to keep his hopes in check but, he had to admit, it felt sad but good to be back at Graceland.

Vernon was out in front of his place, pruning flowers. He saw Ray and walked over to him.

"Ray, good to see you. Thanks for coming," Vernon said, not looking at him.

"My pleasure, sir."

Vernon started walking off with a definite destination in mind. Ray followed.

"I suppose you heard that we moved Elvis's and Gladys's bodies back here last weekend?"

"Yeah. Weren't people trying to dig him up, or something?"

"The world is full of a bunch of crazies, I swear," Vernon said, still not looking at Ray. "He was never going to be safe there. Had to post a twenty-four-hour guard. Stupid. Better they're back here. Belong here anyway. Thought you'd like to see where they're buried."

"I appreciate that," Ray said, truthfully. He was touched by the sentiment. It was nice of Vernon to do this, but why wouldn't he look at Ray? That was a little uncomfortable.

Vernon led Ray to where the graves were and motioned for Ray to go ahead. Vernon stopped. Ray walked alone over to the graves and read their inscriptions. As strange as it was, he appreciated having this opportunity and spent a quiet moment with his brother and his mother.

He was affected for a number of reasons by the inscription Vernon had written for Elvis's marker.

He was a precious gift from God
We cherished and loved dearly.

He had a God-given talent that he shared
With the world. And without a doubt

He became most widely acclaimed;
Capturing the hearts of young and old alike.

He was admired not only as an entertainer,
But as the great humanitarian that he was;
For his generosity, and his kind feelings
For his fellow man.

He revolutionized the field of music and
Received its highest awards.

He became a living legend in his own time,
Earning the respect and love of millions.

God saw that he needed some rest and
Called him home to be with Him.

We miss you, Son and Daddy. I thank God
That He gave us you as our son.

Ray looked back at Vernon, who still wasn't looking at him but seemed quite emotional, like the time when he had to excuse himself from dinner. Ray walked back to him.

"That's really nice, what you wrote," Ray said. Vernon didn't move. Ray wondered if he'd heard him. "Are you all right, Vernon?"

After a moment, Vernon answered, "I wanted to call you earlier, Ray. I almost did it a hundred times, but it was just too hard. I can't look at you and not see Elvis. What might have been . . . regrets. . . . He was my world. I miss him."

"Quite a world it was."

"Amen," Vernon said, looking at the ground. "The Colonel still wants you to stay in the background and I agree. Nothing should take away from the memories Elvis has left with us. Do you agree with that?"

"I don't think anybody could take them away, but I don't want to mess anything up," Ray said, the cold feeling in his stomach coming back.

"I knew you'd feel that way. You're a good boy, too, Ray. You really are. But the memories are precious. Memories are all I have now."

Ray started to say something, then hesitated and decided not to. Since Vernon still wasn't looking at Ray, he didn't notice.

"I don't think we should see each other for a while, Ray," Vernon continued. "I'm too old and it's just too painful. I'm sure you understand." He paused. Ray didn't know if it was for a reply or not. It didn't really matter because he couldn't think of anything to say right then anyway.

"Stay here as long as you like, then let yourself out, all right?" Vernon finally said.

"Yes, sir."

Without ever having looked at Ray once, Vernon walked away. After a few steps, he turned, hesitated, and very deliberately looked up and met Ray's eyes. For a moment, the two stood there, looking at each other. Vernon slowly raised his hand and waved a silent good-bye. It was a small but meaningful good-bye, like an old man might, knowing he will never see the person again.

Vernon then turned and walked away. Ray watched him go, surprised that he felt as bad as he did.

Sheree was in Ray's little kitchen cooking when he arrived, suit coat thrown over his shoulder.

"Hi, hon. How'd it go?"

"I am so damn stupid!"

"That good, eh?"

Ray threw his suit coat on the couch, went to the refrigerator, and got a beer.

"Beer?" he asked Sheree.

"Way ahead of you," she said as she motioned to one by her, trying to be patient, knowing she'd hear about Ray's day when he was ready to tell it.

He plopped down on the couch, took a swig, and started. "Saw Elvis's and Gladys's graves."

"Were they nice?"

"Like what you'd expect—big, glitzy, but nice." The afternoon had been so weird for Ray he didn't exactly know how to tell it.

After a moment, he gave it a try. "Vernon has a tough time dealing with me because I remind him so much of Elvis. He doesn't think we should see each other for a while."

"Is this like the old 'I think we need some alone time'?"

"Seems like."

Sheree knew how much that must hurt from the man he was just beginning to think of as his father. "I'm sorry."

"But do you know how stupid I am? Get this, Vernon was telling me how I still had to stay in the background so I don't screw up any Elvis memories because that's all he's got now. I almost said . . . I even opened my mouth, getting ready . . . I almost said, 'You've still got me.' As if having me for a son, that he's known about for a minute, is somehow going to make it easier to deal with losing a son like Elvis! You ought to read what Vernon wrote about him, it was really nice. Can you believe that? Where was my head?"

Sheree wiped off her hands and walked over to Ray, who stood and held her.

"Probably somewhere close to your heart," she said as she also held him tightly. "It doesn't matter if the world knows it or not. I have the best of the Presley men right here."

The two held on to each other, their love never more apparent.

46

RAY'S TRUCK KICKED UP its usual trail of dust as he drove past his lions on the way home. He noticed that one of them had fallen over and made a mental note to stand it back up. In spite of everything, he'd gotten kind of used to them. He'd even looked "whimsy" up in the dictionary and Sheree was right, he could use some.

His clothes looked like he'd spent the day working, which indeed he had. He was tired, dirty, and wanted a shower and a beer, not necessarily in that order. Entering the trailer, he put down his lunch pail, threw the mail on a table, cleaned up a bit, and treated himself to a cold one.

Ray then grabbed the mail, sat down on the couch, and started going through it, seeing if there was anything important.

A few minutes later, he was still reading when there was a knock at the door. Ray didn't get a lot of unexpected company and looked out the window first. There was a nondescript car in his parking area with a man behind the wheel, waiting. Another was at Ray's door.

He opened it to see a very prim, buttoned-up man holding a file folder.

"Are you Mr. Johnston? Mr. Raymond Johnston?" the man asked.

"Yeah."

"My name is Saltmarsh, Myron Saltmarsh, and I have a delivery for you. Could I see your driver's license and have you sign here, please?" he said, pulling a form out of the folder and offering it and a pen to Ray.

"Sure," Ray said as he stepped outside, took out his wallet, and showed the man his license. "Who from?" he asked, taking the form.

"All in good time," Mr. Saltmarsh said, checking the driver's license as he waited for Ray to sign the form. He then compared the signature to one he had on another paper and seemed satisfied.

"Very good, sir. This way," Mr. Saltmarsh said as he returned Ray's license and led him around to the side of his trailer. Parked there was the most beautiful 1977 maroon Cadillac convertible in the world. It had a fawn-colored top and upholstery. Ray was stunned.

"This is from Mr. Presley. He'd purchased several cars from us over the years. He'd made special arrangements with me for this one specifically, practically a month before his death."

Mr. Saltmarsh handed the keys to a speechless Ray. He looked into the plush opulence of the car and noticed the guitar Ray had played at Graceland in the backseat.

Seeing Ray notice the guitar, Mr. Saltmarsh said, "The guitar was an afterthought. Mr. Presley just brought that by a couple of weeks ago."

Mr. Saltmarsh then walked around to the back of the car. "You should open the trunk."

Ray took the keys and opened it. It was filled with suitcases and duffel bags.

"What is this?" Ray asked.

"As Mr. Presley most colorfully phrased it," Mr. Saltmarsh said, trying to get the inflection just right, "a shit pot full of money."

Ray still had no idea what to say as he closed the trunk in a daze. Mr. Saltmarsh handed him a small envelope. "And this. Please enjoy, Mr. Johnston. If you have any questions, my business card is in the glove box. Good day."

Mr. Saltmarsh walked off before Ray realized that he forgot something. "Uh, thank you very much," he called out but didn't know if Mr. Saltmarsh had heard him. Soon the two men in the other car drove off, leaving Ray with this magnificent car . . . and the envelope.

Ray opened it and took out the card inside.

Ray, *Jesse*

To my big brother.

I love you.

$\mathcal{E}$ —

That did it. Ray was on emotional overload. He wondered what made Elvis change his mind and add "Jesse," but it really didn't matter anymore. Ray looked upward, smiled, and mouthed a heartfelt "thank you." Tears swelled up in his eyes as his attention came back to earth and this magnificent car. He walked around it, looking at it lovingly from all angles. His attention kept going from the car, to the guitar, to the card, then back.

Finally, he crossed his arms on top of the car and practically collapsed as he laid his head down on them. He stayed that way for a long time.

EPILOGUE

Ray and Sheree moved out of Memphis around October 20, 1977 after satisfying all debts and paying in full for Ray's trailer and his one and a half acres.

Their current whereabouts are unknown. Elvis sightings continue to come in from around the world to this day.